THE STRANGER AT THE WEDDING

THE STRANGER AT THE WEDDING

A. E. GAUNTLETT

R A V E N ✦ B O O K S

LONDON · OXFORD · NEW YORK · NEW DELHI · SYDNEY

RAVEN BOOKS
Bloomsbury Publishing Plc
50 Bedford Square, London, WC1B 3DP, UK
29 Earlsfort Terrace, Dublin 2, Ireland

BLOOMSBURY, RAVEN BOOKS and the Raven Books logo are
trademarks of Bloomsbury Publishing Plc

First published in Great Britain 2024

A catalogue record for this book is available from the British Library

ISBN: HB: 978-1-5266-5976-7; TPB: 978-1-5266-5975-0;
eBook: 978-1-5266-5974-3; ePDF: 978-1-5266-5973-6

2 4 6 8 10 9 7 5 3 1

Typeset by Integra Software Services Pvt. Ltd.
Printed and bound in Great Britain by CPI Group (UK) Ltd, Croydon CR0 4YY

To find out more about our authors and books visit www.bloomsbury.com
and sign up for our newsletters

Dedication TK

Once upon a time, or so the story goes, a woman Pandora – the first woman and daughter of Zeus – was forged of clay and breathed into being by the god of fire, Hephaestus. The gods of Mount Olympus gathered at Zeus' behest and bestowed upon her the gifts of language, beauty, emotion and craftsmanship. But Zeus had a gift for her too: the gift of curiosity, so that she may always have her eyes open to the world.

On Earth, Pandora soon fell in love with Epimetheus, the brother of the fire-stealing titan, Prometheus, whereupon Zeus decided the two should marry. And so they did.

As a wedding gift, Zeus gave the couple an ornate box, whose lid had been sealed shut by lock and key.

You must never open this, said Zeus. *Promise me.*

And so they did. They promised him.

Blessed, or else cursed, with the gift of curiosity, Pandora's thoughts would turn with alarming regularity to the box. Her father had said that its contents were not fit for mortal eyes. *But I am Zeus' child*, she reasoned. *Am I strictly mortal?* The thoughts became incessant, overwhelming, until the thick knot of an obsession took hold and she could bear it no longer. She begged and she pleaded with her husband to let her open the box, and still he refused.

One night, as Epimetheus lay sleeping, she stole away to the box, key in hand. *One quick look inside and the thought will be loosed from my head forever. One sharp turn of this key and –*

And so she did.

The key slid in the lock and carefully she prised open the lid. Only she wished she hadn't, for out rushed every sickness, every malady, every force of evil and suffering, every ill of human nature that the world would ever know in a swirling maelstrom of smoke and screeching. Pandora tried desperately to usher the monsters back into their prison, but in vain.

As she lay on the floor weeping, she became distantly aware of a tiny sound echoing within the box. She lifted the lid once more and was cast backwards by a glorious beam of light that shot by her and out into the world. This force was not evil, this force was not ugly; it was beautiful.

It was Hope.

PART ONE

THE WEDDING DAY

1

The room shifts beneath me and the tiny hairs on my arm bristle. There is a happy disquiet in the pit of my stomach.

'Darling, the car will be here soon.'

My mother always calls me darling. I wish she wouldn't. It's a terrible affectation that she cultivated soon after my father died. Gone were the sombre floor-length dresses that she wore every day for six months after his passing; gone the Montecristo cigars that she lit each morning in his name. And hello, single life. The parties, the Altuzarra dresses, the tumbler of gin forever installed at the end of her arm. I don't know who she thinks she is with all this *darling* business.

There are but three opportunities in life to reinvent oneself: secondary school, university and divorce – or else widowhood. I suppose she's taken her final shot, and I don't begrudge her that. Despite her period of mourning though, we're yet to discuss my father's crushing absence.

'Darling …'

My sister throws the blusher she'd just been applying to my cheeks into her vanity box.

'Mum, go fix yourself a drink. You're fussing.'

'I am not *fussing*.' She draws the word out on her tongue as one would a card from an envelope. 'Can't I be excited that a man finally saw fit to make an honest woman of *one* of my daughters?'

Mother has never quite accepted the fact that Karen is a lesbian. My sister once invited her partner to my birthday meal in London and throughout Mother continued to refer to Hannah as *Karen's little friend*. That is until the waitress asked what she wanted for dessert. Karen, exasperated, took one of Hannah's boobs in her hand and asked, calmly and confidently, for the bill. Now Mother doesn't acknowledge Hannah at all.

'Perhaps it's best if you wait downstairs …' I say, my feet shifting nervously beneath my dress. I expect my mother to pounce, to rip the radiator from the wall and launch it at the window, but she doesn't. She simply looks at me, cold, collected, then to Karen, and stalks from the room, the ice clattering loudly in her glass.

'You've been gifted a get-out-of-jail-free card today,' Karen says, smiling.

'It's only 10 a.m. and I've already cashed it in. I've got a whole day ahead of me … I'll end up killing her, or her me. Wouldn't that be something?'

Karen giggles, the glint of a memory in her eye, as she withdraws a deep red lipstick from her vanity box and makes to etch the first line into the curve of my lower lip.

'Perhaps something a little more … or rather a little less …'

'Tarty?'

'I was going to say bold, but we can go with tarty.'

Karen fishes out a pink-terracotta. 'Hold still.'

'Yes, Boss.'

K shoots me a look of faux-reproval. 'Hey, do you remember when Dad took us to see *The Lion King*?'

'How can I forget?' I can see him now, in his oversized denim jacket and khaki corduroys, the sun combing a greyness through his hair.

'We're barely through the door and Dad starts limping as though he's just made it out of the Falklands.'

'It worked, though. They gave us the best seats in the house.'

I'm laughing, but I can feel tears forming in the corners of my eyes.

'Mum's face … she was so embarrassed.'

'We all were. But that was Dad.'

'That was Dad.' A sadness comes over Karen. 'Do you think about him?'

'Every day.'

'Do you think Mum does, too?'

4

'I know she does, but she'll never admit it.'

'No, I don't suppose she will.'

Mother was once so open to the world, to us, but in the time since his passing, she has closed herself off. K and I hope beyond hope, though that hope remains unspoken, the mother we once knew is in there somewhere, waiting to be let out.

Karen crosses to the other side of the room and pulls a pair of silver heels from the shelf, which she deposits before me and eases, one by one, on to my feet. They pinch at the toe. 'Right, let's have a look at you.'

I take my sister's hand and find myself hauled before the mirror, where I'm confronted with an image that is simulta-neously me and not-me; a version of myself that I'd only ever contemplated – and even then, briefly – as a young girl, lemonade in hand and feet dangling precariously into the dyke that abutted our farm. I sat there, peering down at the darkness, and I threw all my hopes and dreams and visions for the future into the great chasm and vowed, one day, when I was older and wiser and that little bit more wizened, to dive in after them.

And now here I am, stood on the edge, and I'm scared. I see the woman before me, smiling out of the mirror, running her hand down the lace brocade of her dress, her feet squeezed into a pair of silver heels, and I'm scared. Not for the threat of the fall or the uncertainty of the blackness that awaits, but because I know I'm about to retrieve what I'd once discarded.

Everyone warned of the first patchwork of nerves that arrived right on schedule, just as I'd climbed out of the bath this morn-ing; of the waxen look that would greet me as I regarded myself and my certain future carefully in the mirror. They warned me of the instinct to run; of the urge to commit some terrible sin before I committed myself to Him. They spoke of the dreads, which I had long thought reserved for sportsmen or actors; of the chicken heart, the white feather, the weak knees. They spoke of cold feet. *Not me*, I thought, *my feet are always cold.*

They told me, too, how I'd look back on all this in years to come and laugh – laugh at the absurdity of my worry, at the notion that there could be any other man for me. And I knew that to be true. For all my fleeting doubt, Mark is the only thing in my life I've ever been sure of.

And it's that thought that enables me to take the step into the unknown, and into the abyss.

'You look beautiful,' Karen says, tugging at the hem of my dress. 'Ready?'

'Ready,' I smile. And just like that, I jump.

*

The farm was a small affair. Four acres of semi-arable land with a chocolate-box farmhouse planted slap-bang in the middle. We moved in when I was eight.

'You're going to love it here,' said Dad, as we drove slowly up the winding gravel path. I'd never seen him so happy. 'There's a pigpen, room enough for us to get a dog and a swing by the pond ...'

'A dog!' gasped Karen, wide-eyed.

'That's right, K. But you'll have to look after it.'

'I will, I promise.'

'I know you will.'

Mother stayed silent. I supposed she was in one of her moods.

'What about me, Dad?' I said.

'Well, it will be your dog, too. What will you name him?'

Karen and I screwed up our faces.

'A boy? Why would we want a boy?'

Dad laughed and I remember thinking how much I loved the way his mouth crinkled at the corners as he did so.

'Fine. Then what will you call *her*?'

'Doggie!' yelled Karen, as though it were the most obvious thing in the world.

'I think you can do a little better than that, K.'

Karen thought for a moment.

'Jessica.'

And just like that, the car's mirth dissipated and Mother began to cry. What started as a small shudder, a crack in a drainpipe, grew and grew with each turn of the wheel and each bend in the path, before erupting – until we found ourselves drowning in its torrent.

Dad tried to rebuild something from the ashes. 'Let's keep thinking, eh?' He placed a big hand on the nape of Mother's neck, leant over and planted a kiss on her wet cheek.

We were not supposed to say that name.

When the car finally came to a rest before the great oak door, excitement got the better of me. I remember rushing out, turning the circular iron handle and running from room to room, sweeping open the faded William Morris-print curtains and marvelling as the crisp light picked out each mote of dust. We were not a tall family, and just as well, for low-slung coffee-coloured wooden beams propped up a ceiling that seemed as though it might fall in at any moment. It wasn't much to look at – mostly bare brick and unvarnished oak floors, but it was charming, and it was home.

Upstairs and hidden to the rear of the house, I found a room drowning in old books. I picked up the nearest one to me, wiped the dust from the spine with the back of my hand and took it to the light of the window. *The Velveteen Rabbit*. I liked the way my tongue rolled the syllables around in my mouth.

I settled on to the hard warmth of the floor, my dress pinioned between my legs, and opened the book as gingerly as one might a clam. And this clam hid a pearl. I remember it clearly, not least as I have read it many times since. A simple story, deceptively so. A stuffed rabbit, given to a young boy one Christmas morning, wonders if he will ever become *Real*. To be Real, a toy horse tells the rabbit, is to be loved. When the boy cannot sleep one evening, his nanny places the rabbit in his bed and the two become inseparable – wherever the boy goes, the rabbit goes, too. And over time, through play and adventure, as the rabbit's hair is loved off, as his whiskers grow threadbare and shabby, the rabbit becomes Real. For the boy loves him. It hurts to be Real, the rabbit learns; but when you're Real, you don't mind being hurt.

I closed the book and looked back up at the room: at its squat ceiling, its peeling paintwork and faded grandeur; at the small flap of wallpaper that hung limply-torn from the wall; at the pockmarked floorboards from which nails protruded irregularly

7

but decisively. It wasn't the room I had in mind, but it was mine; a room of my own at last.

'Annie? Annie, where are you?'

'Just a minute, Mum.' I didn't always call her Mother – not then.

'Annie, down here, please.'

She had that tone: a request concealing an instruction. She meant business. So, I replaced the book carefully and made my way back down the stairs.

At the bottom, Dad stood with a broad smile still plastered across his face. He had slung Karen over his shoulder like a fireman and laughed as she squirmed, her feet beating the air. Finally, he set her down and squatted, placing her cheeks between his wide hands.

'One day,' he said, his weight balanced uncertainly on his haunches, 'you'll want me to pick you up and I won't be able to.'

Karen thought for a moment. I don't think she'd ever reckoned on Dad growing old. In truth, I hadn't either.

'One day,' she said, her face brightening, 'I'll pick *you* up.'

He smiled sweetly. 'Yes, I'm sure you will. But you'll have to get big and strong first. Come on, show me your guns.'

Karen crooked her elbow and strained to flex her muscles.

'Woah, easy there, Tiger. You'll have my eyes out with those things.'

Karen giggled and made to box Dad in the chest, who staggered back each time as though he'd just gone several rounds with Joe Frazier.

'Annie?' Mother walked in, searchingly. 'Oh, good, you're here. Now listen ... you too, Karen ...'

'Yes, Mummy?'

Karen was good at playing the doting daughter. I struggled – I struggle.

'Things will be different here. This is a brand-new start for us all. Isn't that right, David?'

'Yes, but that's not to say –'

'We will build new things. New memories, new friendships, new ideas. The past stays put, you hear?'

The Kent hills are dressed in a riot of autumn colours as we make our slow journey church-bound in a cream-coloured Rolls-Royce, two lavender ribbons fluttering from the outstretched angel on the bonnet. A skylark keeps pace with the car; I watch as its white-frilled wings negotiate the complex ripples of wind on its upward swing, before plunging into the grasslands below. The bird resurfaces, and for the briefest of moments, the outside is alight with song.

Inside the car, there is only silence. Mother sits next to me, quiet, composed. She feels to me, at this moment, a near-perfect stranger. I look over at her as she gazes out absently at the rolling hills, and I see a great emptiness. A vacuum in a void.

The car makes its final turn on to the long, winding drive that leads to the great door of the church, and suddenly I'm back at the farm for the first time: my dad in the front seat, planting a lingering kiss on my mother's cheek. She's crying heavily and Karen, beside me, doesn't seem to understand; she wrestles with a loose stone in the heel of her boot.

The church looms and the past recedes. I wonder how many cars carrying wide-eyed brides have come before me. How many of them nervously set foot on the gravel? How many of them froze? And for the brave, how many of them got their happily-ever-afters?

It's every girl's dream to be a princess, we're told, to be a bride. Not me. I didn't grow up planning my wedding; I grew up planning my career. I wanted to *be* someone, not someone else's. An astronaut, a warrior, a leveller of mountains, an adventurer. I wanted to define myself and for the world to know me and understand me on my own terms, not terms that had been written for me many years ago. If history teaches us anything, it's that bad men have got away with far too much for far too long. History needs more bad women; more Joan of Arcs, more Cleopatras, more Agrippinas; more women who misbehave. Why would you want to be a good woman when you can be a bad one?

The car pulls to a stop and Mother remains unmoved, her arms set like a dinner table in the peak of her lap. I wonder if I'm looking at the woman I will become. *No*, I tell myself, *You will be better. You must be better.*

The driver circles the car and opens the door for me. The birds return, but their song is different now, plaintive. Mother sighs.

'You're a vision, Madam,' says the driver, as he takes my hand and guides me from the car. 'Your intended is a very lucky man.'

'I bet you say that to all the brides.'

He smiles. 'Just the pretty ones.'

'Come on,' says Mother. 'We better get in there – before they suspect a jilting.' She stands tall, back straight, and raises her left arm proudly for me to take. She's trying, and I'm thankful for that. I turn and look at the driver, who leans back against the car bonnet, one ankle crossing the other. He seems to be mouthing something, which I can't quite make out. He tips his cap and ushers me forward with his hands.

Deep breaths, Annie. You've got this.

Inside the church, I'm greeted with a wash of fifty faces. Friends, family, colleagues, well-wishers. They all turn in unison to look at me, little Annie from the farm. Me, who had once dreamed, and dared through my dreaming, to take centre stage, but until now, never had.

I go to move, to make the first tentative step towards my future, but my feet are rooted to the spot. The organ stirs and all I feel is a cold panic that runs down my left leg and into the soles of my silvery shoes. *Help*, I want to scream, but my voice has been taken. A prisoner inside my own body. Then, just when I think I can't do this, just when the crowd weighs too heavy and the organ soars too low, I see Mark at the far end of the aisle in his vintage baby-blue suit. Handsome, dependable, devilish Mark. The only man who could take the trouble from my eyes. And as I place that first step on the threshold of the aisle and feel the tug of an arm bear me forward as a wave bears a lost sailor to shore, I hope beyond hope that I will make him happy, for he has made me Real.

2

Whenever anyone asks me how Mark and I first met, I never quite know what to say. It wasn't a thunderclap or a right hook to the temple; it wasn't a forest fire or an orchestral swelling. No one turned off gravity and the oceans didn't upend. It was gentle. It was slow. It was two cold marbles grazing each other and finding a little warmth.

I'd like to say that we met at a cinema, two lone souls in an empty auditorium, dimly aware of the other's existence until the lights came up and all we saw was each other; or a dropped glove in the manner of Cinderella's glass slipper – retrieved, cherished and returned to the appendage of the rightful owner many years later. But it was far simpler than that. Unremarkable, even. You see, we met on a commuter train. Not the Orient Express or a Bullet Train hurtling to Kyoto for the first *sakura* of spring. No. We met on the 05.38 service to London Bridge, and not a dining car in sight.

'Excuse me. Ma'am?'

I looked up from my window seat to a squat gentleman with horn-rimmed glasses bearing down at me.

'Could you move your bag?'

The man sat down beside me and opened a newspaper, which blew into my face with each gust of wind that caught the carriage.

Up and down the train, bleary-eyed commuters drifted in and out of sleep, their heads gently falling to the windows or to the shoulders of their neighbours. The same old faces dozing in the same old patterns on the same old train, rolling past the same old landscapes. My life, I had to admit, had hit a bump in the road or else a kink in the track – which was mad, for had anyone else been gifted my lot, they would have thought themselves lucky. I had a

11

good job, a small but perfectly formed two-bedroom flat in the city, a place in the country and a handful of close friends.

I *was* lucky, but I wasn't happy and I hated myself for that.

I was beset by the nagging feeling that my life was somehow empty. I tried to fill it as far as possible – I joined a gym, but lacked the motivation; I took up Karate, but couldn't bear to make contact; I'd put a film on, but spend the entire time flicking through dating apps on my phone, awaking to the credits and a red wine puddle soaking into my jeans. I was existing, not living.

So, I guess you could say my life had stalled. But before you go getting visions of Bridget Jones – lone girl in the big old city looking for Mr Right or Mr Right Now – don't. I'd never been one for romance, which I'd long written off as a fiction. Apart from the odd drunken swiping (more left than right), I wasn't looking for love and I'd decided I wouldn't much know what to do with it. Imagine my surprise, then, when love found *me*.

The train pulled into the next station, and amid the crush of commuters fighting for a seat, on he stepped, composed. A long lock of dark-brown hair broke free to graze his forehead, just above his eyebrows. He stood in the middle of the aisle, one arm held aloft, gripping on to the bar for support, as the train sped away from the station and took a sharp bend. There was something in the way he held himself – with a natural grace that spoke of great inner confidence – and the way he smiled gently at a thought that had passed through him, that inspired in me a wealth of feeling that I often struggle to put into words. The more I looked at him, the more I thought I understood him: the job he held, the people he met, the procession of ex-girlfriends who left love-starved voicemails on his phone. He could be whomever I wanted him to be.

The lights went out in the carriage, and when they came back on, the man was looking at me, his genes declaring themselves in the brightest shade of blue I had ever seen. I made to speak, to break the spell, but a gust of wind rattled the length of the carriage and caused my neighbour's newspaper to hit me full in the face.

The man saw. The man smiled.

*

And now I see him as I did in that moment, save that this time he's in his baby-blue suit, standing by the altar, waiting patiently for me. My beautiful bridesmaids – Karen and Laura – are standing opposite in their pastel-pink dresses, each with a clutch of golden lilies pressed to their chests. They smile out at me too, knowing intimately how much I thought this day might never come to pass, and how utterly glad I am that it did. My cold feet have grown warm.

I reach the end of the aisle, stumble a little, nearly fall into him, recover, and find myself passed from mother to future son-in-law as though the two are exchanging goods. Despite the pomp and circumstance – the painted ladies and pretty dresses, the eager attendees, the chauffeur-driven Rolls-Royce out front, the carefully choreographed ceremony and the joyous solemnity of the occasion – in this very moment, and this very moment alone, I feel like cattle. And this is my meat market.

The vicar addresses us, the couple, the church, but the words do not register. This has all happened before and this shall happen again. My parents were married here, and my father's parents before them. Friends, cousins, uncles, aunties have stood here too, in this exact spot, under the mottled light of these stained-glass windows, beside these mighty stone arches, afore the throng of fifty pairs of seated eyes, and have made their vows, pledged their presents, their futures, to one another. They have sworn to live out their remaining years together, and I am about to do the same. Our union is just the latest in a long line of unions – some of which shall remain intact, some of which shall be broken. Not ours. We shall remain strong; Mark and I shall prosper. We have each, individually, weathered so very much. We shall both, together, weather so much more.

As Mark reaches up to my face and gently lifts my veil, I want to cry. I fight hard to hold back, but I catch myself. *Oh, no, you don't, Annie. Almost there.* I try to shake these last self-sabotaging thoughts from my head and look to the room, to the faces staring back at me – to Karen, who has loved and will always love me; to Mother, who cannot love; to dear patient Laura, who only wanted the best for me; to Mark's father and Jean, his wife; to

13

all our friends and colleagues, who sit there with bushy-tailed anticipation.

Until I see a face that is stark for its unfamiliarity. This man is all angles – high, prominent cheekbones, a severe pointed chin and slick dark hair swept from temple to temple above a furrowed forehead. His clavicles stand proud against his shirt. He regards me now with a cool, detached stare, as though he is looking right through me and has seen something that he doesn't like, something that has fired a bitterness in his mouth.

Mark gently takes my hand in his and I turn to him. 'I'm terrified,' he says quietly as the vicar gestures for the church to fall silent.

The stranger regards me still.

'Me too,' I whisper.

3

I began seeing the man on the train each morning on my commute. We wouldn't talk – we'd always be a few seats apart – but we'd share a look here or an eye roll there at the expense of an obnoxious fellow commuter.

'You've got to do something, Annie. He's all you ever talk about.'

Laura sat on the terrace, casting ash to the street below. She had come over, ostensibly to pick up a scarf she'd left some months previously, but I knew that wasn't the real reason. She was here to check on me.

'Like what?' I said, projecting my voice from the kitchen, where I sat forcing a wedge of pitta into a tub of week-old hummus.

'Like fucking talk to the guy.'

My face shrivelled. 'I can't. I – It's like I lose all sense of myself. I become …'

'An idiot? It's a crush, Annie. We've all been there.'

'No. It's more than that, it's …'

Laura laughed and threw her cigarette butt into the neighbour's back garden.

'I wish you wouldn't do that.'

'Oh, stop being so precious.' Laura slid her small frame through the gap in the sliding door to the kitchen and helped herself to some pitta.

'Was it always this hard?' I said.

'The pitta?'

I looked at her as I might a petulant child throwing a shit-fit in a supermarket.

'Dating.'

'We're not at school any more. You can't wait for the class clown to tug on your pigtails or staple your dress to a notebook before he finally plucks up the courage to persuade one of his mates to ask you out on his behalf. You have to go get them. You want something, you take it.'

Laura demonstrated by tearing off another strip of pitta, rolling it into a cigar and forcing it into her mouth. She smiled through bulging cheeks.

'See?'

I rolled my eyes.

'We just need a game plan,' said Laura. 'A plan of attack. Like when Danny Matthews tried to talk Mrs Holliday into going to the Sixth Form prom with him. He didn't blunder in half-cocked; he had it all mapped out. The rose petals in the top drawer of her desk, the vomit-inducing messages scrawled on the dirt-encrusted bonnet of her car ...'

'It didn't work though.'

'Didn't it?'

'No, he wasn't at the prom that night.'

'You're right, he wasn't – because he was at Mrs Holliday's house instead.'

'You're lying,' I said in utter disbelief.

'Maybe. Maybe not.'

Laura had a habit of embellishing the past. She was never one to let the truth get in the way of a good story.

'Fine. So, what do you suggest I do, oh wise one?'

'A note.'

A bus from the darkening street below seemed to hiss and sigh as it unloaded its weary passengers into their evenings.

'A note? You're taking this school analogy a bit too far.'

'Think about it. Your only chance is on a crowded train – the eyes of a hundred commuters on you. You don't want to make him uncomfortable. Keep it cool; slip him a note just before the doors open and walk off. Very nice, very classy.'

'And then what?'

'And then you wait.'

16

Laura caught her half-reflection in the glass frame of a Vermeer print I had found at a car-boot sale one summer in Devon. With quiet abandon, she adjusted her hair and ran a tidying finger around the gloss that had overshot the edges of her upper lip.

'But it's not me, is it? When have I ever been so forward with a guy?'

Laura turned back, remembering herself, remembering me. 'Why should the man always have to make the first move? What happened to Little Miss Independent?'

I hated to admit it, but she had a point. And waiting for men to approach *me* hadn't exactly worked out.

'OK, say I do it. What if he doesn't call?'

'Then you have your answer. Sink or swim. Lord knows I can't put up with your lovesick moping for much longer. If you won't do it for yourself, do it for me.'

With that, Laura scooped her jacket from the kitchen counter, planted a kiss on my forehead and made for the door. She had a date, but then when didn't she?

'Aren't you forgetting something?' I held out the scarf to her.

'No, you keep it. Never much cared for cashmere anyway. Too decadent.'

When Laura had gone, I poured myself a large glass of wine and sat staring down at a blank scrap of paper. Its emptiness taunted me. How could I distil a thumping array of feelings, feelings I had no right to – I didn't even know the man – into a pithy and blasé note? *Is this silly?* Then I thought back to Danny Matthews – his daring in the face of near-certain defeat, regardless of the outcome. So, I wrote it, climbed on to the sofa and fell asleep with the candles still burning.

You should do one silly thing each day; this is mine for the year. Drink?

The next morning, as the train approached his stop, and I fought hard to suppress all the voices in my head that told me such an endeavour was foolish, that he was bound to say *no*, that he was too good for me, I confess to feeling a little giddy. For the first time in my life, I was taking action.

The train stopped and the carriage filled with the usual crush of bodies. I was beginning to recognise these people – there was Lady-of-the-Manner, her nose always tilted towards one o'clock; Marcel-Marceau with his face like flour; Mr Pug; and, finally, Sir Cough-a-Lot, Arthur's most irritating knight, whose only power, as far as I could see, was an acute ability to pepper others with his germs. But the man I was looking for, the only one who mattered, was nowhere to be seen.

My heart sank as the station receded and I felt as though the platform had contracted into the pit of my stomach. I straightened myself out. *He must be sick*, I thought. *That's it. Day off work. Nothing more. He'll be back tomorrow. Wednesday it is.*

But Wednesday it wasn't. Or the day after that.

Two weeks went by.

He must be on holiday, I told myself. *A fortnight in Sicily – Taormina first, then on to the south coast and Syracuse, no doubt.* He seemed the type to travel a great deal, I reasoned.

After five weeks had passed, I had to concede that I'd lost him. That was that.

He'd left my life just as quickly as he'd entered it.

*

The vicar's words wash over me, and the church itself seems to shift on its foundations.

If any man can show just cause, why they may not lawfully be joined together, let him now speak, or else hereafter for ever hold his peace.

I turn to look out over the sea of faces again. The familiarity comforts me. Until it doesn't. Until I see that angular man, the stranger in the room, the man who could unhem all that is being sewn today. But he does not speak out. He does not motion. He simply sits there with a knowing look, a raw grin forming at the edges of his mouth.

Mark Anthony Lane, do you take Annie Marie Clark to be your wedded wife, to live together in marriage?

Do you promise to love her, comfort her, honour and keep her for better or worse, for richer or poorer, in sickness and health, and forsaking all others, be faithful only to her, for as long as you both shall live?

The building shifts once more as the vicar moves to seal our whirlwind romance under the eyes of God. I wonder whether Mark knows what he's going through with. I don't deserve him.

'I do,' says Mark. Two little words that wash out the old and birth the new. *We will build new things. New memories, new friendships, new ideas. The past stays put.* And that is for the best.

And then it is my turn to make my pledge. There is not a doubt in my mind, no other consideration and nothing left to say but *I do.*

The rings?

Mark's best man steps forward with a red velvet cushion, embroidered with two small letters: *A + M*. Mark reaches to the cushion and takes the smaller ring; his hands shake slightly as he slides it into position on my fourth finger. He is claiming me, and I am happy to be claimed.

I give you this ring as a sign of our marriage. With my body I honour you, all that I am I give to you, and all that I have I share with you.

Mark's words track the vicar's, then mine track Mark's. I slide the larger ring into place on his finger. He turns to the congregation – to our friends, our families – and holds his hand up for all the world to see. I too have claimed him and he wants everyone to know it.

And by the powers vested in me, I now pronounce you husband and wife.

There is a swelling in the church, an outpouring of joy. *Kiss her*, shouts someone.

Mark moves towards me.

Wait for it, cautions the vicar wryly. A pause. And then … *You may now kiss the bride.*

Hands clasp hands and laughter rings out. Mark grabs me with a force I have never known him capable; his lips meet mine and we fit. Our love is finally sealed for all to see. Mark is my only. And I am only his.

People stand and clap and cheer. There is laughter and there are tears too, but the right kind. The happy kind. Even Mother looks on adoringly. I do not want to forget this moment.

As I stand here at the altar, Mark before me and my eyes held in his, I notice in my periphery, just beyond Mark's shoulder, a sombre dot among a riot of colour.

The stranger in the crowd, the uninvited guest, smiles. He sits there, and he smiles.

And that smile belies a great, rotten truth: something wicked this way comes.

4

'Hear ye, hear ye, Lords and Ladies of the fairer land, peasants of the marshes, townspeople from beyond the verges and all gentle hill folk. We have been gathered here in the name of Princess Karen who has chosen on this most auspicious day to be wed to noble Sir Kenneth Carson, the whitest knight with the blackest steed in all of Albion.'

Dad gestured to a topless Ken doll stood in the centre of the garden table. Around him sat a medley of stuffed animals, many of whom had seen better days. Rupert Bear was missing a button eye, his red cable-knit coming apart at the seams; Cookie Monster was short a handful of blue fur, ripped from him during a tussle with our bellicose one-year-old former neighbour; and Tinky Winky's coat-hanger-shaped antenna was hanging on by a mere thread.

'As father of the bride, it is incumbent upon me to offer a few words in celebration of this most magical union.'

Dad was not a man of facts and figures, of statistics or algorithms. He couldn't read the stock market or file his own taxes. Those things didn't interest him; storytelling did. He was a born raconteur, possessed of a vivid imagination, which is perhaps why he found his natural calling as a copywriter. *People don't buy products*, he once told me. *They buy stories.* It was a sentiment that was pressed into him long ago by his father, an ad-man who turned a small advertising agency into a global player. With one simple slogan that came to be plastered on trains, lorries, billboards, ships, phone boxes and mountain tops – you might have even seen it yourself and not given it a second thought – a slogan that travelled around the world many times over and still refused to stop, still refuses to stop. *A slogan can change lives*, my grand-dad said. And he was right: it had changed my Dad's and it had changed ours.

A calm June breeze rattled the spoon in Dad's teacup as he looked to K who stood knock-kneed in a frilly little dress with a red ribbon around the waist that Mother had found in the local charity shop.

'Good people,' Dad continued, 'I have known young Karen for six full summers and during that time I have seen her blossom like the peonies around us. She was often a difficult child – crying *off with his head!* at the slightest show of impudence ...'

'Stop being silly, Daddy!' shouted Karen. She was glowing. Anyone would be forgiven for thinking that this was all for real.

Mother smiled at me. It had been a while since she'd done that.

'Very well ... But she was, as she continues to be to this day, a gentle, nurturing soul. I sometimes wonder who has raised whom.'

Dad stumbled slightly and a thunderclap flashed across his face. His head dipped a little. These episodes were becoming more frequent. He went on, but lighter now, wavering, as though the moment was slowly being stolen from him.

'And, dear Sir Kenneth, whom my daughter has chosen among all the other suitors – and there were many – I beseech you now to love my daughter as she deserves to be loved and to protect her always.'

Dad coughed heavily into a handkerchief and his whole body shook, his shoulders shifting angrily up and down like piston engines. He tried to stuff the hanky back into his pocket quickly, but I could see that it was spotted dark-red. He drew the back of his hand across his lips, and looked up through watered eyes to Mother, who could only muster an encouraging smile in response. Despite the arguing, these two still knew a love that most think an impossibility. It was there, even if you couldn't always see it.

'Now if you will all kindly raise your finest china.'

He lifted the blue-and-white patterned teacup with one trembling hand and Mother and I joined him in the toast.

'To Princess Karen and Sir Kenneth.'

'To the happy couple,' we followed.

'What do you mean I'm not giving a speech?'

'Mother, go sit down – they'll be starting soon.'

'I will not move from this spot until you answer me.' The scent of gin on her lips is overwhelming.

'We've been through this.'

'We have not.'

'Yes, we have,' I plead. 'You also promised you'd behave yourself.'

Mother shrugs her shoulders. 'I say a lot of things.' In one swift, practised motion, she throws her head back and empties the contents of her glass before gesturing to a waiter for a refill. I grab the hilt of her hand. 'Oh, don't be such a bore, Annie; you're getting like your sister.'

'Go. Sit. Down ... Now.' She looks at me askance down the barrel of her nose, testing my resolve. But I won't budge. And she knows that.

'Very well.' On the way back to her table, she swipes a fresh champagne flute from a passing tray. Karen sidles up beside me and wraps a comforting hand around my waist.

'I give up,' I say.

'Oh, come on. It's only your bloody wedding day. This'll all be a distant memory tomorrow when you wake up for the very first time as Mrs Mark Lane.' She plucks each syllable like a guitar string.

'I'm worried about her, K.'

'Why?' Karen looks over her shoulder to Mother, now in thrall to Mark's 22-year-old nephew. She seems to be stroking his arm.

'That's why.'

'Let her enjoy herself. So long as she doesn't do anything silly.' We share a look. 'Just leave her to me. You enjoy your day – and your night.' She winks.

'If you're watching her, who's watching you?'

Karen mock-laughs. 'Very funny.' She turns to take her seat.

'K ...'

'Yes?'

'There's a man here –'

'There are lots of men here.'

I roll my eyes. 'Slicked-down hair, dark eyes. Spindly.'

'Sounds just your type.'

'K, I'm serious. Have you seen him?'

She senses the gravity in my voice. 'No. No, I haven't. But I'll ask around. Who is he?'

'I'm not sure exactly.'

A loud clinking sound rings out as Mark's father gets to his feet and taps his flute with a butter knife, causing a hush to descend upon the room.

'We'll talk after,' I whisper to K before scampering to my seat under the cover of Mother's call for Mark's father to *Get on with it*. Heckling. Good start.

'As you'll all be aware, sadly Annie's father couldn't be here today, so the honour has fallen to me, the father of the groom, to lead the toasts. Sorry, Mark.' The room titters. 'I just hope, Annie, that wherever your father is – smiling down on us today, no doubt – that I do him proud, and honour you both in turn.'

I promised myself I wouldn't cry this early on. But I'm smiling too.

'Thank you all for joining us today. Frankly, even I'm a little surprised to be here. When Mark came to me and told me of the happy news, that he was engaged … Well, to call it a shock would be an understatement.' More titters. 'I couldn't believe he had it in him again.'

Mark winces beside me, and there is a flash of anger there too. It is a reminder, today of all days, that he could have done without, that we both could have done without. I catch Mother's eye across the table. Her brow wrinkles and she mouths, *Again?* Karen appears to jab her in the side.

'My father once said to me on my wedding day, many years ago, mind you, that *a boy is not a man until he knows the love of a good woman*. Well, this morning I had the privilege of echoing my father's words to my son. Today, my boy is all grown-up.'

Mark's mother, Jean looks up at her husband adoringly, and then to her son. Jean is the kind of mother that any child would wish for. She's doting, she's caring, she's brimming with energy and compassion, and when she *knows best* she truly does know best. When we first met, *she* was the open arms, the washer of hands, the bouquet of flowers, the welcoming committee that I so desperately sought. The warmth I failed to find in his father, I found in his mother. And I like to think that she found something in me – not quite the daughter she never had, but the one she never knew she wanted. I smile at her now and she beams back with the punch of a thousand headlights.

'There are many paths to love, and marriage is but one of them. But let us be clear: marriage is not for everyone. Marriage is hard. Marriage is tough. Marriage is a long climb up a steep cliff, knowing that at any moment there might be a sheer drop ahead. But marriage is also the power to face the unsurmountable, the strength to forge on despite all the obstacles that lie in wait. Marriage is the wayfinder. Marriage is the beacon.'

I catch Laura's eye as she mimes shoving two fingers down her throat. *Joking*, she mouths. But she isn't. Laura has always struggled with public declarations of love.

'I won't go on; I'm under strict orders not to start telling my old army jokes. I guess that leaves me just one thing to say. I'm so glad that these two kids found happiness together and I wish them all the love in the world and an everlasting marriage. Now if you would all join me in raising your glasses ...' Fifty flutes are thrust into the air. ' ... to Mark and Annie. May you find your summit. To the happy couple!'

My heart is fit to burst as I look out at the light playing through the columns of champagne, at the chorus of well-wishers and the pastel-hued dried-flower centrepieces that adorn each table. I am grateful for this day, grateful that I found the steel to go through with it, that I didn't run, that I didn't stray from the path. I am grateful for his words. I am grateful for his restraint, whatever he may think of me privately. But more than that: I am grateful for everyone who has taken time out of their lives to celebrate us. There is no greater endorsement of our love.

But it is only when Mark takes his stand to deliver his toast that I remember not everyone here wishes us well.

'I'm sure Pete – yup, grinning like a child over there; thanks, Pete – is just itching to tear into me with a few revelations that I'd rather keep to myself –' The room laughs. '– but before he does, and I'll keep this brief, scout's honour, I'd like to thank everyone who has put this day together, centrepiece by centrepiece; I'd like to thank the bridesmaids who, I hope you'll all agree, look absolutely stunning – here's to you – and, finally –' Mark turns to look at me with those bright blue eyes. '– I'd be grateful if you would all indulge me while I share a few words about my lovely wife.'

'On our fourth date – and if this doesn't tell you everything you need to know about Annie, I don't know what will – she gave me this.' Mark fishes from under the table a paperback copy of *Misery*, which he displays proudly. 'I vaguely remembered the film: James Caan as a famed writer held captive by a deranged fan struggling to come to terms with the death of her favourite fictional heroine. But what this should have to do with Annie and me … So I asked her why, why this book.' He adopts a voice; not disparaging, but not his own. Shrill, a little intemperate. Me, I suppose. '*I thought it might cheer you up.*'

Everyone laughs; his father is in hysterics. I don't think I've ever seen him laugh so hard before. To an outsider, to one who couldn't see our love, it might seem as though Mark was belittling me. I shake the thought loose and smile for the photographer circling the room.

'Now there are many things that might cheer me up – a warm summer's day, a child's laughter, that first pint – but this book is not one of them. For a long while it puzzled me. I wondered what she was trying to say. And then I read it. Halfway through, Annie had scrawled a note on a yellow Post-it: *Mark, I'm your number one fan.*'

The loudest, the proudest collective *aww* rings out through the room and at a stroke Mark has redeemed himself.

'It was then I realised that this enigma … this sweet, sexy, intelligent woman who could floor me with a single look, who would seek to cheer me up with misery … this was the woman I wanted to be with.' He turns to me again. 'Annie, I …' His voice chokes and his confidence falters for the briefest moment, but he collects himself so quickly it may never have happened. 'I'm not sure of the man I was before I met you. I'm not sure I would recognise that man, in fact. To most, rock bottom is just an expression but for me, for a time, it was a physical place.'

A few guests share uneasy glances. *Where's this going?* mouths Laura.

'I've come a long way since then and … I guess what I'm trying to say in my own bumbling way is: I couldn't have done it without you. It takes a remarkable woman to do what you have done; to have turned this old, grizzled, horror novel into an enchanting tale; to have transformed this crotchety, bad-tempered, foul-mouthed old frog into a prince; and to have convinced that frog to love again. And today … well, today marks the start of a brand-new story; a happier story; a story that we'll write each word at a time, each chapter and verse; a story that I know will have a happy ending.

'Our happy ending.'

5

'Annie, you've been quiet today. Something on your mind?'

James looked at me with those poacher eyes. I always hated it when he did that. He liked to draw from us that which we fought hard to suppress. But he underestimated our resolve.

I shook my head.

'You won't get the most from these sessions unless you're willing to share. We're all here for you.'

I looked around the room at the twelve haunted expressions, each one dissembling a tragedy, each one suffering in their own private, unmanageable way. *I don't need to be here*, I would tell myself, but that was a lie. I did. I needed to be there more than anyone can know. I just didn't always have the strength to speak. And on the few occasions I dug deep, ferreted around for something, anything, I came up short. That thing that I'd buried, I'd buried so deeply that it was as if it was no longer there. But it was, and it would always be. And so I kept coming back to the group – every Wednesday at 7 p.m. for six months now. In a curious way, listening to the suffering of others made my load that bit lighter.

James beat a hasty retreat. 'I won't press you if you're not ready. But I hope, one day ...' The room became a little smaller and the air a little thicker.

'No ... I'm ...'

People looked to me in surprise; no one expected me to speak. I had become part of the furniture in these sessions, and as with all furniture, the upholstery was starting to go.

Caroline sat opposite me. Two years ago, during a rare family holiday to the Algarve, she'd lost her nine-year-old son. He ran on to the beach at night, a game of hide-and-seek in the thick of summer. She reported him missing, and a manhunt ensued. They never found him, never found the body, not a trace, and Caroline has never had her closure. Worse, she still thinks him alive.

Watching her then, my story seemed insignificant. Anything I said would have seemed trivial. How could my tragedy possibly compare with hers? I felt foolish for thinking I had any right to participate in this.

'I'm sorry. Let's move on.'

Caroline looked up at me, her eyes blistered red. 'Please,' she said.

Her petition was signed by the faces of those in the circle. Dark, encouraging eyes pleaded with me to continue, to share something in which they too might recognise a jot of their own suffering.

So, I took a deep breath. Some stories become real in the telling.

'When I was a little girl, my sister and I would play a game – a silly game, really. When our parents were asleep, we'd creep down the stairs and chase rabbits after dark. We'd wait by the fence at the end of our drive, our little faces pressed to the slats, and we'd stun any rabbits out foraging with the lights of our torches. They'd get this strange, dazed expression in their eyes, as though hit by lightning – then my sister would try to catch them with a butterfly net. She never did, of course. They were too quick for her.

'We stopped abruptly one day. For years, I could never recall why, until last week a dream brought it all crashing back. One night, we'd gone to the end of the drive as usual and … It was cold. Did I mention it was cold?'

I looked to James for reassurance. 'Go on, Annie,' he said gently.

'We were at the end of the drive, by the gate, and Karen – that's my sister – saw a rabbit make a run for it across the road. Right on cue, I took out my torch and stunned it. Karen made to catch the rabbit in her net, but before she had the chance …'

I was acutely aware that these people were hanging on my every word. I could say anything and they'd go along for the ride. But only the truth would do.

'Before she had the chance, a car swept around the corner, full speed. The rabbit was so stunned it couldn't react. The driver tried to swerve but it was too late, and the rabbit, it …'

Tears were coming now, thick and fast, but I wasn't sure precisely why. I hadn't cried in a very long time. My emotions were often just out of reach.

'Annie, do you feel responsible?'

I nodded. It hurt to talk then.

'OK, thank you, everyone,' said James. 'I think we'll leave it here for today. A good session. Annie, why don't you stay behind for a moment.'

I looked over at Caroline once more, half expecting to find disappointment there. But no. Instead, she came over and threw her arms around me. She drew my body tightly to hers as though trying to wring every breath from us both. 'Thank you,' she whispered. And just like that, she left. That was the last time I saw her.

Outside, the air was biting. The door fell shut heavily on its hinges and I lit up a cigarette. I smoked a little back then. Not enough to declare myself a Smoker, but just enough to take the edge off life's sharper moments.

A light rain was beginning to spread across the blackness of the car park – deserted save for one car, its headlights on, its interior dark. The car seemed abandoned but the engine hummed.

I moved closer to get a better look. There was a face in there, a face that seemed to be looking beyond this world. The man stared straight ahead. A prospective member of the group, I assumed, one unable to take that first step on the long road to recovery. How long had he been sitting here, willing himself to enter but struggling to find his feet?

'Hello?'

Nothing. The man sat stock-still as a shadow played across the architecture of his face. The brightness of the headlights still prevented me from seeing inside clearly but, from what little I could make out, I thought this man haunted, his expression drawn.

I tapped on the window. One, two, three times. On the third knock he turned to look at me with those blue eyes, those eyes I once knew – from the train. They were no longer bright but darkened. Black.

6

The room is knitted in laughter as Mark's best man sits back down, having taken us on a journey through the early years of their friendship – the joints smoked on the playing fields, the girl-friends fought over, the knickers planted in rucksacks ... These stories were new. Mark has never liked to talk about the past, not with me. *You're my future*, he once said, *let's focus on us*. And yet through the years, Pete has remained a constant in Mark's life and so the past has never really gone away.

Then, just as the toasts draw to a comforting close, Mother stands up, champagne in hand. She seems unsteady on her legs.

Oh, god.

K tries to pull Mother back down to her seat, but she bats her arm away.

'If I could have your attention, please,' she says, her voice wavering, her hand gesticulating wildly.

Two of Mark's colleagues continue to whisper at the back.

'Kind Sirs. If you wouldn't mind.'

They don't seem to have heard her.

'Oh, will you both just shut the fuck up.'

That did it.

'Thank you. Now, I have a very, very important announcement to make.' She pauses for a moment to drink in the quiet and takes a large sip of her champagne. 'Would the owner of a 1995 green Ford Mondeo parked outside, please move your car immediately; it's hideous.'

Mother sits back down triumphantly. Nobody knows quite what to say, and the room falls into a stunned silence. A few awkward coughs ring out before Mark clambers to his feet. I'm mortified.

'Thank you all for coming,' he says, 'and for … helping to make today so *memorable*.' The awkward coughs become awkward laughs. Mark gives Mother a look – long enough to carry weight. 'Now if you'd all like to make your way through to the dance floor, we have a little surprise for you: some truly awful dancing.'

As the guests start to disperse, I grab Mother, barely containing my anger. Karen looks sheepish. 'What was all that about?' I say.

'I thought you could do with a little colour. It was all so frightfully drab. Dare say we had more fun at your father's funeral.'

There it was: after nearly two decades, she finally acknowledged it, acknowledged that he was gone. Her timing has always been impeccable.

'Mother –'

'Oh, what. Let me have my fun.'

'Stop it,' I say. 'This is my day. For once, this is not about you.'

'Oh, Annie darling, it's never about *me*. When has it ever been about *me*. You couldn't even be bothered to tell your own mother that your husband has been married before.'

She is testing me, feeling her way to my limit. I take a deep breath, feel the air balloon in my chest.

'If you can't control yourself, I don't want you –'

And then I see him, the man from the church, the dark stranger, strolling across the floor towards me. He's so comfortable in himself, with himself. His gait says he owns the floor, the roof, the building; he owns the space between us. He exudes surety, certainty. He could put a million pounds on black and never even blink an eye.

'Annie?' Despite his severe features, he's charming, disarming even. Up close, he's older than I first suspected, but there's a softness in his voice that belies his age.

'Yes …'

'I just wanted to offer my congratulations. Mark's a wonderful guy, and you two make for an excellent couple. Just the other day Frank was –'

'Sorry … Don't think me rude but who are you exactly?'

A body of water forms between us. K hastily guides Mother away.

'Where are my manners. Cameron. I'm a friend of your father-in-law.' He extends a hand in greeting that goes unanswered. The hand drops slowly back to his side.

'From the army?'

'Not exactly.'

The water freezes, and there's nothing but ice around for miles.

'From where then?'

Cameron's head tilts to one side as if he is considering his next move. He's looking for a checkmate or else an escape route. But he doesn't seem the running type.

'It's a long story,' he says charily.

'And one that I should love to hear.'

'It can wait. Besides, I get the feeling that we'll be seeing a lot more of one another. Congratulations again.' With that he disappeared into the sea of guests abandoning their tables in a fog of wine.

Laura rushes up beside me. 'Who was that?'

'I've no idea,' I say, bewildered. 'He said he was a friend of Mark's father.'

She fakes a full-body shiver. 'Gives me the right creeps.'

'Do you think he –?'

'Forget about him. Seriously. Right,' says Laura as she hooks her arm through mine, 'let's get you to the dance floor.'

I groan.

'You'll be fine. Just don't do that starting-a-lawnmower dance you tried at your hen. No one wants to see that.'

Mark and I stand silently in the middle of the hall, waiting for the music to start for our first dance as husband and wife. The guests stand around us too, watching our every move, trying to catch a glimpse of our love.

In the gaping pause as the DJ rushes to find the right track, Mark runs a reassuring hand through my hair and tucks a stray strand behind my ear. I smile at the warmth of his palm.

'I love you,' I mouth.

'I love you too.'

He must sense in me a disquiet, a nervousness.

'Are you OK?' he says tenderly.

'Really wishing I'd taken those dance lessons now,' I reply.

He laughs. 'Two minutes and it's over.'

I pout playfully, my lower lip hanging out. 'Two minutes and everyone will know I can't dance.'

'What makes you think they don't know that already?'

I hit him lightly on his arm as the music starts at last.

'Follow my lead,' he says, as he steps forward and places his head next to mine. I can smell the cologne I bought him for his birthday. Rich, mellow, oud. That scent takes me back to our first date, to the day it all began. 'And try not to get your heel caught,' he whispers in my ear. A little in-joke, ours. No one else's. The spectacle is theirs, but this moment is ours.

7

The guests dance on in a tableau of interlocking arms, contorted bodies and stolen kisses, as I slip outside for some fresh air. Today has been glorious, and yet at times it has all felt a little much. You can spend your life craving the spotlight, and then the moment you get it, you realise the space beneath is too hot and the glare too bright. I needed a moment to myself again.

So here I sit in the late summer air, thinking not of Mark, not of the man now careening around the dance floor with all the grace of a built-in wardrobe, but of the men who have come before. The ones who didn't quite make it, but were it for a change of timings or circumstances, could be through those glass doors instead.

First there was Lucas, my primary school boyfriend. Short, pug-nosed, with milk-bottle glasses, a mop of matted blond hair, a face full of freckles and a head devoid of ideas. And then there was Josh. Father was a banker, mother was a diplomat. Huge sense of entitlement that would often manifest itself in what Laura affectionately termed 'bitch fits' when he didn't get his way. Then came Andrew, and Luke, and Connor. A string of distractions in my early twenties; none of them lasted much more than two months. I was young, I was naïve, and I was selfish. I was adamant that I had to learn to be happy alone before I could be happy with someone else.

And then, finally, there was Edward. Ed is the one that got away, the close-but-no-cigar. To think of Ed now, my heart stops and a cold chill runs the length of my forearm. I adored him, but it wasn't to be. I'm not entirely sure what happened – I'm not sure if it even matters – but I think, as time wore on and we stripped away layer upon layer, we came to see each other, to really see each other. And I don't think he liked what he saw. He broke up with me, and then he left, my heart in a million little pieces on the kitchen floor of my sister's flat.

On the face of it, I could have married any of these men. For we could end up with any number of people; we can love any number of people. The difference between them and Mark? Timing. Mark came into my life at a time when I was ready to give myself fully, and were you to ask him the same, I'm sure he'd agree. Timing is everything. Had we started dating when I first saw him on that train, we might not be together now; he might be with someone else entirely, and I might still be sat on my sofa, alone, swiping my way through a swamp of potential digital soulmates.

'Here you are,' says Laura, closing the door to the pit of noise behind her. 'Fag?'

I take a stick from the pack, run a match the length of the coarse strip and feel my whole body rage with adrenaline. I'm a naughty schoolgirl again.

'Pete's looking cute tonight.'

I look at her as if to say *this is new*.

'Do you think he's up for it?'

I laugh. 'How should I know?'

'Well, he is Mark's best mate. He hasn't said anything to you?'

I think for a moment. 'No.'

'But he's single?'

My eyes are drawn to two shadowed figures in the distance; one has the other pushed up against a tree, his hand riding the hem of her gown, her hand in his hair.

'Annie?'

'Pete might be a little *preoccupied*.' I gesture to the tree.

'Fuck.'

'Fuck indeed.'

'Back to the drawing board, then.' She takes a long drag on her cigarette. 'Couldn't even scare up a date to my best friend's wedding. How sad is that.'

'Laura, come on –'

'Oh, no, you don't! Stop that. Stop those pity eyes.'

'What pity eyes?'

'*Those* pity eyes. I've seen them before ... When Jason dumped me last June, a week before my birthday ... Incompatible, my fucking arse. He just much preferred his dick in someone else.' Laura checks herself mid-rant, turns to me and grins. A false grin. 'Having a lovely day?'

I laugh. 'Oh, shut up.'

'Suit yourself.' Laura begins to fidget with a loose thread on her dress. She wraps it around her index finger, then unwraps it again. 'Still, there's always that handsome older man.'

'What handsome older man?'

'Dark, brooding, slightly creepy in a sexy way,' she says playfully, but I'm not laughing. 'Asking an awful lot of questions.'

'Laura, what questions.'

She looks startled, eyes wide, pupils swimming in wine. 'I don't know –'

I lean forward and grab her wrist a little more forcefully than I intend. 'Listen to me. I need you to tell me exactly what he said.'

'OK, calm down. Let me think ... He said he knew Frank, and Mark; that he was a joiner by trade ...'

'A joiner?'

Laura seems irritated by my interruption. 'Yes, a joiner. Like a carpenter, I guess.'

'And what did he ask you?'

'All pretty innocuous stuff: how we met, where you went to school, about Karen, Jessica ...'

A dull panic rushes through me and places its ugly hand around my throat. *How on earth could he know about Jessica?*

'Where is he now?'

Laura reaches for her wine and takes a sip. Her lips are stained red.

'Last I saw: with your mother.'

8

'Just who the hell are you?'

I find Cameron and Mother sitting together in the corner of the banquet hall. They're startled by my interruption.

'Darling, what is this?' Mother waves an arm through the air dismissively.

The stranger sits there, unyielding. He crosses one leg over the other and a perfectly manicured hand – a detail that belies his advanced years – rests, insouciant, on the walnut arm of his chair. A platinum wedding ring encircles his fourth finger.

'I could ask you the same thing.'

'Oh, don't be silly.'

'Then who is he?'

'How should I know. We just met.' She turns to Cameron, who is rising from his chair. 'What did you say your name was?'

He opens his mouth to speak, to defend himself, but I won't give him the chance.

'Look, I don't know who you are, who invited you, or what on earth you think you're doing here, but you are not welcome. I'd like you to leave.'

'Annie –' Cameron goes to place his hand on my arm.

'Don't.'

'I didn't mean –' Cameron takes a step back. He looks at me, regards me coolly. I think I see his mouth curl up into a smirk.

'Stop it. Stop it now. You are not welcome. You were never welcome. So take your little notepad, take your little pen and please leave.'

Mother rises to her feet, wobbles slightly and takes another sip from her martini.

'Darling, you're being hysterical.'

'Mother?'

'Yes?'

'Zip it.' And to my amazement, she does.

'Well ...' Cameron appears lost for words. A man seemingly so used to being in control, has found himself out of it. 'I was invited by Frank, and Mark ... Please forgive me if my presence here has caused you any distress; that was certainly not my intention. I don't wish to intrude further, so I shall, as you suggest, be on my way.'

Cameron pauses. He clearly doesn't know whether to go on, whether there's anything else to be said. He bows his head ever so slightly, his steel gaze fixed firmly on me, and then leaves, prompting all the oxygen in the world to abandon my body in one giant exhale.

'What's going on?' Mark has heard the commotion and arrives to take me into those big wide arms of his; my head finds its natural place on his chest and I can breathe again, so I breathe *him*. He smells like home.

'Annie took against your friend Cameron,' says Mother.

'Cameron?'

'Yes, he said he was a friend of you and your father.'

'He's no friend of mine. Dad!'

Frank waves from the corridor and Mark gestures for him to join us.

'Something the matter?' Frank looks at me, and there's concern there, genuine concern.

'Do you know a Cameron?' asks Mark.

His father thinks for a moment and runs a finger across his lower lip. 'I knew a Clinton once.'

'But a Cameron?'

'Never.' Frank is emphatic. 'Why?'

Mother interjects. 'There was a man here – black hair, a little on the short side – said you invited him.'

'I did no such thing. The guest list is perfectly none of my business.'

Mark raises my head from his chest and runs a tender finger around the sweep of my chin. A loose hair breaks from the nest for the second time today, so he tucks it behind my ear again.

'Guys.' Karen arrives out of breath. 'They're ready for you outside. The car's here.'

'It can wait,' says Mark before turning to me again. 'Whoever he was, he's gone now. Are you OK?'

I nod.

'What's happened?' asks K sheepishly.

Our mother drains the remainder of her drink. 'Wedding crasher. And a bloody good one at that.'

Mark takes my arm and guides me to a bench in the corridor. The world disappears. We remain.

'It's been a long day,' he says, rubbing his eyes with both palms, his tie loosened around his neck. As he sits beside me, the hems of his suit trousers rise up just enough to reveal grey socks with a tiny owl in silhouette. A gift from me in the early days of our romance.

'Well, it's not *exactly* how I'd pictured it.'

Mark looks at me, surprised. 'You mean you *didn't* want a heckling, pissed-as-a-fart mother, a photographer who seems more interested in Laura's cleavage than capturing our day and a strange gatecrasher at your wedding?'

We laugh and I brighten – just enough to subdue the shaking. That man is with me still.

'So we had a little hitch. OK, a few hitches,' says Mark. 'It really doesn't matter. When we fly out tonight, on that plane –'

'I'll be sat beside my husband.'

Mark kisses me gently, tenderly. I can taste the whole story of our relationship on his lips.

'No,' I concede, 'I don't suppose it does – matter, that is.'

Mark and I stand poised, votive offerings, aware of a swelling beyond the door, where friends, family, well-wishers are gathered for our big send-off. It's dark now, pitch-black, and the flood-lights previously trained on the marquee have been switched off. Despite the glass door separating us from the crowd, us from them, the present from the future, the future from the past, I can only sense their existence from the frisson of excitement, the quiet chattering of lips; I can't see a thing. I can barely see Mark, who has slipped his hand inside mine in an act of reassurance or solidarity – I can't say which. Perhaps both.

'I wonder what they have in store,' he says, a new weariness in his voice. 'Pete wouldn't tell.'

I squeeze his hand in response. He squeezes back, tighter still. But there is a nervousness in the gesture, as though this time he is trying to reassure himself, not me. His hand shakes faintly and he shifts his weight from one foot to the other. Is he anxious or uncertain? Have his cold feet arrived too late?

'Ready?' he says.

I want to say *Always*, that I've been waiting for this moment my entire life – the end of the beginning of me and the beginning of the start of us. But I don't; my heart is beating too heavily, my mouth too dry, my legs too weak. So Mark opens the door and guides me on to the stone steps outside.

Everywhere is black, all black, as though the night has wrapped itself around us. There is a pause, followed by the dull beat of a single drum. A cello joins, a violin too. And then, in a flash, a hundred sparklers are thrust into the darkness and the sky is aflame. The light forms a tunnel either side of us, leading us down the drive to a vintage car that waits to speed us to our honeymoon, and the start of our next adventure, together.

Mark pulls me forward and we start running – running so fast I worry I might trip on the stones, so fast that my thoughts stumble over themselves, so fast that the broken tunnel of sparklers becomes a solid whole. There's chanting and yelling and clapping and laughing. The light dances and my vision swims. Here and there I catch a shadowed face I think I recognise – a colleague, a friend perhaps, but I can't be sure, for the light disappears just as quickly as it arrives. Everybody might as well be perfect strangers, but they're my strangers, perfect or otherwise, holding aloft a hundred sparklers just for me, for us, in the name of new beginnings, and love, always love.

When we finally reach the car, my heart molten in my chest, Mark opens the door and looks up, expectantly. He is every bit the man from the train, every bit the man I imagined him to be. And just as I planted my flag in my room that first day at the farmhouse, just as I claimed that space for my own, I realise, as he looks at me through those shiny blue marbles, that I have planted my flag in him.

'Wait,' I say and run back towards the storm of light once more.

I look down at my bouquet, down at tradition, down at a set of rules. Part of me wants to keep it or else to throw it to the ground, but it's too late; a group of women are running forward too, all hands, all hungry. But there is a face among them, just one, and I'm taken aback, for it looks just like *her* were she still with us, were her branch not cut short. I smile at the woman, at the likeness, at the vision, and she smiles back. The past has stepped into the present.

I throw the flowers into the air.

As the bouquet tosses and turns, a ballerina against the sparkler-lit darkness, and the sea of hopefuls edges ever forward to claim their prize, to claim their futures, I watch the once vibrant reds and purples and whites and greens, start to fade. As the bouquet enters its downward arc, the petals come loose, the stems break up, and the whole begins to rot. It rots, and as it rots, it disintegrates as a rocket ship might, having re-entered the earth's atmosphere at too steep an angle. But as it falls further, and the outstretched hands reach through dying embers, there's nothing left to catch. The bouquet has turned to soil, and it is falling between their fingers, falling and falling and falling until it seems as though it might never land. But that brief eternity passes too and the soil rains down on to a box, in a pit, with scores of tumid, bereft faces looking down upon it, and handfuls of dirt raised against the blue sky.

Mark's cousin Fran leaps into the air and catches the intact bouquet before landing clumsily amidst a crush of bodies. She smiles out at me, delighted with her prize.

Laura's hand on my shoulder ushers me towards the waiting car, where Mark stands. But he is not alone. There is a figure there.

Who, I cannot be sure, for the darkness clings to them like a cloak.

Their lips are pressed to Mark's ear and their words seem to cast a pallor across his face. The redness flees his cheeks and the blueness his eyes. The figure recedes and disappears among the crowd as I draw near, and for a moment I wonder if there had been anyone there at all.

But as soon as we step into that car, something changes in him, and I don't know what. It's as though for the past eighteen months, Mark has been looking at a painting, but he has been looking too

45

close – at the detail, the brushstrokes, the gentle dimpling of paint amassed on the surface of a hand, the silken texture of a nose, the surprise of a single spot of black in a sea of white. Up close there was only beauty: terrifying, all-consuming beauty that made it very difficult to imagine anything else, to think that there might have *been* anything else beyond that single scene. But then, at some point, he must have stepped back and allowed himself a moment to consider the whole; he must have removed himself from the frame and seen at a clap that the painting was ugly. Not just in subject and form, but at its essence, in its belly.

To speak of it terrifies me, for I am forced to examine this event, the beginning of the end, in which it all starts to crumble – this edifice of mutual trust and adoration and affection that we have erected steadily. No matter how much I review the day, this day, I can't identify the precise reason the music stopped, but this much I know: Mark waves from the window to Frank and then to Jean, who waves back with a single tear in her eye; I wave to Laura, to K, to the slip of faces that seem to press themselves as one.

But as the car emerges at the end of the driveway into a stream of oncoming headlights, as the figures recede into the night and the waving stops, Mark and I turn to one another, alone at last, the past dead and buried, the future unfurling before us, dancing out into the distance with big, wide, open arms, and we find that we have nothing left to say. Not a word. The day has bound us together, and it has bound our lips too.

When the dark road is lit once more with orange and white lights from airplanes landing and taking off, when the car stops beside the terminal and our chauffeur circles behind to remove our luggage, Mark holds his head in his hands.

'Annie,' he says, as he draws his finger and thumb across his forehead.

I turn to him, eyes wide, waiting for whatever terrible thing he has to say, waiting for him to dispel the magic of the day, to bring the fairy tale of us, of our whirlwind romance, to an inglorious end. And then he says it: sharp, brutal, a surgeon's knife cutting deep and striking bone.

'I think we need to talk.'

PART TWO

THE PROPOSAL

Six months earlier ...

9

Cameron was not a morning person, had never been a morning person, would never be a morning person. And yet his wife would insist on his being awake before 7 a.m. to greet the day.

'Caaaaaam.'

Yes, all right, he thought, as he turned on his pillow, his very soft and very warm pillow, to look at the world sideways, as though for the first time. Squinting, he could just discern the outline of a black sack on the roof of his neighbour's shed. He'd have to have a word with Gary again. But the last time had been such a to-do that he dreaded the thought.

It had been a tough year. Not financially – business was booming and the glut of referrals he'd received in the wake of the Kellerson job would see him through to the New Year. Busy is as busy does. No, it had been a tough year for other reasons. Sophie had suffered her third miscarriage, and it had taken its toll on both of them.

Cameron righted himself with a strength that he did not know his abs still possessed, threw his legs over the edge of the bed – *why did she choose such a bloody high mattress* – and hopped into a soft pair of slippers, which he'd taken the trouble to arrange neatly the night before, side by side, exactly fifteen centimetres from the bed, with only the suggestion of a gap between them. Cameron was a man who liked, no *cherished*, order. As far as he saw it, it was the one and only defence against the gathering forces of chaos. Order was power, order was control. And he liked to be in control – well, with one exception …

'Caaaaaam!'

'Yes, yes. I'm coming.'

'You have a visitor.'

A visitor? Cameron never had visitors, not to his home, and not at this time of the morning. The last visitor he had was a care worker to inform him that his dad had passed away, and she too was a visitor he could have done without. No news given or received before 7 a.m. is good news.

As he pulled his faded blue dressing gown around him and fastened the belt at the waist, he was reminded of a film he had seen not a month before. A man – an insurance broker he thinks, but he can't be sure – opens his front door in the dead of night to be confronted with a masked assailant, who poses no questions that can't be answered with his gun. The insurance guy never sees the morning.

Cameron turned the handle on the bedroom door, and gingerly poked his head over the bannister into the living room below, hoping beyond hope that the film hadn't spilt over into real life. *Don't be silly*, he reasoned. Cameron had always been troubled by a vivid imagination, he knew that. One of these days it was bound to get him into trouble, serious trouble, but hopefully today was not that day.

His head poked ever further over until a face that he dimly recognised, taut and weather-beaten and severely aged since he last clapped eyes on it, beamed up at him. 'Hello, Cam,' it said. 'Long time.'

And at a clap, Cameron found himself back in the changing rooms, back amongst the sweat and bravado, the adolescent braying and intimidatory schoolyard politics. Back in the thick of trauma, and back at the mercy of a predatory pack of prepubescents. Cameron hated school.

He was not a particularly fat child, not a thin one either; not too tall, not too short. His unremarkable stature, coupled with his distinctly average intellect, *should* have conferred upon him an unremarkable status. He *should* have been the boy nobody saw, the one who slipped under the radar, unnoticed by anyone other than his closest coterie of similarly unremarkable friends. And that might well have been the case, were it not for one incident.

A dreary day of rugby practice bled into a very long and very hot communal shower. He must have been dreaming, half-dozing from the heat, for when he remembered himself and came to, a number of the other boys were standing around him, pointing.

Cameron's got a boner, they chanted, as though as part of a ritual – and ritual it was: ritual humiliation. Never mind that it was a perfectly natural, healthy even, bodily response, especially at that age; the boys were out for blood and they were going to get it. And who had been at the head of the pack? Who had raised the first pitchfork with that primitive cry? Who else: Frank.

And so for the rest of his school career, and indeed several years beyond, he was known as BBC: Boner Boy Cameron. It followed him around, weighed him down; a great, big, invisible albatross about his neck, the likes of which the Ancient Mariner had never seen.

Cameron knew then, more than anyone, how a single event had the potential to irrevocably shape the course of one's life. To a degree, though he had done well to break free of that past, to slip that skin, he had lived a life that had been authored for him. Until he met Sophie, sweet, beautiful Sophie. *She's too young for you*, his friends had said at first, *it'll never last*. But some fifteen years later, here they were, and he'd never looked back.

At the foot of the stairs, Cameron found an outstretched hand waiting for him, which he shook. There's no point balling up the past and allowing it to rot and tangle within, he told himself. Who does that help? He'd been through enough in his own life to know that everyone deserved a second chance, even Frank. And from the cut of his clothes and the precision telegraphed in his movements, Cam wagered that Frank was, or had been, a military man. And the military changes a person, one way or the other. It will make you, or it will break you.

'How have you been, Cam?' Frank removed his green tweed cap to reveal a gleaming monk's tonsure. His baldness secretly delighted Cam.

'Really well. Thank you. How long's it been?'

'Forty years.'

'Forty years ...' Cameron became distant and a vast silence opened up in the room. Coming to, he remembered his manners. 'Forgive me – you've met my wife, Sophie.'

The two exchanged an awkward *how-do-you-do*, which did nothing to puncture the quiet.

'Well,' said Sophie finally. 'You must have a great deal to catch up on, so I'll leave you both to it. Let me know what you want to do about breakfast, honey, OK?' With that, she pulled her jacket on, slipped out and peeled off in her red Audi. Cameron had hoped for their usual morning kiss, but Sophie had never been a fan of Public Displays of Affection.

Frank was the first to speak. 'You've done well for yourself, Cam.'

'She's great, isn't she?'

'No, I meant all this –' He gestured around the house, which was not especially big, or flashy, but was, as the most fastidious of interior decorators would have to concede, beautifully appointed.

'Oh.'

'But Sophie's great too.' Frank broadcast an unsettling grin, and then slapped Cameron playfully on the shoulder, which sent him back to that shower, if only for a moment. Frank's grin dissipated; first the arches of the lips, and then the teeth. 'May we?' This time Frank's gesture was to the sofas.

'Please.'

The two men sat opposite one another. Cameron noted that Frank had still to remove his jacket; he clearly didn't intend to stay long.

'I haven't come here for a catch-up. But you probably guessed that.'

'You want something.'

Frank fiddled with his tweed cap, feeding it through his palms as one might a steering wheel. Cameron amused himself with the image of Frank, quite literally, *cap in hand*.

'I need to find someone. *We* need to find someone.'

'Ah.'

'Ah indeed.'

'Look, Frank. I'm very grateful to you for coming but I haven't done that kind of work in years. I don't know who told you –'

'I bumped into Max. He mentioned you'd dabbled in a *side-line*, as he put it. He gave me this.'

Frank waved a little scrap of paper marked with Cameron's address.

'He shouldn't have done that.'

'Perhaps not, but he meant well.'

Cameron stood up abruptly, and for the first time ever in the company of Frank, *he* felt in control. 'I'm sorry you've had a wasted trip but I'm afraid I really can't help.'

Frank looked up with the helpless eyes of a child.

'Please. It's my son ...' Frank trailed off, and his emotion got the better of him. His guard slipped, his steel veneer shattered, and the military man became a civilian.

Cameron stood there uneasily. He feared the next four words to leave Frank's mouth would be *Do you have kids?* But he reminded himself, for the second time this morning, that this was not the movies. And yet he couldn't dismiss the tragedy in Frank's eyes. This man was hurting – for his son or on behalf of his son, he couldn't be sure. But Cameron's father had not taught him to turn his back on suffering. And here was suffering.

With a sigh, Cam lowered himself back on to the sofa opposite, acutely aware of a stiffness gathering in his left leg. He grabbed a notebook and pen from the coffee table before him.

'When you're ready ...' Cameron clicked his pen.

'My son's wife, my daughter-in-law, has gone missing.'

Cameron's pen hovered over the page. He thought for a moment, for a good long moment, and then closed his notebook.

'This is really a job for the police.'

'You don't understand – this was eighteen months ago.'

'Eighteen months?'

'The police have given up the ghost – perhaps justifiably. You see, there's evidence to suggest she may have ... vanished herself.'

'Evidence?'

'A note, written in her own hand.'

'But you doubt that?'

'In it she doesn't just suggest that she's leaving Mark; she suggests she's leaving all of us.'

Cameron noted Frank's use of the present tense. She was clearly very much still alive to him.

'Suicide?'

'Yes. Well, no.' Frank cast around for coherency. 'The implication was subtle, throwaway. But I just don't buy it. It's not the woman I knew.'

'I guess no one ever truly knows quite what someone's going through.'

Frank sighed heavily now.

'It just doesn't add up. Eight years of marriage, a happy marriage, and she just walks out one day, or worse, without so much as a *thanks for the memories*.' He leaned in as though to whisper, but sat back again, bolt upright. 'There's more to it.'

'What makes you say that?'

'Mark's a good kid but –' Frank stopped as though unsure of how to proceed, or else fearful of revealing anything incriminating. 'He's a good kid. Let's leave it at that.'

'You mean your son? Frank, I'm going to need all the facts if I'm to take the job, even if those facts are ... *unpalatable*.'

Frank rubbed his palm nervously across his lips and then once through his fringe of hair.

'Mark has had his fair share of troubles, sure. What boy doesn't, growing up?'

At this, the two shared an awkward look. Rather than acknowledge the elephant of their shared history, they concealed it, wallpapering over the beast.

'Any history of strange behaviour?'

'Strange?'

'Odd. Out of the ordinary.'

'He quit his job. Before she disappeared. He had a steady gig, a surgeon. Very good money, solid career progression, top of his field, and he just upped and left. I guess that's something the marriage shared.' Frank managed a wry smile.

'Anything else?'

'Mark's always been a *thinker*. Introspective, you might call it. But before she disappeared ... Mark became *removed*.'

'As in not returning your calls, removed?'

'As in you could be talking to him but nothing would register, removed. He was somewhere else.'

'Maybe he was unhappy in the marriage, but didn't know how to tell you.'

'Yes ... Jean thinks the same thing.' Frank freed himself momentarily from his train of thought. 'Sorry – Jean's my wife.'

'I see.' Cameron wrote *Mother/Jean* on his pad and underlined it twice.

'A part of me,' Frank ventured, 'small though it is, wonders whether Mark knows a little more than he's letting on.'

Cameron hated to ask, but it was the other elephant in the room, and there was no concealing this one.

'Do you think he killed her?'

In his agitation, Frank accidentally knocked his hand into the Anglepoise lamp stood beside the sofa, 'God, no. What a thing to say.'

'We must consider all lines of enquiry.'

'Yes, but not him. Mark wouldn't –'

'But you've entertained the possibility that she may no longer be with us?'

Frank seemed not to hear, or want to hear, the question. Instead, he fished for a photograph in his jacket, which he then pushed across the coffee table to Cameron, who looked but did not touch – to touch would have been to commit, and he couldn't be sure this was a part of his life that he wished to revisit.

'This her?'

Frank nodded

'She's pretty.'

The photograph showed a blonde woman sitting on a park bench, her head partially thrown back in laughter. She seemed to be looking at something far beyond the camera. Was there a hint of fear in her eyes?

'You can keep that copy, if you like,' said Frank.

'I haven't agreed to this yet.'

Frank looked down at his cap, which had come to a rest over the hook of his knee, and turning it over, he opened a compartment secured with a silver button and removed a roll of notes.

'I was rather hoping this would lead your thinking.'

Cameron looked at the money, which Frank held aloft – his own olive branch, palm frond – between thumb and forefinger.

'It's not much, but you'll get double again on completion. Plus expenses, of course.'

'She meant a lot to you, didn't she, Frank?'

'To all of us. She was a good person, a beautiful soul. Sometimes I wonder … I wonder whether she was too good for Mark, and if that, perhaps, was the problem.'

'How's Mark coping?'

'About as well as could be expected. It devastated him for a long time. There was a moment when we worried if he'd ever move on. And then he did. Just like that.'

'He's seeing someone new?'

'Engaged,' said Frank with a disapproving look. 'They marry in six months.'

'Was there any *crossover*?'

Frank looked shocked. 'No. Not that I'm aware of. But it didn't take him long to get back on the horse. His wife's gone barely four months and he's out on his first date. Nine months later and boom: he's down on one knee, wants to do it all over again.'

Cameron's mind raced, but he did not dare articulate what he was really thinking, not yet. 'Well, I guess we all heal in different ways. We cannot grieve forever.'

Frank nodded solemnly. 'I didn't even know someone could remarry that quickly without a body to divorce, so to speak.'

'It's possible if the surviving spouse applies to the High Court based on a presumption of death. It's usually a seven-year wait, unless –'

'Unless what?'

'Unless there is good reason to believe the missing spouse is dead.'

'The note,' said Frank.

'Yes,' said Cameron. 'The High Court must have believed whatever was in that note to be definitive, or as close to definitive as can be given the circumstances.'

Cameron's supplicant fell silent again, disbelieving.

'So why you, Frank?'

'What do you mean?'

'Doesn't she have parents? Or siblings? Why aren't they out there looking for her?'

'Her mother died when she was young, and she never even knew her father. She has a sister, but they're estranged.'

'For any particular reason?'

'Addict. Only ever came calling for money – that is, until Mark told her to stop coming by the house. But that was years ago. Her family are very much out of the picture.'

Cameron restated the question that seemed to puzzle him most. 'So why you?'

Frank thought for a long moment before his face softened as though he was chasing a memory.

'I never had a daughter, Cam. But if I had, I'd like to think she would have been a little something like her.'

Cameron nodded to himself and stood up again. 'I need some time. Keep your money for now. I'll be in touch if I think I can be of use.'

Frank stood too this time, and secured the cap on his head. He looked ten years younger.

'Good to see you, Cam. I'm sorry about – well, everything.'

Cameron smiled weakly. 'Thank you.'

Frank made for the door and turned back in the hallway. 'You don't have kids, do you, Cam?' *There it was.* 'Not a single photograph of young ones about the place.' He winked. 'You're not the only one with an eye for detail.'

'Thank you for coming, Frank.'

'Well, if you'll forgive me for saying, I think you've dodged a bullet. More trouble than they're worth.'

And with that he left.

10

A wedding is not a beginning, but an end. I see that now. All those wonderful things that we promised to do together, all those adventures – the walking holidays, the wine tastings, the operas, the ballets, the fun – fell away the moment we made our pledges. I, Hope Marie Hedger, take thee Mark Anthony Lane, to be my wedded husband, to have and to hold from this day forward, for better, for worse. Well, this is definitely worse, and I'm not entirely sure now if there was ever a better.

I ran a bath earlier. Salts, a lavender-scented candle, a glass of red wine perched precariously on the lid of the loo seat beside me, while Mark busied himself downstairs with the dinner. I wondered how different my life would have been had I never met him. Would he have been happier? Would I?

Somewhere out there, in a world not too dissimilar to our own, there are versions of us whose orbits never collided, and I would like to meet those people, to see how things might have been. Are we married to other people? Are we alone? Do we have kids? Do we even want them?

I think back to when he proposed. I was dumbstruck. We'd been together ten glorious months. There were ups and downs, but he loved me – of that I was certain. Ever the romantic, he whisked me away to Rome, to the cathedrals and late-night light shows, and then proposed to me on the sweep of the Spanish Steps as a lone violin player packed up his stall for the evening. He was a different man then, and he is a different man now.

The warm scent of cacio e pepe joined me in the bath. There was a time when Mark would have joined me too, slipped in behind me, run long fingers all down my back, kissed the nape of my neck. Like he did in Rome. But not now.

Any yet I must remember. I must. It wasn't always like this. It wasn't. He was once the man I knew him to be, the man my mother adored before she passed. She could rest easy, she said, knowing I had someone caring for me. If he cares still, he doesn't show it. I wonder if he has forgotten how.

Dinner's ready, called a voice from the foot of the stairs. But I didn't want to answer, for I knew what awaited me down there: a man who is no longer my husband.

So instead, I closed my eyes, shut them tight against the world, and I slipped beneath the bubbles. Would he even notice I was gone?

11

'Come on, just let me set you up with him. He's great – own flat, stable career, easy on the eye and, crucially, sane. Very sane. Scout's honour.' Laura raised her left hand to her temple.

'He'll call, I know he will.'

'You gave him your number weeks ago, and nothing ... What makes you think he'll call?'

'A feeling.'

'Oh, good, a feeling. And there was me starting to worry.' Laura spread herself across the full length of the sofa in a playful fit of histrionics. 'A *feeling*, she says. For fuck's sake.'

'Oh ye of little faith.'

A beat and Laura sat bolt upright again, a quizzical look flashing across her features. 'What aren't you telling me?'

'Nothing.'

'Hardly. Your face is betraying you; you're smiling.'

'Am not.' I fought hard to supress the grin that was working its way through the tiny muscles in the corners of my mouth.

'Nice try. Come on – spill.'

'OK. Well ... And don't be mad ... he may or may not have already called.' I braced myself for Laura's reaction.

'Bullshit.' She looked at me long and hard.

'I'm seeing him Sunday.'

Laura, exasperated, returned to her supine position, and stared at the faded concentric patterns of the Artex ceiling. From time to time, when I was bored or despairing, I liked to do the same; I would imagine myself as a tiny ant in a giant, crazy-paved hedge maze of Artex. Sometimes there would be a route out; other times, every exit led to a dead end, every path a full stop. I was trapped.

'Then why all the secrecy?' asked Laura after some time.

'Because I know you don't approve.'

Laura wrinkled her nose. 'It matters very little whether I approve or not. Annie has always done what Annie has wanted to do. This time will be no different. Though I will say this: call me crazy but it's probably best not to date people you meet at therapy. Rule 1, if you like.'

I hated to admit it, but she had a point.

'Technically, he never made it to therapy. The car park is as close as he got. Besides, we met before; you know that.'

Laura stifled a laugh. 'Yeah, I do. Does he?'

'Not yet.'

A silence passed between us.

'What? I don't want him to think I'm a stalker.'

'I fear that ship has sailed.'

'Not my fault the Fates are smiling down on us.'

'God, you're so fucking smug. It's irritating.'

'If it helps, I know a great guy – own flat, stable career, easy on the eye and, crucially, sane. Very sane. Scout's honour.' I went to raise my hand to my temple but Laura threw a cushion at me. 'All right, I deserved that.'

Laura laughed and scooped up her phone from the floor. She held it above her head and scrolled endlessly, as I lay there listening to the wind force its way through the narrow gap in the sash window.

'OK, so where is Lover Boy taking you?'

'It's a surprise.'

'For me or for you?'

'Both.'

'Fine, well, I won't probe. Just be careful.'

'Of what?'

'There are a lot of strange men out there.'

'Strange women, too,' I added.

'And what finer poster children than us.'

'Speak for yourself.'

Laura leant over and shoved her phone in my face

'I've just matched with this guy,' she said. 'James, investment banker, from Balham. Do you think he's the sort that might try to milk a cat?'

We met at 4 p.m. in Holland Park on a crisp Sunday in spring. It was Mother's Day. I sat there in a long black coat with a faux-fur collar, on a bench at the southern end of the park, my feet alive with nervous anticipation as I watched children playing on the swings opposite. The sight inspired in me a deep longing.

I'd spent my whole life convinced that I was not cut out to be a mother, that any child would be cursed to have me for a protector, for a provider. As far as I was concerned, I had no *maternal instincts*. And yet in the year or so that preceded my first date with Mark, I'd started to look upon kids, on my having them someday, very differently. You could easily chalk up this newfound ache to the ticking biological clock but it wasn't that simple. My life seemed to be missing something that a romantic relationship could not account for.

And so as I looked upon the kids opposite with the newly appointed eye of a prospective mother, I found myself pining, if only briefly, for my very own Mother's Day. If not with Mark – the second rule of dating, according to Laura, is under no circumstances to mention children – then with someone. But not just *anyone*. I didn't want kids for the sake of having them, I wanted them as the ultimate expression of love.

In my reverie, I barely noticed the man who had sat down beside me, barely noticed the liberally sprayed oud or the coffee that he sipped on decisively. I barely noticed any of this – not until he spoke.

'This is one of my favourite places in the world,' he said softly, slowly, almost wistfully, and in a manner that commanded attention. 'When anyone thinks of the great London parks, it's always Hyde or Regent's or Richmond, at a push. But they never think of Holland Park. Some of the best things in life fly under the radar.'

He turned to me then and I saw the sadness in his eyes had yet to shift.

'You look nice,' he said.

'I know,' I replied, my tongue planted firmly in my cheek.

'I wish I had your humility.'

'Don't,' I said, 'it's a real drag.'

The blackness in his eyes shifted slightly and he laughed. He actually laughed.

'Shall we?' He jumped to his feet and held his arm out for me, so I took it.

We walked up past the cricket grounds and tennis courts, past the hordes of dog walkers with their pampered Kensington pooches, up past the bombed shell of Holland House and open-air opera marquee, round to the Lord Holland statue, and back down and around through the giant chess sets where yet more kids gathered and jostled and cajoled. We talked little, except to comment on some of the more rambunctious dogs (or kids) and their extroverted owners (parents), and we shared a wealth of silence, comfortable silence. I felt, in that moment, that I had known this man for a very long time. I think he felt the same.

'I don't mind telling you that I was pretty nervous this morning,' he said. 'You know ... Dating again. It's been a while.'

'They haven't changed it, if that's what you're worried about.'

'It?'

'Sex,' I replied. 'Though, I'm sorry to report it's no longer a *lie back and think of England* affair.'

Mark went balloon-red.

'God, you're easy,' I commented.

'I might be forgiven for making the same observation.'

I punched him on the arm playfully. *Was he flirting?*

'We should pay our respects to the peacocks,' he said, as we stood outside the charming stone and glass Orangery. A wedding reception was taking place inside. The bride was beaming.

'The what?'

'Peacocks.'

I must have still looked confused, for he grabbed my hand in a rush of pure electricity and led me to a small enclosure. The sign read: *Kyoto Garden*.

Beyond was the most enchanting sight I had ever seen. Water cascaded down carefully staggered plateaus of rock, down between a riot of colour – reds, lilacs, pastel pinks and greens – past perfectly manicured lawns into a great pond where giant koi carp swam in and out of the ripples of water. Stone lanterns and Japanese maple trees ringed the pond as silent sentries; adventure playgrounds for a scurry of grey squirrels. The garden was an oasis of calm and tranquillity in a city that was otherwise an incessant, ever-revolving wall of noise. It seemed to me that nothing very bad could happen to you here.

We took a seat on a bench looking out over the western fringe of the pond.

'It's lovely,' I said. 'But I don't see any peacocks.'

Mark put his finger to his lips. *Shh*.

We listened together, two microphones held up to the static, and amidst the rushing water, amidst the whispers of wind through leaves, came a drum-roll-like rustle, followed by an ear-shattering cry.

Two kids, no older than five, came tearing around the corner in a tangle of limbs, running from an unseen danger. A peacock tore around the corner after them, but their father was too quick; he scooped them both up in his arms and shooed the waspish bird with his foot. Mark laughed as I winced. The peacock retreated.

'They generally like to be left alone,' said Mark.

'I can relate to that.'

'You don't strike me as the strong, silent type.'

'Strong, yes; silent, no. But we all need a little time to recharge.'

'Well, this is where I come to recharge,' he said. 'Some days I need it more than others.'

'It does seem the sort of place I could come and have a good cry,' I joked, but Mark wasn't laughing.

He nodded absently and ran his thumb down the line of his jaw. He was thinking about something. And whatever that something was, it had prompted a black cloud to hover over him and threaten rain. The mood changed, and I could feel it, like a sudden drop in temperature or a lift speeding downwards. The floor had come away from us both. He seemed at that moment a man with more on his mind than in it.

'Are you OK?' I asked.

'I —' He rubbed his hands together as you might to generate heat, but it wasn't exactly cold. 'Sorry. It's just the last time I was here, I was with —'

Here he stopped but I didn't wish to press. I placed my hand in his, a gentle reassurance, a thumbs-up across a playing field.

'Whatever it is, it's none of my business — not yet.' I laughed, and this time he laughed too, sort of.

'No,' he said. 'I've been keeping it inside for too long, and it's done me no good there. Besides, maybe it'll make more sense to you than it does to me.'

So he told me, and the edifice crumbled.

He was married before, which hardly surprised me. Mark was a handsome man.

'For how long?' I asked.

Eight years, he said, but it felt as though they had known each other for far longer. I asked after her — the woman before, the woman to which every future love interest would be compared. He seemed reluctant to answer at first; perhaps he feared that in revealing her, he would be gifting me a peek behind the curtain, a look at the barometer, a look at the test itself.

'You don't have to talk about her if you don't want to,' I assured him.

This seemed to do the trick. Men are funny creatures: the more you want something from them, the more you push and demand it, the more stubborn they become and the less likely you are to get to the crux of the matter. Yet feign indifference and you uncork the well. They'll often give you more than you ever wanted, or needed, to know. Mark, in this respect, was every man. It disappointed me a little.

And so as he spoke, freely and at length. I learned that she was blonde, a yoga instructor — though not originally, she trained as a nurse, which is how they met. She was loving, caring, a smile that could light up a room and banish the darkness.

'She wanted kids, really wanted them,' he said, 'and she would have been a terrific mother.'

My stomach lurched. The more he told me about her, the bigger the shoes to fill.

'And you?' I asked.

'What about me?'

'Kids. Were they on your vision board?'

Mark smiled, sort of. The joke had fallen flat.

'I wanted a family too; I just wasn't sure whether I'd make a very good father. I guess it doesn't matter,' he said. 'For one reason or another, it didn't happen for us.'

She was close with Mark's family, I learned, but had no real family of her own. She was lean, athletic, always running somewhere or other, always plugged into her bloody music, always existing firmly within herself. She wore her hair in a ponytail because she thought it made her cheekbones stand out more. I learnt about each and every freckle on her face; he had mapped them all.

'So what happened? If you don't mind me –'

'She left.'

'For another man?'

'No idea. She walked out one day last year and I haven't heard from her since. It's as though she vanished into thin air. No money missing from our account, her credit cards inactive. She left me a note, but that's it. Didn't even come back to collect her things.'

I didn't know what to say. I wanted to put the cork back in.

'So that's why you were there, that evening, at the Richmond Centre ...'

'Yes. Though I couldn't bring myself to go in. I've found it very hard to share this with my own family, let alone a group of strangers who all have their own crosses to bear.' I was thankful that he didn't enquire after mine. 'I just –' He hung his head in his hands and tapped his forehead rhythmically. 'I just don't understand.'

'Why she left?'

Mark drew his long, slender fingers through the wisps of hair above his ears.

'I mean, things were tough at the time. We were arguing, more than I care to admit. And work had me in theatre at all hours. I wasn't the perfect husband, far from it. I would snap at her over the smallest things, but I was tired, and I ... Why didn't she try to talk to me?'

'Maybe she didn't feel she could.'

'I was her husband,' he cried out involuntarily, prompting a passer-by to stop and mouth to me, *You OK?*

I had started to wonder at that moment if this had all been a terrible mistake, if Mark was ready, if he was the man I thought he was, or if I had forced upon him an image of perfection that he couldn't possibly live up to. But before the thought had a chance to gain purchase and reach its logical conclusion, Mark remembered himself.

'I'm sorry. Again.' He laughed absently. 'I've been out of the dating game for a while.'

I could have resented him for opening up quite so much, but I didn't. Instead I told him there was nothing to apologise for; that it was a huge thing, a life-altering event over which lesser men would have shuttered themselves away for an eternity; how brave he was to be dating again, and so soon. He bridled at the last comment. I don't think he'd considered for a minute that he was, in fact, moving on, or else taking the first step on a very long, very uncertain path. And I could see that it scared him, for to move on meant leaving eight years behind.

'So can you top that?'

'Oh, no,' I said. 'I think you've cornered the market on depressing stories. You win.'

'I'd like to say it was a closely fought contest, but –'

'But what?'

'But you give very little away. There could be a lifetime of horrors in there.' He pointed to my head, 'And I'd never know.'

Just then my phone vibrated in my pocket. It was Laura.

And ...?

Mark saw, his face a Cheshire cat. 'Well, don't leave the woman hanging.'

I replied, quite deliberately, in full view of Mark.

Jury's out.

'Right,' he beamed, 'We can't have this. I have some jurors to impress.'

We walked up and out the northern end of the park, along past Notting Hill Gate, and on to Portobello, where the last of the Sunday traders were packing away their stalls.

As we wandered the fast-emptying streets, I thought of Hugh Grant and Julia Roberts in that film and wondered if their romance had transcended the cameras, the set, the screen; I thought of the race riots and the carnivals, of Chesterton and Rachman, of the wide-eyed Influencers who posed in the name of social media outside the variegated pastel townhouses and the brunch spots *du jour*; but mostly I thought of Dad, and how he had brought us here many years ago, me and K, the heavens open, one umbrella between the three of us; how we had fought over the last slice of chocolate cake in a rundown café off Golborne Road; how Dad had turned to me and pretended to pull a fifty-pence piece from behind my ear to K's amazement and my embarrassment; and how, when it was time to go, time to catch the train back to Kent, he paused in the doorway of a mother-and-baby shop, where, suspended in the window on a small white hangar, there was a tiny blue jumper with a pink 'J' embroidered on the front.

Eventually, Mark and I found a pub along the main drag, and settled into a quiet booth in the corner. The hours passed and we discussed just about everything: religion, politics, life, love, the universe. He told me about work, how he'd quit the hospital to spend a little time on himself, how a series of shrewd rental investments and the odd bit of cash-in-hand garden work continued to sustain him. The latter, he did not for the money but for the love of the great outdoors. It gave him a space to think, to recentre. The stress of surgery had become a distant memory, and there it would stay. For now.

'And you?' he asked with genuine interest.

'Me? I lecture disaffected, hungover students on the ancients – Greece, Rome. I'm sure they all blur into one the-morning-after a vodka-fuelled night.'

'Well, if it helps, I'd sign up to your module.'

'You would?'

He smiled cheekily. 'I said I'd sign up; I didn't say I'd go.'

I thought I'd never get bored with his voice, of its warming baritone, its grit and poise. He told me about his fishing trips with his best friend, Pete, who sounded, for all intents and purposes a bit of a lad. But they grew up together, he said, and intimated that, contrary to popular belief, often you cannot choose your friends; that we're simply thrown together with people at random. I disagreed. I said we have a choice in all things and that we can choose friendship just as easily as we can reject it. And quite right too, for often it is friendship, not romance, that redeems us; sometimes friends can heal in a way that a partner cannot.

My phone vibrated again.

It's a date, Annie, not Twelve Angry Men. Have Fun x

As we talked, I started to open up a little, which unnerved me, for there was always the distinct possibility that I could let something slip – that I could allow something out into the world with no way of putting it back again. I told him about the university, about the farm and how exciting the move had been. I told him about the stream; the tyre swing slung from the old oak tree; and *The Velveteen Rabbit*, which he hadn't heard of. *No matter*, I said, there are plenty of other books. We talked briefly of Mother – he thought it odd I called her Mother too. He said he could hear the capitalisation in my voice.

And then, inevitably, conversation turned to Dad. *You haven't mentioned him*, he said. But I deflected and changed the subject; I wasn't ready to share that. He noticed but was too polite to say. I decided then that he was the gentleman I'd known him to be. He was gentle.

'Where are you based?' asked Mark.

'London during the week; Kent on the weekends, usually.'

'Well, la-di-da, Miss Two-Homes.'

'It's not like that. God, you must think me spoilt.'

'Not a chance,' he smiled. 'Do I get to visit?'

'Maybe.'

'Maybe, huh?'

'If you behave yourself …'

By the time we'd left, the streets were a Munch sketch: dark and desolate. He walked me back to the tube through a warren of side streets, us stopping every now and again to admire the looming Georgian buildings with their stucco-white frontages and their occasional Juliet balconies. I imagined then the view from above – what anyone might have seen looking down on us, two tiny wayward specks in their long coats, longing to connect but neither quite brave enough to break cover.

When we came to Westbourne Grove, by the roundabout in front of the church, he held me under the strength of a street light, and we kissed. I melted into him, and he into me. I went on to tiptoes and his hands found their place on the small of my back.

A homeless woman walked past at that moment. *Young love*, she muttered to herself, before moving on. *Yes*, I wanted to reply. *I think it might be.*

Mark drew back and held my head between his hands.

'Come back with me,' he said. There was an urgency in his eyes. 'You don't have to think of England. You can think of me instead.'

'I want to –'

'Here comes the "but".'

'*But* I have an early lecture tomorrow.'

'An early lecture,' he repeated. 'She has an early lecture.' The whisky still had him in its grip.

'Next time?' I offered.

He kissed me again. 'Next time.'

I like to imagine that Mark went home that evening with a little skip in his step; that as he drew his bath, poured himself a nip of whisky and carefully set his favourite Leonard Cohen LP on his record player, his mind turned with persistent and alarming regularity to me, to our wonderful, whirlwind afternoon together; that even from our very first date, he knew I was the woman who could, if not replace her wholesale, then plug the gaping hole left by the woman before; that, perhaps, I could begin to make him happy again.

I like to imagine that he turned out the light that evening, excited, for the first time in months, for the future, for our future, and that as he turned over on his pillow, to look at the cold, empty pillow beside him, the last reminder of a cold and empty love, he reached down under the covers, under the soft silk of his boxers, and masturbated over the thought of me. For that night, as *I* slipped under the duvet and turned out the light and clamped a warm pillow between my thighs, I masturbated over the thought of him, and the chance that he could soon be mine.

71

12

Cameron couldn't remember the last time he was ill. He was, even in his advanced years, a fit and sprightly man; which was just as well really, because he hated hospitals, all hospitals. Each and every visit set his teeth on edge. It was the possibility, he supposed, that one day he would enter one and never truly leave. And so it was with some considerable anxiety that Cameron set foot in the Royal Free, not in the service of his own health – he had to keep reminding himself of this fact – but in pursuit of a missing woman.

After Frank had left his house that day, Cameron, for reasons he would struggle to explain if asked, found himself drawn to the photograph of the young blonde woman on the bench. *What had prompted that fear in her eyes? And what could cause a person to walk out on a long and seemingly happy marriage?* It didn't add up.

Frank was delighted, of course, when Cameron called to accept the job; so delighted he doubled his fee from the outset.

'That's more than I could possibly acc—'

'Nonsense,' said Frank. 'I have it on good authority that you're worth every penny.'

'I don't know what to say.'

'*Thank you* is usually a good start.'

Silence reigned on Cameron's end of the line. He was grateful – for both the money and the vote of confidence – but he was not in the business of genuflecting, not any more.

'For the price, I'd like weekly reports,' said Frank.

'Of course.'

'And let's try to keep this between us. I don't want to worry Jean.' More white noise before Frank rounded off the call. 'Bring her back, Cam.' A pause, pregnant this time. 'If she's still out there.'

Those words rang in his ear like church bells as he entered the Royal Free that day and made his way to reception.

'Forgive me but is there someone I can speak to about Dr Lane? Mark Lane?'

The receptionist, lost in a hail of typing, did not look up, which bothered Cameron. It shouldn't have, but it did.

'Miss ...'

'It's Mrs actually,' she said curtly, still typing, her angular head focused on the screen in front of her.

'Well, Miss, Mrs, Mr, whatever, I'd be grateful if –'

'Down the hall, second door on the right.' The receptionist waved her arm as though directing traffic. 'Ask for Mr Rahman. He's on break.'

As he made his way past a mass of bodies without beds, Cameron realised, for the first time that morning, that Sophie didn't talk much last night. She didn't kiss him goodnight, she didn't press into him in the dawn hours, and she didn't run her hand down the length of his leg. *Was she ... angry with him?* Yes, he probably, arguably, should have consulted her before taking the job, but he was his own man. Well, except when he wasn't.

Down the hall, Cameron knocked on the prescribed door. No answer. Having knocked a second time, and having distinctly heard the movements of a person, or persons, on the other side, he decided to try his luck. He inched open the door, and, sure enough, there sat a man in full blue scrubs, a white surgical mask slung low around his jaw.

'Who are you?'

'Forgive the intrusion ... I'm a friend of Dr Lane.'

The man looked surprised. He thought for a moment, took a final sip of the coffee in his hand and closed the newspaper resting on his crossed legs. 'In that case you'd better come in.'

'Mr Rahman, I presume?'

The man extended his hand in welcome to Cameron, who looked at the hand but didn't meet it with his own. 'Usman.'

'I'd rather not if you don't mind. Hospitals … Germs …'

'Understood. My wife won't even look at me until she's fetched the pressure hose.'

The two men shared a smile.

'Please, take a seat. Though I should warn you I'm wanted in theatre shortly.'

'You're a surgeon too?'

Usman nodded. 'Orthopaedics.' Frank must have drawn a blank, for he added, 'Spinal – that kind of thing.'

'Yes, of course,' said Frank. But there was no *of course*. He hadn't the foggiest. 'It's about Mark.'

'Yes, how is he? It's been a while – haven't seen him since he left.'

'He's –' Cameron hated this bit: the subterfuge, the lies. '– not great.' But they were necessary evils.

'I'm sorry to hear that. He did seem to be … struggling in his last few months here.'

'Because of his wife's disappearance?'

'Well, yes … and no. It started before then. We all knew he had a problem. Well, not everyone.'

'Problem?'

'Sorry, *how* do you know Mark exactly?'

Cameron found himself on the operating table. One false word and the good doctor, one of his few leads in a case that was surely littered with dead ends, would close up like a clam defending its pearl.

'His father and I go way back.' Cameron thought this might be enough, but the man's silence said otherwise. He continued: 'I've known Mark since he was a little boy; practically part of the family.' The second statement was harder to utter. Cameron hoped Rahman hadn't noticed him stifle a swallow as the words fought their way out.

The surgeon eyed his questioner with suspicion, but something in the way Cameron held himself – with a fulsome confidence that belied his great untruths – lowered Rahman's guard.

'Mark's drinking, mainly. At an early op for a road traffic accident, Mark showed up in a complete state and –' Rahman checks himself, cuts the story short. 'I sent him home. The late scrub-ins were one thing, but the booze ... He could have been struck off.'

'But he wasn't?'

'No. But if he had stayed ... If he hadn't have left when he did ...'

Rahman became aware of his interrogator once more. 'How do you know Mark's father?'

Cameron's thoughts flashed back to the showers – boys laughing, pointing, baying, closing in as one. Wild dogs circling wounded prey. 'We were at school together,' he said finally.

Rahman laughed. 'Poor you. By all accounts his dad was a grizzled old warthog.'

'He was,' agreed Cameron. *He is*, he wanted to add.

'But you didn't come here to talk about Frank.'

Cameron shook his head.

'So what can I do for you?' asked Rahman, checking his watch.

'I'm trying to track down Mark's wife.'

The doctor's cheeks filled and then expelled a violent blast of air. 'Good luck.'

'You don't think she's out there?'

'Oh, she's out there all right. Who hasn't, in their more fanciful moments, or after a particularly bad day, contemplated a brief break from their partner? The difference is, she went all in. Not so much a break as an amputation.' He smirked. 'And the lengths she went to ... she doesn't want to be found. The police couldn't manage it.'

'I'm not the police.'

There followed an uncomfortable silence, which Rahman ended with a second look at his watch. 'Two more minutes.'

'Did you ever meet?'

'Sure. She was a nurse here, several years back now, and a very good one – friendly, well-liked. She left after a while, of course; started teaching one of those stretching classes.'

'Yoga?'

'Might have been.' Rahman mused to himself, 'I guess you could say Mark had a type.'

'More specifically?'

The surgeon leant in. 'Nurses. She wasn't the first, and she wasn't the last.'

'Mark was having an affair?' Cameron made a note on his pad.

'Look, it's really not my place to say, but by all accounts it wasn't the happiest marriage.'

'How so?'

Mr Rahman took a deep breath. His instinct was clearly to conceal, to maintain a veneer of professionalism, as he'd been trained to do.

'Please,' petitioned Cameron. 'It could really help.'

'Mark said they'd been struggling to conceive.'

A sharpness ran through Cameron's gut. This was all heading a little too close to home now. He had known that struggle himself, had held Sophie's hand as she received the news that all was lost, had watched her destroyed in a word.

'I believe there was even talk of surrogacy, adoption, potentially. I don't know the details. Mark gave very little away.'

Calling Mr Rahman to Room 5. Mr Rahman to Room 5. Thank you.

'I'm sorry,' he said, and stood up sharply. 'I need to go.' Just before he left the room, he added, 'Talk to his best friend, Pete. Never liked that guy, but he could probably tell you more than me.'

The door closed and Cameron was left alone in the break room.

I should call Sophie, he thought.

13

1st March

I'm not sure what's worse: that we haven't made love in eight weeks or that we've stopped trying. Gone are the days when our bed was our home, when Mark made me his home. When he would rush in from work, lift me up so high that my hair might brush the ceiling; when I might wrap my legs around his waist, knot them together behind his back. Gone are the days when we tried to make something more than love, something greater. Gone are the days when we tried, when we tried to grow our love into a family.

Each month, when my fertility was at its peak, Mark and I would find stolen moments to try for the child that never came. Lunchtimes, when we'd each rush home from work for five minutes before having to rush back out again. Evenings, when the romance of the occasion would be lost to its necessity. Sunday mornings, when the distant sound of the church bells would soundtrack our bodies colliding. But as the months passed and once the doctors had confirmed what we'd long suspected, the intimacy, our intimacy, left this house for good. I had seemingly lost my hunger, and he his. The shame didn't help, of course; the heavy burden of failure we each felt. The clock that was once ticking had now stopped at two seconds to midnight. Our forever happiness was just moments away, but forever out of reach.

I suggested IVF. No, he said. He'd seen first-hand the strain this could put on a couple. He didn't want that for me; he didn't want that for us. We'd been through enough already.

Adoption perhaps? No words this time. He just shook his head. But I knew what he was thinking: it would never be his, could never be his. Not really.

And so we continue in this stasis. No longer trying and forgetting how to. I still want the child that never came, but most of all I want Mark and the intimacy that we once shared. Our bodies may have failed us, but I refuse to allow us to fail one another. There is – there was – too much goodness here.

Last night I came home early, cooked him his favourite – beef bourguignon with all the trimmings – decanted two glasses of Beaune and slipped into a little black dress. I turned in front of the hallway mirror and thrilled to see the soft, weightless silk shimmer its way down and over the arch of my bum. I wore that dress on our third date, but it didn't stay on long. Three hours later and it took up permanent residence on the floor of his bachelor flat. I don't think I've worn it since.

I was lighting the candles in the dining room when I heard the familiar jangle of keys in the door. He was home. While the lock turned and a footstep ventured into the darkened hallway, I positioned myself in the door frame of the dining room, the candles behind casting me in silhouette. I was in character: the alluring homemaker, the sexy mistress, the devilish wife of a dear friend. I was willing to be whatever, whomever, he wanted me to be. Just like the old days, the good old days, when our passion burnt as bright as the candles.

Hey, honey, I said, as I leant back seductively against the door jamb. I hoped that the light behind might reveal that I wasn't wearing any underwear. That I was ready for him. That I had been ready for eight long weeks.

Mark entered the sitting room and stared across at me. A look of disdain crept into his tired face. He drew near through the dark, inched closer to study the scene before his eyes. The closer he came, the stronger the scent of alcohol. The stronger the scent of perfume too. Not mine.

What on earth are you wearing? he said finally, as he pushed past me into the dining room. You're not twenty-five any more.

14

'No. You have to do it like this!' Karen crouched gingerly by the creek at the foot of the farm and began to place sticks fortified with mud in the centre. 'Dad knew how to do it.'

I let the comment go.

'OK, let me try.'

'You'll ruin it,' said K.

'I won't. Give me one.'

Karen stood up straight and looked from her hand to me, from me to her hand.

'Please?'

'If you ruin it, we'll have to start all over again,' she said, handing me a stick caked in mud. '*And* you'll owe me ice cream. Chocolate ice cream.'

'I best be careful then.'

Her little eyes narrowed at me as I hovered above the stream and gently started to place a newly mud-caked stick with several of its wet kin. *Steady now. Steady.*

The farm was a darker place after his passing. A long black shadow grew from the large oak tree by the hawthorn hedge, down past the weir, and trailed all the way up the gently sloping hill to the farmhouse itself. A pall lay over all that we did, all that we were, and that pall wouldn't shift; the shadow remained for months. It swallowed us whole.

Mother took to her bed the day after he died. Karen and I tried, as much as two kids could, to console her, but she was beyond reach, seemingly unaware that we too might need consoling. And so it was that we sought to entertain ourselves with games, if only to take our minds off the deafening absence and not look up and acknowledge the black sheet draped above our heads. We knew it was there, but we knew it was the thing we must not look at. The moment Mother had looked up was the moment she decided her bed was the best place for her.

As I went to place the stick, K's eyes burning holes in the back of my head, I must have come in at an awkward angle for no sooner had I lowered it into the cluster than the tower of cards crumbled and the makeshift dam fell apart. The creek continued unstirred.

K was thunder. She balled her little fists so tight that she might have crushed a walnut and stamped her foot so hard that a jet of mud splattered up my cream dress.

'Now look what you've done! It's only a game, K!'

Karen knew at once she'd gone too far. She began to cry.

'Oh, K, I'm sorry,' I said, pulling her in for a hug. 'I didn't mean to snap.'

Her small body folded into mine. 'He said he'd never leave.'

'He didn't have a choice. You know that, right?'

I felt the weight of her head bury into my shoulder.

Perhaps sensing we were all that we had now, we held each other. Not a molecule or an atom or a gluon existed in the space between. We held each other in a way we never had before. The stream bubbled on, the long grass bowed in the breeze, and the light began to fade until all that remained was the dim glow from the canopy of stars above our heads.

'Girls! What are you two doing down here? Dinner is almost ready.'

Soon after Mother's Black Period hit, we had a visitor to the farm – a visitor who came in on the wind and never really left. But Mary Poppins she was not. There was a hardness to her, a steeliness that made Mother, by contrast, appear a kindly Cistercian monk. Having met our grandma, you could forgive Mother her foibles entirely. As K and I were raised in our mother's shadow, so too was our mother raised in hers.

Grandma valued many things – cleanliness, godliness, good manners, obduracy, resourcefulness – but gentleness was not one of them. And yet what we saw as hard, Grandma saw as durable.

You either get tough or get torn. And make no mistake about it: this world cares not a bean for your suffering. She loved us though, in her own funny way, I'm sure of it. Loved us more than perhaps we understood at the time. As I've grown older and the years have started to hang on me like pleats in a silk skirt, I've come to realise that some people love through the carrot and some through the stick.

'Just look at the state of your dress.' She was angry, really angry. 'Is this your doing, Karen?'

K looked sheepish as she wiped away the last of her tears. Grandma didn't much care for tears – didn't understand them, didn't know what to do with them.

'Well, I –' Grandma looked at us both, raised her best scalding-finger, and then slowly lowered it again. The redness blooming in her cheeks withered and the veins firing at her temples lost their charge. It was as if she'd decided we'd been through enough. And in that moment she taught me something valuable: sometimes love is letting those you care about get away with murder. 'Come on, let's get you cleaned up.'

As we made our way up the hill to the house, my eyes fell to the neighbouring field. There so far hidden by the rope of trees that lined our own farm, and now having shed their leaves for the slow crawl into winter, squatted a great stone structure, unmolested save for a lick of white paint on its southern wall, which some landowner had thought to apply many decades ago. Its wide, solid brick frame was broken up only by two slim, horizontal, rectangular openings, which you could be forgiven for mistaking for eyes.

K stopped too, having followed my gaze. 'Nan, what's that?'

Grandma drew up several paces in front and turned, her hands buried deep in her apron.

'What's what?'

K's extended finger drew an arrow to our sight line.

'That's a pillbox.'

'For medicine?' asked K. 'To make people better?'

Grandma laughed, for what felt like the first time. 'No, to make them dead.'

'Who?' I asked.

'The Nazis, of course.' She said it so matter-of-factly. *Nazi*. I'd heard the word at school, and always in connection with *a very bad man*, but, in truth, I didn't have the faintest idea what a Nazi was. Not then.

'Can we go play there tomorrow?' asked K.

Grandma shook her head. 'It's dirty and dangerous. You must never go in there. You hear me?'

K nodded and Grandma grabbed her hand as they walked on towards the warm glow of the house. But I didn't follow. Instead, I stood there transfixed by this brick monolith, this bit of history, this slice of the past that sat in our own time, out of time, until, having stood there long enough, I saw the field, our farm and our lives there as a piece of paper that had been written on, and written over, time and time again. The thought was at once terrifying and liberating. And still the pillbox faced me, silent.

'Annie. I'm going to count to three. Ooooone. Twooooo –'

'Coming!'

The house had changed since Grandma's arrival.

'How is anyone to move on when the past is everywhere,' she said as soon as she first set foot inside. The sentiment sounded familiar. 'No, this won't do at all.'

So down came the whimsical ornaments that Dad had picked up from flea markets the length of France as he travelled with school friends in his youth; down his territorial army service medals that adorned the mantelpiece above the open fire; and down his watercolour drawings of the deeper, wooded recesses of the farm that once hung serenely in the hallway. We'd always teased Dad over these, but they were actually quite good, if quaint, and they made him happy. He would paint and he would be happy. They were his escape, until he managed the real thing.

In their place, up went reproduction prints from the Arts and Crafts scene that Grandma so loved; up went a muted triptych of the Madonna and Child; and, crucially, up went the blinds. As Mother's Black Period took hold, light filled the house once more, even if it couldn't quite find its way into her heart.

When Grandma had finished, the house had taken on a different energy. One phase of our life had been snipped off, and another, brighter one was taking root; only I didn't know it at the time. Everything was changing, and I was scared, we were scared.

'Karen, have you set the table?' Grandma was standing over the range, stirring a vat of soup. The steam was turning her face a deep beetroot.

'Yes, Nanny.'

'Good. Annie, go fetch your mum.'

K and I looked at one another in a stunned silence. We hadn't seen Mother in two weeks. She wasn't coming; we both knew that.

Grandma dropped the wooden spoon into the pan and untied her apron. 'I guess I have to do everything myself around here. Annie,' she shouted back from the stairs. 'Stir that soup, you hear?'

And so I stirred.

Five minutes later, Grandma returned, alone.

'Take your seats, girls. We have a guest of honour this evening.'

This time K's mouth fell open just enough to see the small chip on her tooth where Tim Heeley had clocked her with a toy truck in preschool. Her lower lip had swelled to the thickness of a Hollywood starlet.

'Go on. Places.'

As we sat there, picking at the loose threads on the bamboo table mats, we heard a foot on the stairs, which, had we not been waiting, had our attentions been trained on anything else, we might never have heard at all. The stair creaked softly, and the source of the weight paused, pondered. A second, a third step followed. Then nothing. Grandma, K and I all looked up to the ceiling, but we needn't. Mother was in the room with us.

'Welcome to the land of the living,' said Grandma. 'Hope you're hungry – there's enough here to feed a small nation.'

Mother slipped into her chair at the head of the table and nodded weakly before allowing her head to drift to the empty space beside her. Dad's chair. Mother looked pale, etiolated, helped not a jot by her jet-black robe. I had expected Grandma to admonish her for not dressing for dinner, but she didn't. Likely because we could all see, as clear as day, the last two weeks had been especially cruel to her. Mother had aged beyond her years. And the will to go on, the will to fight, was seeping from her before our very eyes. I didn't know just how much she loved him, not until he was gone.

'Karen, the parsnips please,' said Grandma. K passed the bowl and screwed up her nose at its contents. 'So, Annie dear, how's school?'

I didn't understand why we were carrying on as though nothing had happened – I hadn't been to school in weeks. I wanted to scream.

'It's OK, I guess.'

'OK?' Said Grandma. 'I called your teacher. She said you were a model student, best grades, top of the class …' She waved her hand to indicate etc. etc. 'Must be a damn sight better than OK.'

I didn't know what to say, so I shrugged.

'Cat got your tongue.'

'We don't have a cat,' said K.

'It's an expression, Karen.'

But K was too busy acting out how a cat might try to pull her tongue from her mouth. All the while, Mother remained silent and continued to push her food from one side of her plate to the other. No one was acknowledging her, no one was acknowledging the vacuum. It was infuriating.

'Mum, how are you feeling?' I asked.

Grandma dropped her fork, and I knew then I should have kept my mouth shut. 'She's fine. Aren't you, dear?'

She wasn't fine. Nothing about this was fine.

Karen joined the chorus. 'Mummy looks sad.'

Grandma sensed she was fighting a losing battle.

'Mummy just needs our support right now, especially tomorrow. I want both you girls on your best behaviour, OK? We have a long day ahead of us.'

Mother burst into tears – the kind of tears born only of total and utter heartbreak. *Tomorrow* was the funeral.

'Your mother is just tired.'

And that was it: the proverbial straw. I could tell from the shaking that began at the tip of her fork and finished at the soles of her feet, that Mother was touching the void. The anterior shifts in the topsoil before a landslide, the first winds of a new hurricane.

'I. Am. Not. Tired.'

And then she screamed. A scream so violent, so wretched, so monstrous, that it hurts me now to think of it. A scream of pure agony, of a soul leaving the body and peering across the frontier. It was all we could do to clamp our hands over our ears and yet still the dreadful sound got in.

Grandma pulled Mother's head into her bosom as the wailing went on. 'Girls,' she said gently, 'why don't you both get ready for bed? I'll be up soon.'

And so we left them. A mother cradling her child. And no one to cradle us.

'She did look tired,' added K, once we'd left the room. 'Maybe she just needs a good nap. I know I'm cranky when I'm sleepy too.'

'I don't think a nap will solve this one.'

As we reached the upstairs landing, K nudged me in the ribs. 'Annie, look.'

The door to Mother's bedroom was open. From the glint in her eye, I could see what K intended.

'No, we mustn't. Come on.' I made to grab her by the hand, but she shook loose. I knew why she wanted to enter; with the rest of the house exorcised of Dad's ghost, the final vestiges of his belongings would have been shored up behind that door. Grandma may have been ready to let the past go, but Mother wasn't.

'I'll just be a minute.'

Before I could argue, her little body had slipped between the door and its frame without disturbing the air between. I had no choice but to follow.

I had expected chaos – tissues here, letters there, old photographs lying in collage – but we found only order. The bed was made, her spare dressing gown was on its hook behind the door, the armchair was clear, the side tables were dusted, and the single cup of coffee was on its coaster. No clutter in sight. There didn't seem to be any trace of Dad either.

K walked over to the patterned dressing table by the window – its top-right drawer was open just a crack. Something had prevented it from closing fully. But despite her small stature, K was determined; she pulled at it, pulled at the stuck object, and the drawer gave way in an almighty crash, emptying the entire contents on to the spotless floor.

'Shush, K. They're going to have heard –' But before I could finish, our eyes had alighted on the object, a jumper, no bigger than a hand's breadth, a little 'J' beautifully embroidered in pink cotton on the front. Karen turned to me, her thumbs caressing the soft blue fabric. Her eyes were wide.

'Was this – ?'

But we both knew: it was Jessica's. Dad had bought it for her second birthday, a birthday that was to be her last.

'It's so pretty. Can I keep it?'

'No, K. You need to put it back where you found it.'

'But I'll look after it.'

'I'm sure you would but it doesn't belong to you.'

'But –'

'No buts. Put it back.'

Grudgingly, K replaced the jumper, along with the rest of the drawer's contents, and slid it home into the gaping hole in the table.

'Come on, let's get out of here before Mum finds us.'

'Do you think Dad is with Jessica now?' K's eyes were full of spirit, full of hope.

I smiled – not because I wished to encourage the thought, but simply because I didn't know the answer.

15

That first date seemed to come and go as though it hadn't come at all. For a few days after, he didn't contact me and I didn't contact him.

I've always found it odd, this dance people do. We are each in search of the one who just might be the answer we never knew we needed, who just might complete us, who just might make this whole sorry affair bearable, and we spend that search, the first tentative moments, feigning abject indifference for fear the other might just get an inkling that yes, we like them too. And yet dance we do, dance we must; that way we might never get hurt, we might never reveal too much of ourselves until we absolutely have to. And by that point, it's too late, the ship will be sinking, and we'll be going down together, Jack and Rose, in a sea of mutual feeling. At least, that's the hope.

'You're allowed to call him, you know,' said K, as we made our way to lunch with Mother.

'I know.'

'So what's stopping you?'

'I'll give it to the end of the week. If he hasn't called me then, I'll –'

'Ignore him some more?' K rolled her eyes at me.

'But what if he's not interested? What if he's had second thoughts?' Self-doubt had infiltrated not just my thinking, but my voice too; it quavered.

K softened. 'Then he's had second thoughts. He's allowed to.'

'I guess.'

'You guess nothing. Call him tonight.'

We drove on through the narrow, single-track country lanes. Every now and then, I stared out the passenger window and watched as a strong breeze, the first stirrings of a storm, would flatten the beds of long grass that lined the edges of the unmarked roads, revealing, as though in boast, a world hidden among the overgrowth. As we rounded one corner at speed, I spied a lone rabbit darting into the hawthorn. I don't think K saw.

'Enough about me. How's Hannah?'

Karen fell silent.

'Oh, dear,' I said.

'Oh, dear, indeed. She moved out last week.'

'I'm sorry, K. I didn't know things were that bad.'

K sighed. 'Neither did I. I think it's temporary – at least I hope it is.'

'Have you told Mother?'

'You kidding?' K momentarily took her eyes off the road and looked at me. 'She'll be over the moon. I could do without that right now. And not a word from you either.'

'Cross my heart, hope to die, stick a needle in my eye.'

We met Mother in a small gastropub on the outskirts of the village.

'Is this really the hill you want to die on?' I had to hand it to her: it was a hell of an opener. 'It's my birthday and you choose here of all places?'

'We thought you might prefer something a little more low-key this year,' said Karen, ever the stateswoman.

'Well, you thought wrong, darling. Very wrong.' Mother softened, seemed to briefly stand outside herself and realise how ridiculous, how ungrateful she was being. 'Still, I guess we're here now. Might as well make the most of it.' She went to sit down at a table. 'But next year –'

She wasn't always like this; before Dad died, she was loving. She was firm, but she was loving. Every now and again we still catch glimpses of that woman. She might appear in an unscripted gesture or tender phrase, an artless laugh or kindly smile. But she doesn't seem to visit as often as she once did. As the years go by,

as Mother falls deeper and deeper into this adopted persona –
a defence mechanism, I suppose, erected in the wake of great
trauma – I fear that good woman we once knew, who loved in her
own special way and we loved in turn, may be lost to us forever.

'Yes, Mum,' said K. 'Next year. Whatever you like.'

Mother clapped her hands together. 'Wonderful. Now what are
we all drinking? We're celebrating after all – and not just my
birthday.'

K looked to me. I shrugged.

'Oh, girls, come on now. All in good time.'

Mother ordered a bottle of champagne and hustled us into a
cheers.

'So … Where were we … Glasses at the ready. I have a little
announcement to make. Well, not quite a *little* announcement, a
big one.' Mother, never one to miss an opportunity to pause for
dramatic effect, looked at us each in turn. 'Derek and I are getting
a divorce.'

Derek was Mother's second husband, whom she met a year or
two after Dad passed, and whom can be credited, in part if not
wholly, with kickstarting Mother's regrettable transformation
from grieving widow to a faded, jaded Holly Golightly.

At Grandma's insistence to shake her out of her funk, Mother
had joined a ramblers group, which would convene every Sunday
atop the southernmost tip of the Sussex Downs before tracing the
undulations of the hills direct to the foot of a pub. It was a struggle to get Mother there at first – she would come up with every
excuse under the sun – but after a few months, a few late starts
and curtains dragged open at dawn, not only was Mother going
of her own free will, and leaving early to boot, she was returning
with a silly smile plastered across her face.

Who is he? Asked Grandma, to which Mother replied *Who?*
But Grandma could see through the thickest of fabrics. *Oh, all
right*, said Mother, before spilling all. Derek was an older man,
about twenty years her senior, and handsome in an understated
way. He had made his money, a small fortune, in property and
since his wife had died and there lingered a question mark over
his own mortal thread, he was looking for someone to help spend

it – both his time and his money. Enter Mother. But years later, the money had started to dry up, and he hadn't. That, fundamentally, was the problem.

'Oh, Mum, I'm sorry to hear that,' said Karen.

'Why?' said Mother. 'I'm not. Finally free of the old ratbag. God knows that man caused me enough grief. We hadn't had sex in two years. *Two* years. Do you have any idea what that does to a woman?'

I wanted to say, *Well, yes, actually, I do.* But I didn't.

'Of course, he's keeping the villa in Antibes – I shall miss that place – but he's leaving the rest. Whatever's left, that is, after the debts are settled. Speaking of which – homes, not debts – how's the farmhouse, Annie? Taking good care of it?'

'Yes, Mother.'

'Good. But it's a family place, deserving of a family.'

'I'm working on it,' I said, exasperation having got the better of me.

Mother raised an eyebrow and seemed to take an interest in what someone else had to say for the first time that afternoon.

'Annie's met someone,' said K impulsively. I know she didn't mean to drop me in it; she wouldn't wish that inquisition on anyone.

Thanks a lot, I said in a look.

'Do tell,' said Mother.

'Well, it's very early days ...'

'That's the best bit,' said Mother. 'So who is he?'

I told her he was a surgeon, emphasis on *was*.

'What does he do now?'

'He's ... taking some time for himself.'

'Taking some time for himself. I see. What a luxury.'

The irony of this, coming from a woman who hadn't worked in twenty years, seemed lost on her.

'Come on then, how did you meet? Tell me everything.'

I neglected to mention our meeting outside the Richmond Centre – that might have caused her to raise the other eyebrow. One eyebrow is intrigue; two eyebrows is a disaster. So I told her about our first date, its genesis, its romance. She had a lot of questions.

'Who are his parents?' 'Where does he live?' 'When are you seeing him again?'

The last I couldn't answer.

'Oh, Annie darling,' she said. 'Your sister's right: if you feel this way about him, then call. We regret the things in life we don't do, the ones we didn't run after. Don't let another one slip through your fingers, for all our sakes.'

The truth of the matter is: I did call Mark later that evening, and I'm glad I did. For too long, I'd been relying on the man to take the lead, but there is no real reason why they should.

I was a bag of nerves as I dialled, but I needn't have been. He picked up, breathless. I thought I heard another voice in the background, an interloper to our conversation, but he was alone, he insisted, recently up from a nap. He sounded tired.

He'd been meaning to call me, he said, but life had got in the way.

I know the feeling, I sympathised.

He made some silly joke about peacocks, I forget what, and intimated that he was very sorry to have left me that night.

Me too, I said.

Can he see me again? Soon?

I'd like that.

And in checking my pride at the door, there followed a procession of dates, trysts, adventures. With each one, I found myself falling for him, the real Mark. There was an easiness about him, a casualness to his manner, a spontaneity that appealed to the Type-B person locked inside me. Where I was methodical, regimented, order itself, he was unbidden, impulsive, chaos, pure chaos. He was the wild-growing hedge, the hawthorn, the bracken; I was the gardener bearing the clipper. I remember reading somewhere about the importance of order and disorder existing simultaneously, and how we should all embrace both; we should place one foot in order, and one in chaos. Yin and yang. Order is your rock, your anchor on the real world, your bond to structure, to precedent, to the known. Chaos is the thing from which new things grow. Chaos is not always danger – sometimes it is – but chaos is

93

also where possibility lies in all its shimmering uncertainty. Mark was chaos, and it thrilled me.

On our second date, we met on the South Bank. The wind was whipping across the river and driving water into the foreshore. I stood there in front of the Tate Modern, gazing up and out towards the magnificent dome of St Paul's. A teacher once told me that there are several points in London from which it is illegal to block the view of the cathedral. Standing there, in that moment, I wondered why anyone would ever wish to try. What a gift that building is to us all. Mark was late, but when he did arrive, he did so bearing gifts. Well, a gift; a candle, more specifically. We sat on a bench facing the gathering storm, and we talked, before getting up, walking some more, and talking some more. We ended up walking all the way to Battersea, where we just about made it into the park before the heavens opened. A jazz group continued to play on the bandstand in the centre of the park as the rest of us sought shelter under nearby trees. Mark pulled me to him and he kissed me. Finally, I had my movie moment.

After that, our meetings came thick and fast. We couldn't get enough of one another. Each day we spent together, the sadness lifted ever more from his eyes. Soon, they were blue again, blistering blue. If this *were* a movie, a romantic comedy with some suave-yet-diffident lead (Mark) in hot pursuit of a liberated city girl with a small-town heart (me), this would undoubtedly be the part in the movie with the montage, for all good rom-coms must have a montage, and the boy must get the girl. This girl.

We went to London Zoo and the Aquarium, then a crazy-golf place where he let me win and I chided him for it. There was the palm reader he surprised me with in a townhouse in Pimlico; the bar at the top of a multi-storey car park in Peckham; the flower market on Columbia Road; and the bao restaurant, where I managed to drink a whole bottle of sake and catch my heel in a drain on the way out. Mark, the all-conquering hero, bent down, clasped my foot between his hands and released me from my trap. I gave Mark a copy of *Misery* that day. I wanted him to know that I was his number one fan, drain or no drain.

Once, we stopped into the Royal Academy and found a gallery, desolate save for two dozen busts of famous and not-so-famous faces. Pink pads and pencils resting on benches at the perimeter encouraged visitors to sketch the figures, so we took up our pencils and we sketched. When we were finished, we had to guess which bust the other had drawn, or, perhaps more accurately, attempted to draw, as artistic talent did not reside in either of us. I guessed his subject immediately – mostly because I had been watching him as he faced, intently, a specific pocket of air. Mark was unable to guess mine, but then that was inevitable; I had cheated. I had been drawing him.

On our sixth date, he took me to see *Annie Hall* in a small independent cinema just off Shaftesbury Avenue. *The other Annie* in my life, he said, as we settled into our seats, the lights burning low and popcorn piled high. I confess that it was my first time seeing the film. Despite meeting the apparent love of her life, and falling in and out of love, Annie remained a fiercely independent spirit – in dress, in speech, in life, in love. I admired that about her; admired her will to put herself before all others, her courage to cut her own swath. She was, in every sense, a thoroughly modern woman making her own way in a thoroughly modern world. She didn't depend on the affection or adoration of men. Men were not necessities; they were playthings, momentary distractions. She loved Alvy, I'm sure she did, but she didn't need him; she didn't need anybody. I turned to look at Mark, watched his eyes glisten at the final line, the parting shot, and I wondered then what he wanted from me. Did he want this Annie, or that one?

We went back together for the first time that evening, to his place. We fell into one another as he fumbled for the keys in his pocket. Inside, he pushed me up against the unlit fireplace in the darkness of the sitting room. His hands pinned mine to the wall while his mouth, his warm breath, traced delicate patterns on my neck.

How many others have there been?

'Let's go up,' he said, slipping a hand down the waistband of my jeans.

Is this what I want? Am I the Annie he wants? I bit my lip.

He led me upstairs and pushed me back on the bed. My jeans came off, my top too, and before I knew it his head was buried between my legs, his tongue tracing the curvature of my inner thigh. It had been a while since I'd felt like that, some time since any man had caused me to feel. In that moment, I panicked slightly. I told myself I didn't deserve to feel that way.

'Stop,' I said.

'What's wrong?'

I grabbed him by the hair and pulled him up level with me, face to face with all his sculptural perfection. I removed the remainder of his clothes, piece by piece, thinking as I did that his billowy shirts had betrayed the body beneath for far too long. I put my hand around his neck, squeezed a little, not too much, feeling with my clawed fingers his quickening pulse and tightening my grip on the desire that ran through us both.

'You first,' I said, before flipping him on to his back, at which those little marbles of his rolled firmly into his head. And there they stayed.

I awoke in Mark's house in the dead of night, my heart racing, with that feeling you get upon coming to in an unfamiliar place. I lay there, staring at the ceiling in the dark, haunted by the prospect of work the next day. Another lecture on another senator that no student was interested in. Sometimes it felt like a futile battle, a thankless task; I was Sisyphus, pushing that boulder up the hill, only for life to kick it back to the bottom again. Tomorrow would be a new climb.

My mouth was dry, so I peeled back the duvet, careful not to rouse the sleeping mass beside me, wrestled on my jeans and felt my way downstairs to the kitchen. Groping my way around the walls, I found a switch, which, once flicked, cast out a blinding ball of light. I ran the tap a little longer to get the really cold stuff, and filled a glass, emptying it just as quickly.

As I went to turn out the light, something caught my eye in the living room. Perched on a sideboard was a photograph of a bride and groom in front of a church, bridesmaids to either side and a page boy kneeling mischievously in the foreground. I drew closer and lifted the frame to the light. At the centre, smiling, happiness itself, was Mark and his wife. I had been right: she was pretty, but in the moment, I didn't wish to concede that. This was their perfect day, and here it was, the photograph a trophy on the mantelpiece. I'm not sure what I felt then. I want to say jealousy, but anger seems more appropriate. I wanted to know why it was still there – why it was still proudly on display for all to see, for him to look at in times of despair.

Something overtook me then, a wretched impulse that started as a whisper and rose to a chorus. I began pulling out the drawers in the sideboard in a frenzy, in a sleep-starved rage. I don't know what I was looking for, I don't know what I was hoping to find. Maybe I was hoping that photograph was all that remained, that he had buried her for good, discarded her along with the eight years of marriage; perhaps I was looking for proof that he had moved on, that he had chosen me, that the photograph was just a blip, a mistake. But instead I found the touchpaper that would light a thousand questions and burn a thousand answers, for there, in the second drawer down, hidden under a patchwork of unfinished knitting, was a diary, *her* diary. I opened it and began to flick through, and as I did so a piece of paper, folded several times, drifted slowly to the floor. Lined paper, blue ink.

Writing this is one of the hardest things I've ever had to do, but the alternative, to not speak my truth, to stay in this paralysis, is harder. I hurt, Mark. I've been hurting for some time, and I just can't keep pretending any more. I want the pain to stop. I still love you, but it is all too much.

The handwriting was shaky, and there was a tearstain at the bottom right – his or hers, I couldn't be sure. *Why has he kept this?* I thought.

Just then I heard a sound above, the sound of someone turning over on an old mattress, the sound of someone waking.

I slipped the note back into the diary and the diary into my jeans, so that I might better understand their relationship, so that I might better know how to prevent ours from suffering the same fate. The drawers held nothing further of value, so I closed them and made sure to replace the photograph in its original footprint. I turned out the light, crept upstairs, back into the safe warmth of Mark's arms, and I watched him sleep for a while.

I watched him and I wondered if he had wanted me to see that photograph. I wondered if he wanted me to find her diary, her note. I wondered if he wished to parade his past before me, so that I would come to know what I too could lose were I to take his love for granted. I wondered if he would ever understand this Annie, the real Annie, just as I have come to understand the real Mark, the sleeping giant beside me who has failed to look behind the curtain.

16

4th March

Sleep doesn't come as easily as it once did. I'll read a book, draw a bath or listen to a podcast in the hope that my mind will turn itself off. But it never does. It runs and it runs and it runs. I can't remember the last time sleep visited me uninterrupted. On the few occasions I have been able to close my eyes and drift off for a pure moment, I'm back in the old house, in that cupboard, Tess laughing outside, tears streaming down my cheeks. She knew I was terrified of small spaces, she knew. And still she did it to me, and laughed.

I tried to tell Mark about the dream, but he doesn't want to know. He's stressed, he says. He needs some space, he says. He has too many of his own problems to shoulder any of mine. You're smart, was his solution, You'll work it out. But there's nothing to work out – I just want him to listen. All I've ever wanted is for him to listen, and perhaps to understand. I want to feel understood and I want to feel seen. But as time wears on, Mark has proven himself incapable of either. I wonder if his love for me is drying up, or if he's stopped storing it here. I fear it is elsewhere, I fear it is in that hospital. He can tell me all he likes that it is work keeping him there at all hours, but ...

Last week I found a lipstick stain. Purple, not mine. He denies it, of course, says I'm being ridiculous, jumping to conclusions. He tells me he loves me, that he could never do that, and holds me as though he believes it. But I don't. I don't believe it. The girls say I should leave him, that I deserve better. They're right, I do. And yet I can't imagine a future without him, not one that I would want to live in. So for now I endure. I say nothing and life goes on, as it always has.

This morning I found him sitting in the armchair in the living room, his head lolled to one side, his mouth open. I could smell the vodka on his breath; I could see it in the dirtiness of his clothes. He looked like he hadn't been home in days. I asked him where he was last night. Out with Pete, he said. I'm allowed a life beyond you, he said. But I've never denied him that. The accusation stung. I went to call the hospital on his behalf, to tell them he's sick and won't be able to make it to surgery today, but as I dialled, he slapped the phone from my hand. It fell and the screen cracked on the kitchen floor. Leave it, he said. Stop meddling. You love to meddle.

I'd like to say that this was a one-off, but it's happened before, and I think it might happen again. He's drinking more and his behaviour is becoming increasingly erratic. Sometimes he scares me. But then I remind myself that he has given up a lot for me, that he is still the man I fell in love with all those years ago. I must be thankful. That man is still inside him, somewhere, and I shall find him again, as I found him before.

17

'I don't hear from you in years and you call up for a favour?'

Cameron found himself on the back foot. He thought she'd be pleased to hear from him at the very least, albeit reluctant to grant his request. She was still the strong, intemperate presence he'd remembered, and in that instant, she reminded him a little of his father.

'Has it really been that long?'

'Longer.'

Cameron thought for a moment, considered the gulf of time that stretched from him leaving the police to now, and all that had happened in between.

'I've had a lot to contend with,' he said, a little too meekly for his liking.

The voice on the other end of the phone softened in response. 'Yes,' DCI Vernon sighed. 'I'm sorry about your father – a horrible thing to have to go through.'

'I'm sorry too.'

'For leaving?'

'For not leaving sooner.'

The woman laughed. 'Was I really that bad a boss?'

'It wasn't you. It was –'

'The job.'

'The job,' Cameron agreed. Twenty years in the Force had taken its toll, and he had no regrets about getting out when he did. Every so often DCI Vernon would get in touch, try to lure him back, unsuccessfully. But, barring the odd bit of private detective work, he held firm. It wasn't a life that he found agreeable. But now here he was, dipping his toes uncertainly back into ice-cold water that was not fit for swimming. He told himself he was doing it for the money, but, in truth, he knew that it was to see if he still could.

DCI Vernon sneezed down the line.

'See,' said Cameron. 'Even you're allergic to it.'

'I'm allergic to *favours*. My body is worried what you might ask of me. So come on then ... Out with it.'

'I'm doing a little investigative work for an old friend whose daughter-in-law went missing just over eighteen months ago, presumed dead. You lot have given up the ghost; so too, it seems, has her husband.'

Cameron was greeted by a long silence on the other end of the line. DCI Vernon had a habit of letting people speak until they fashioned a noose for themselves with their words. Having worked with her for so long – too many years to count – Cameron was wise to it, so he stood his ground and let the silence consume *her*. Until ...

'You know I can't give you the case files. You're no longer on the payroll.'

'It's not that.'

'Well?'

'I gather she and her husband might have tried to adopt a kid shortly before she went missing. I could be clutching at straws, but I need to explore every avenue. Can you run a search of all the applications lodged with state adoption agencies over the past three years?'

'Cam, if you suspect the husband is behind her disappearance, then it's really a police matter. Do you have any other evidence to support this?'

Cameron flushed a little; thankfully, DCI Vernon wasn't there to witness it. 'Well, actually, no. But it can't hurt to rule him out. What was it you used to say? Look to the husband and the truth is never far behind.'

'Cam, I dunno. It's –'

'The first and only time. I promise. I won't ask again.'

DCI Vernon sounded reluctant. 'I'll see what I can do, but I make no promises. Name?'

'Either Hope Marie Hedger or Hope Marie Lane. And thank you – I owe you one.'

'I'll keep it in my bottom drawer with the others.'

*

Cameron found Pete sitting alone on a wall at the northern tip of Battersea Park. The river passed untroubled behind him.

'Your assistant told me I might find you here. Cameron,' he said, offering his hand.

Pete, dressed in a smart pinstripe suit and oxblood loafers, looked up at this stranger, confused. His sandwich hovered mid-air as, seemingly, he tried to place him – somewhere, anywhere. Did he think Cameron a client? An old friend? Pete took the stranger's hand anyway.

'We haven't met, have we?' asked Pete, dusting the breadcrumbs from his lip and wiping the heels of his hands on a napkin.

'Oh, I don't think we'd have much cause to meet. Unless you were very badly behaved in a past life.'

'I'm very badly behaved now,' Pete laughed, but it dissipated the moment he realised he was the only one laughing.

'You'll be relieved to know that's not why I'm here.'

'Are you a cop? Undercover?'

'No.'

'Then who are you?'

Cameron smiled wryly. 'A concerned citizen.'

Pete leaned back and crossed one bent leg over the other knee. 'Well, what's concerning you today? And what does it have to do with me and my lunch break.'

Cameron had never liked estate agents – and this one was no different. All bravado and oleaginous charm wrapped in a suit. An ego that soared as high as the pagoda that stood behind him. But he was not here to like him; he was here to learn from him.

'I'm concerned about a blonde woman, about so high –' Cameron drew his flat hand up level with his neck '– who went missing one day and not a peep since.'

Pete went white as a sheet. 'Look, I know nothing about Hope. If that's what you came here for, you're wasting your time.'

'But you did *know* Hope, did you not? It would surprise me if you didn't given you're, by all accounts, Mark's closest friend.'

'Of course I knew her. But I don't know why she left.'

'But you could hazard a guess, I'm sure?'

Pete stayed silent, lost for words.

'Why don't we start with the affairs.'

Pete's jaw fell open. 'Me and Hope? I would never –'

'I was thinking more of Mark's affairs, but we can tackle yours too if you like.'

'Oh. Mark.' Cameron noted the slight fall in Pete's shoulders, the long exhale of breath.

'He was seeing someone, wasn't he? Or more than one perhaps?'

Pete's shoulders hardened now against his interrogator, his lips pursed.

'You don't want to talk?' Cameron pressed.

'You can talk, I can eat,' Pete replied as he bit pointedly into his sandwich.

One of the first lessons DCI Vernon ever taught Cameron was not to continue to apply pressure to an uncooperative subject; that would only lead to a dead line of enquiry. Instead, a good detective should reframe the conversation, befriend them, understand them, catch the subject off guard.

'Cheese and ham?'

Pete stopped eating and looked up at Cameron.

'The sandwich,' Cameron gestured.

Pete nodded.

'May I?'

But without waiting for a response, Cameron's hand reached into the wrapper nestled on Pete's lap and withdrew the other half of the sandwich. He held it aloft.

'When I was a little boy, each day before school, my mum would wake up early and make me a cheese and ham sandwich. Sometimes with pickle, cucumber, a spot of mustard or whatever else she might have had to hand that week.'

Pete, not a little irritated by this stranger who had helped himself to his lunch, looked on incredulous, but said nothing.

'And do you know what I did? Every day, on my walk to school, I put that sandwich in the bin by the post office. I hadn't the heart to tell her that I didn't even like cheese and ham – never had. Even now, I still think of the love, care and attention that my mum would invest in everything she did, and I still think of those sandwiches.'

Pete leans forward, re-engages. 'Why didn't you just tell her?'

'Somehow it seemed easier not to. But I wish I had. If my years in the police taught me anything, it's that the truth stings for a little while; lies sting for a lifetime.'

Pete and Cameron exchanged a look that said more than any words could have, and as they did so, Cameron dropped the cheese and ham sandwich he was holding into the bin beside them.

Pete sighed. 'I knew there were problems. In the marriage.'

'Mark and Hope?'

Pete nodded. 'Mark mentioned another woman once, when he'd had a little too much to drink. But he never confided in me, not about that stuff. He knew what a difficult position it'd put me in, having to see Hope all the time, look her in the eye.'

'His drinking. You're aware he had a problem then?'

'I knew he drank too much, but it wasn't out of control. Or so I thought ...'

'Until he left the hospital?'

Pete snorted. 'Jumped before he was pushed. Before any blot was put on his copybook.'

'Do you know why he started drinking? Why he changed?'

'He's never said, but if you ask me –' Pete looked around him, as though checking that no one was witness to the conversation. His eyes finally alighted on the pagoda, now lit up in the full glow of the afternoon sun. 'None of this will get back to him, will it?'

'I will treat whatever you tell me with the utmost discretion.'

Pete, reassured, confided in the stranger quizzing him. 'If you ask me, he felt stuck. Stuck in his relationship.'

Cameron made a note on his pad. 'You think he wanted out?'

'That's for you to determine.'

Just then, Cameron felt his phone vibrate in his pocket. He took a quick glance. The screen read: Marianne Vernon.

'One moment,' he said to Pete, before walking out of earshot. 'Mari? How are you?'

'I made a few calls ...' *She still hated small talk then.* 'An application was lodged by Hope Marie Lane with the Hillcrest Adoption Agency in South-east London.'

'Was it successful?'

'No.'

'They were rejected?'

'Not exactly.'

'Was it pulled? Change of heart?'

'It didn't even get that far. It was submitted with only one signatory, and they needed two – one for each parent.'

'Whose signature was missing?'

'Her husband's.'

18

My virginity was lost to me before I had cause to give it up. It was lost to me on the playing fields, in the corridors, the lunch halls and classrooms. It was lost to me in the car parks and narrow alleyways where false whispers were currency amongst the school leavers and new starters. It was lost to me in the rumours that lit up the showers and the texts that flooded students' phones. It was lost to me before I'd had the chance to find it, to understand it, to hold its meaning. It was lost to me in the words of my peers.

By the time I did come to have sex for the first time, it seemed a day like any other for an experience I was sure I'd have again. I was seventeen and the world was just opening up to me: I could smoke, I could drive, and next year I'd be off to university – the first in the family to go. I felt grown-up in a way I never had before. Except for one thing, one little word, three little letters. I had started to feel ashamed and afraid that I was being left behind by my peers. It seemed everyone had done it but me. To hear them talk of it, it was transformational, spiritual; it was the pulling back of a veil to a new world, which, once glimpsed, could not be unseen. And then it happened. Except it was none of those things. It was not significant, it was not romantic, and it was not particularly pleasant. It was, in a word, a much longer word, *disappointing*.

His name was Jon, but it didn't have to be. He could have been anyone. I remember very little of it – perhaps just as well – save waking up afterwards in his mum's bed as he lay there, comatose, wearing a grin. *He'd have something to tell his mates tomorrow*, I supposed as I got up quietly, gathered my things and made for the door. There I came face to face with his mum, who had a look of horror on her face, a look that told me I was worth so very little. A few years later, I saw Jon at a house party, cigarettes in our hands and cider cans around our feet. I asked him what happened, why he never told a soul of our encounter, I was a little hurt that he didn't. He held up a wrist to me in answer. Little round scars pockmarked his skin. His mother was Catholic, he explained; he had brought shame upon the family. *But we were kids*, I said. *We still are.*

That first night with Mark was different; it was special. It was the first time I'd always hoped for but never got. That night sparked something in me. I came alive. For days afterwards, I could do little but picture our bodies entwined; every branch on a tree became a limb embroiled in another; every drop of dew a bead of perspiration.

'Trees as limbs? You need help,' Laura said wearily, as we met for brunch in a café in Peckham. I was competing with her phone for attention, or what little she had to give. A hangover had taken root in her.

'No,' I said. 'I need Mark.'

Laura looked up and put the phone down on the table. 'So it's serious?'

I smiled. 'I think it might be, yeah.'

'You *think*, or you *know*?'

'I know.'

A young couple, mid-thirties, walked arm in arm on the pavement before us. She carried a bouquet of pampas grass in her spare hand; he held a bottle of orange wine in his.

'Oh, God. Then it's worse than I thought.'

'What?'

'You love him.'

I blushed. 'I do not ...'

'Go on, complete that sentence. I dare you.'

But it was no good. I feared that any moment my blush would colonise every inch of my face.

'I can't,' I conceded.

Laura was enjoying this. 'Because ...'

'Because I love him.'

'The truth will out. Does he know?'

'I haven't told him if that's what you mean. But I think he does. And I think he feels the same way. Though he can be pretty inscrutable sometimes.'

Laura wiped a gloop of mascara from the corner of her eye. 'You know what they say about inscrutable men.'

'They're terribly interesting?' I asked playfully.

Laura shot me a matronly look. 'They're often hiding something.'

'Thanks, Mum.'

'I mean it, Annie. It all seems to be happening pretty fast. I've said it before and I'll say it until I'm blue in the face: be careful.'

*

Mark called me later that night as I emerged from the shower, one towel clung to my body and the other wrapped snake-like about my head.

'Hello?' I said as I collapsed on my bed. My feet dangled off the end of the mattress.

'Is that the London Owl Sanctuary for lost owls?'

I often joked that Mark looked like a little owl when he wore his reading glasses. They were large, round, steel-rimmed; his prescription made his eyes look ever so small, but no less sparkling.

'At your service,' I said.

'Hoot hoot,' he replied, to which the only reasonable response could be: *Hoot hoot.*

Far too many men take themselves far too seriously. They're so desperate to embody power, dominance, learning, that they forget to be vulnerable. They're so desperate to be men that they forget to be the boys they once were. I loved that Mark was playful. I loved that he wasn't afraid to be vulnerable.

'So what can I do for you?'

'You can tell me where I might find a nice, kind, young lady to give me shelter from the storm.' It was raining outside and a thin mist was starting to spread across the Common.

'I don't know about kind, or nice, or even young for that matter, but I can offer you shelter. What time will you be here?'

Mark broke character, a little abruptly. 'Oh, shoot. I promised I'd go help Pete move a fireplace in the morning.'

'A fireplace?'

'I appreciate this sounds like a terrible excuse – so terrible it's surely believable. He's remodelling his flat and … yada yada … I won't bore you with the details. Rain check?'

'Rain check.'

'What are you doing tomorrow afternoon?'

'I'll be in Kent.'

'Why don't I drive down? I'd love to see the place.'

It felt like a big step, and one I was excited to take. But it was also a scary step. *Was it too soon?* I worried Laura was right; maybe this was moving too fast.

'I'd love to show it to you,' I said evenly. If I was nervous at the prospect, Mark need never know.

'Then it's a date. Right, I better run; it's starting to chuck it down now. This little owl will be drenched.'

'See you tomorrow,' I said.

'Hoot hoot,' he replied.

19

'It's beautiful,' Mark said the next day as we emerged from our respective cars and stood side by side on the loose gravel path, the farmhouse before us and the fields rolling away beyond our shoulders.

'Yeah?' I said, secretly pleased that he was impressed by this.

'Yeah,' he said, turning to look at me. 'It's all yours?'

'Well, mine and my sister's. But I live here for all intents and purposes.'

'At weekends,' Mark reminded me. He wanted to show me he had been listening.

'At weekends,' I agreed.

Mark turned and looked out over the fields, down past the pillbox to the creek where K and I played as kids.

'When you said you grew up on a farm, I was picturing something altogether more –'

'Ramshackle?'

'I was going to say *rustic*.'

'It's a farm in name only. Although we did have some chickens.'

'Had?'

'A girl's gotta eat.'

Mark laughed. 'I'm not sure those chickens would agree with you.'

'I didn't know you'd suddenly turned vegetarian?'

'Well, I woke up this morning, stuck my finger in the air and decided I needed a cause.'

'And vegetarianism is it?'

'For today, yes.' Mark's blue eyes twinkled.

'And tomorrow?'

'That depends. Do you have any immediate plans to frack gas in South Sudan?'

'No immediate plans, per se.'

'Then tomorrow remains undecided.'

I liked his silliness. I liked the way he brought me out of my shell. I liked the Annie I became around him. It was me, still me, but confident, brighter. He shone and I absorbed his light.

'I'm curious. Why do you bother living in London, if you have all this here?' he asked.

'Sometimes I ask myself the same question.'

'And the answer?'

'That it would be terribly lonely here by myself.'

'I'm sure you won't be by yourself forever,' he smiled. 'Pretty girl like you.'

That was the first hint, the first suggestion that he saw us as something more than a fling; that he might just be in this for the long haul. I was anxious about bringing him here, worried that he might feel it too much, too soon. But no, he surprised me with his good grace.

'So do I get the grand tour?' he said, stepping up to the great oak door.

'You will get the not-so-grand-tour,' I said, teasing.

'Right, I suppose you reserve the red carpet treatment for the King.'

'If then,' I said, poking him in the back as I turned the iron handle.

His eyes lit up once more the moment we crossed the threshold. 'It's just so *quaint*,' he said, half in awe, half in jest. 'Little quaint Annie's little quaint farmhouse.' He was teasing me now.

'I'm sorry, ladies and gentleman,' I said. 'This tour has come to an end.'

With that, Mark drew me to him, and kissed me full on the lips. A hotness spread up and down my body; his kiss the match that lit the flame. Then my pale skin must have blushed, for he pinched my right cheek.

'You're cute when you're not even trying.'

'And when I try?'

He kissed me again. 'Unbearable.'

I led him through the house, room to room, hallway to hallway. He stopped every now and again to marvel at some trinket, or some photograph of me, of K, of the family that was. In the living room, Mark's eyes fell upon a picture of Dad, dressed in a suit and tie, smiling out of the frame. Mother stood beside him in a billowy dress, which must have caught the wind at precisely the moment the picture was taken. She looked radiant. And they looked happy.

'This your dad?' Mark said, lifting the frame for a closer look.

'Yes,' I said.

'He looks smart.'

'He was.'

'And kind.'

'He was that too.'

My gaze fell on the armchair in the corner of the room, his chair.

'He used to sit here,' I said. 'It was his favourite. When he'd get up to make a sandwich or go to the loo, K and I would rush up and sit in it. The moment he was back, he'd pick us both up and plonk us right back down on the floor, by the fire.'

I looked up at the clock on the mantelpiece. Its ticking grew louder and louder and louder, until I felt I might burst, until the ticking became me and me it.

Mark gently repositioned the photo frame and placed a reassuring hand on the nape of my neck, just as Dad would do to Mother. 'I'm sorry,' he said. 'I didn't mean to upset you.'

I wiped an errant tear from the bridge of my nose. 'You didn't,' I said softly. 'It was a happy memory. I seem to recall less and less of them these days. I'm thankful for the ones I can.'

'It's hard,' Mark said almost absently, 'living among the past. Every object, every room, every doorway a potential reminder.'

He was thinking about her: the woman who had quit his life so spectacularly. I wondered then if he'd ever stop thinking about her, or whether he might even want to. A lump formed in his throat, but he turned to me and smiled, as if in defiance of this emotion that threatened to rise up within him. But whether it was sadness, or regret, I could not be sure. Whatever it was passed from the room just as quickly as it entered.

'You still have her things?' I asked.

He nodded. 'I'm not sure what to do with them. Most have been boxed up, ready to go to charity, or to her friends, but I ... I need a little push in the right direction.'

I took his hand with a rapidity that caused him to look at me, to really look at me. I felt like, in that moment, we were finally starting to understand one another; finally beginning to forge a connection that ran far deeper than any well. I was not pushing him, I was drawing him to me.

'If you're not ready,' I said, 'then that's fine.'

'It's not that ...'

'Then what?'

'When she went, I didn't just lose my wife, I lost my best friend. And I lost my mind. I didn't know who I was without her.'

'And now?'

'It's got easier. But for a long period, I lost myself a little. In truth, perhaps I lost myself before I lost her.'

Mark pulled his hand from mine and paced distractedly through the living room. Whatever he was thinking about now, it wasn't her. It was him.

'Mark?'

He stopped and looked at me.

'I think there's something you should know ... If this, if we're ...' He scrambled for the words. 'If this is going somewhere, and I hope it is. Because, Annie, you've made me the happiest I've been in a long time. If this is going somewhere then ... there's something I need to tell you ...'

My chest tightened. Surely no good can ever come of those words.

'Work got too much – long hours, patients I couldn't help. I guess I withdrew. Stopped being the husband I should have been, the husband she needed. I started drinking. Just a little at first to erase the stresses of the day. But then that wasn't enough; I drank to erase the day itself. I knew I had a problem, but my problem was also my solution. And before too long my relation-ships started to suffer, and so did my job.'

'What happened?'

'I came to work one morning, scrubbed in, stood in theatre with three pairs of eyes on me, and my hand was shaking. A nurse passed me a scalpel but I couldn't take it. I just kept shaking. Thankfully, a colleague sent me home before any real damage was done. But I hated myself for it, vowed to kick the drink. And I did, for a time, but I couldn't go back to work. It scared me to lose control like that. But I'm not the me I once was. I'm in control now; the drink does not control me. And a large part of that is because of *you*, and how happy you make me.'

Such an admission should have raised red flags, but it didn't; it's the truth that isn't spoken that should concern us most. The fact that he told me, that he opened up a darker part of his history, and that he trusted me with it, comforted me beyond measure.

'And Hope?'

'What about her?'

'Do you think that's why she left?'

Mark sighed heavily. 'I wish I knew.'

'Did you try to find her?'

He shook his head ruefully. 'I did at first – drove to every place that I thought she might be holed up, rang everyone who might have seen her. Nothing. I didn't sleep for weeks, stopped eating. At some point, my parents became concerned, checked me into a clinic where nurses monitored me, fed me, washed me.' He looked at me then with mild embarrassment. 'By the time I emerged, I realised it was hopeless. It was pretty clear she didn't want to be found, and she certainly didn't want me to follow her. So I gave up. For what she put up with, it's the least she was due. A release.'

'From you?'

'From us.'

Mark looked at the carriage clock on the mantelpiece as it counted out our silence. Neither he nor I knew quite what to say. Just as I thought we were growing closer, that sharing might bring us a new understanding, we seemed further apart than ever.

'I better go,' he said finally, picking up his jacket from the sofa and gesturing towards the door.

I tried to rescue the moment. 'But it's only early; I thought we could grab some dinner later, perhaps go for a walk –'

'No, really.' The answer was firm. 'I must get going. Thank you though, and thank you for the tour.'

He turned, kissed me coldly on the cheek and left. He seemed to take my heart with him but refused to leave me his. I wondered if I would ever see him again.

20

There comes a time in any fledgling courtship when the balance of power shifts. The texts, which once came in great floods, slow to a trickle. The rhythm sways, alters and finds a new equilibrium. A wide, cavernous space opens, and into that space steps paranoia and doubt.

At such times, reasonable people come to do unreasonable things as they are forced to contend with a wellspring of emotion underpinned by the thought that all that has been built could be undone in an instant; that just as quickly as they came to fall for you, they could right themselves and pretend they'd never fallen in the first place. And it is a thought not without foundation. In the blink of an eye, they have the power to erase those feelings, erase everything you had, erase the whirlwind dates and sweaty nights, erase all traces of your touch from their body, erase their ever having met you. They could cut you off as a chef discards gristle and never think of you again.

To an extent, it was ever thus. But this new age, this modern age, where you are only ever a swipe away from the *next best thing*, has dispensed with the old adage: *the grass isn't always greener*. And yet, maybe, just maybe, the adage is wrong. Maybe it is time we reappraised it, threw out the old rulebook. For, as much as we may try to convince ourselves otherwise, sometimes the grass *is* greener on the other side. Sometimes there *is* a better match for us. A ring can seem to fit the finger perfectly, but it's only when you try on a different size that you realise the ring had been too tight all along, too constrictive, and that those marks left on the finger, those indents and impressions, were the aggregation of your inexperience. But switch out the ring and those marks will fade in time. The wrong choices, too, will be lost to us.

Mark fell silent after nearly nine months together. The *good morning* and *goodnight* texts came to an end; he no longer called me, no longer took my calls. I wondered if it had something to do with Hope – whether she was holding him back in some way, whether he felt that he couldn't truly give himself to another while she was still out there, wherever *there* was. Maybe as things got more and more serious between us, as his feelings for me grew, he panicked. Maybe he thought the same might happen with us; that I might leave him one day and tear apart the life he'd only just rebuilt. Maybe he was scared.

For all my speculation, I knew the real reason, of course, deep down: he'd lost interest. Our short romance had come to an end, and he hadn't even had the decency to let me know. I was hurt, I was upset, but most of all, I was angry. I was grieving for a relationship that had never been given the chance to take flight. I was grieving for a future that was never mine.

I had resigned myself to this fact, with not a little heaviness in my heart, when several weeks later, as I was delivering a lecture on Empire to a group of bored students, unnoticed by everyone but me, a small figure slipped into the back of the hall. I had to squint, to really focus my attention on the back, but sure enough, there he was: it was Mark, smiling, at me. He was happy.

'Lord Elgin's imprimatur from Sultan Selim III to begin excavation of the Parthenon Frieze has been called into question by a great number of prominent individuals and organisations. Invariably the issue, at heart, is inextricably bound with questions of empire, power and legitimacy. *Who has the right to rule?*'

A bell sounded to signal the end of lecture and the hall exploded into sound.

'OK, everyone. Enjoy your weekends and see you next week. Oh, and don't forget your reading.'

The place emptied, save for Mark, who, once the last student had left, stood up and made his slow descent down the steps towards me with a bouquet of flowers in hand. There was an excited, boyish look in his eyes.

'I know it's terribly conventional of me,' he said, as he planted a lingering kiss on my lips and handed me the flowers.

'There is absolutely nothing conventional about you,' I smile.

After all, who else would ghost someone and then ask what he was about to ask me.

'You ready?' he said.

'For what?'

'Well, it wouldn't be a surprise if I told you, would it?'

'But where are we –'

Mark placed a finger to my lips. 'Suitcase packed, car out front. Everything's taken care of. All that's missing is you.'

*

Nine months after the funeral, Mother moved out, leaving K and me in the care of Grandma, and the farmhouse in the care of us, deeds and all. But I wasn't ready for that kind of responsibility, surface or otherwise; I was just a kid.

Grandma said Mother left because the farmhouse reminded her too much of him, of the man who encouraged our move there in the first place, but that wasn't it at all. Mother left because *we* reminded her too much of him. Each time she looked at her own children, she saw loss, and love became an impossibility.

'Annie, grab your things. We're going,' called a voice from the drive.

At that time, as my difficult teenage years took root, I'd taken to hiding away around the back of the pillbox in the neighbouring field. There, in the wild peace and quiet, looking out towards the weir, I could think and dream undisturbed; I could read and imagine all the places I would and would not see in my lifetime; I could plan the wars I would wage against mythical tyrants and great injustices; and I could plot the course of my own life like a badly written novel. But most of all, in that suspension of time and place, I could smoke, and Grandma would be none the wiser.

'Annie, I will count. You know I will.'

I stubbed out my cigarette on the heel of my shoe, pulled my jumper over my head and shook it into the wind so as to dispel the scent of scorched tobacco. By the time I reached the drive, Grandma was at the wheel of her car, straw boater pulled low on her forehead, and giant sunglasses perched at the tip of her nose. She looked over the lenses at me.

'You can stay here if you'd rather. Karen and I are chasing the sun. Isn't that right, K?'

'You betcha.' K was sat in the passenger seat, looking like a doll propped up in a dining chair.

'I didn't say that.'

'Then stop dilly-dallying and get in. If we leave now, we can be at Camber by midday. The tides wait for no man.'

'Don't you mean wo-man?'

Grandma threw me what she would call 'an old-fashioned look'.

'You're supposed to warn me when you're being funny,' she said. 'That way I'll always know when to laugh.'

When I think of that day now, I think of leathered bodies turning like rotisserie chickens in the warm glare of the sun; of a carpet of cinnamon sand undulating in neatly arranged peaks as far as the eye could see; of ice-cream salesmen ringing their bells and wringing their hands once the stock ran low; of parasols and deckchairs, buckets and spades, sun hats and suncream. I think of Grandma, and I think of the little drowning girl.

'Karen, take this and get us a good spot – not too near the water mind you.'

Grandma handed K an oversized parasol, which she dutifully hoisted on her shoulder. Without another word to us, she struck out across the beach, her little feet struggling to find purchase in the shifting sand.

'Annie, take these –' I was gifted two chairs and a cool box. '– and I'll follow with the rest. Oh, and catch up with your sister. Make sure she doesn't take anyone's eye out with that thing.'

A little way down the beach, I found K trying to drive the parasol deep into the sand.

'Here, let me.'

'I can do it,' she said. And she could. Once, twice … third time lucky as the end of the parasol took root in the sand and held at last. She flexed her arms to me and smiled. But that smile disappeared as she realised the last person she'd performed that gesture for, was Dad.

'Good spot, Karen, and by the groyne too. Grandma likes to hold on to them as she gets into the sea.'

Grandma did that sometimes – speak in the third person. I used to find it annoying but I confess it had grown on me. She had grown on me. The steeliness I had perceived in her when she first arrived at the farm wasn't steeliness at all; it was resilience, it was fortitude, it was love born of a desire to instil in us the grit to weather any coming storm.

But there were no storms that day. The sky was a wide open expanse of blue.

'Here,' said Grandma as she passed me a crisp ten-pound note. 'Go make yourself useful and fetch us some ice creams.'

Time stretched out on that beach, unwound with the rest of us. I can't say if we were there five minutes or an hour. It didn't matter. We laughed and played, waded into the sea to cool off when the heat grew too oppressive, and listened to Grandma's old stories of Grandpa. He died before either of us was born, and we'd heard so very little of him. What we did know – that he was a village chemist, tall, dark and handsome, with a penchant for Turkish Delight – came from Grandma. Mother rarely talked about her father, but she didn't have to; he was alive in her, just as she shall always be alive in us, for better or worse.

'When did you know you would be with him forever and ever and ever?'

K had a way of asking the questions I couldn't, or didn't think to, ask.

'Well,' said Grandma, a sparkle creeping into her eyes, 'we'd been on several dates, shall we say – though we didn't have much money back then, so they were nothing fancy – and one night, a bit too late for him to be out really, he knocked on my mother's door and asked to speak to me ... My mother, your great-grandmother, was very angry. Fuming, she was. He'd woken her up, curlers in her hair and everything. But your grandpa was persistent – you have a bit of him in you, K.'

'I do?'

'Oh, yes. You have his heart.'

K folded her arms across her chest and smiled to herself.

'There and then he told my mother, in no uncertain terms, that he'd walked all the way from Chislehurst and he wasn't leaving until he'd seen me. He had something to ask me, something that couldn't wait until morning. My mother could have slammed the door in his face at that moment – in hindsight, she probably wished she had – but she didn't. She called me downstairs in my nightgown, bleary-eyed, no make-up ... I was so excited to see him. Have I told you both how handsome he was? Broad shoulders, big arms. All the girls fancied him, of course, but he wasn't interested in them. It was me he liked, and I liked him too.'

'Then what happened?'

'So I'm standing there on the doorstep, my mother behind me, and before I know it, he gets down on one knee, takes a tiny little box out of his pocket and says, *Eileen Bertha Taylor, will you marry me?* There was no other answer in the world to me than *Yes!*'

'What if you'd said *no*?' I asked. 'He'd have been so hurt.'

'If Grandma had said *no*, we wouldn't be here,' said K wistfully.

Grandma looked at me and K with the eye of an antiques appraiser and answered firmly, 'Best decision I ever made.'

As the heat of the midday sun gave way to a cool and gentle breeze; as Karen filled, emptied and refilled her blue bucket with sand; as Grandma's snoring found its own soft, syncopated rhythm; and as I fought hard against the heaviness in my eyelids, a sudden cry went up and rent the air.

Grandma awoke with a start, thinking, as I did in that moment, that it was Karen. But it wasn't. Karen was sat, as before, with her bucket and spade, looking out to where we were all now looking, and the focus of the screaming that surrounded us: the figure of a young girl struggling against the tide.

I clambered to my feet as the entire beach swarmed forward – everyone desperate to reach the drowning girl. The more I looked, the more I saw the panic in her features, the water invading her lungs, the colour draining from her skin, the more convinced I became that it was her. She was older, but it was *her*.

A certain fear crept up and into my legs, fixing them to the spot; it would be a fear that would visit me time and time again, for it was then that it started. It was the first time I saw her since her death, since the accident, and she has visited me ever since. She has grown as I've grown, aged as I've aged. She's there in the shower, there when I cross the road, there as I sit idly on the tube, there when I close my eyes. She comes in the waves of elderly women or the drowning faces of little children. And she comes to remind me, lest I forget, of that ice-cold night. I know she's not there, not really. I know it's all in my mind, a figment of my imagination, a manifestation of my guilt, but that doesn't stop her.

I shake my head, shut my eyes fast against the vision, and still she comes. Jessica will always come. My happiness troubles her.

Two men reach the girl at the same time. One wraps his arm around her neck and drags her backwards to the shore, while the other, glory snatched from him, grabs her wayward raft. After a few tense minutes as the rescuer fights against the rip tide, the girl's lifeless body is borne to the beach and laid out across the hot sand. *She's not breathing* is the cry from the gathered crowd. *Is there a doctor?* A man pushes through, bends down over her and begins to administer CPR. But she doesn't respond. People hold their hands over their mouths. They're terrified, and yet thankful it's not their own child.

Just as the man seems on the verge of giving up, just as the crowd seems ready to abandon all hope, the young girl coughs. One last push on her ribs and her body convulses, prompting a jet of water to erupt from her lungs like a whale surfacing. Relief is palpable. The girl's mother scrambles to her side, cradles her head in her hands and sobs at what might have been.

'Let that be a lesson to you both,' said Grandma, and then growing mournful: 'Not that you needed one.'

*

The car took a series of hairpin bends as we descended into the picture-postcard town of Polperro under the glare of the low-slung winter sun.

After a long drive, we pulled up at a small guest house seemingly in the middle of nowhere. While Mark wrested the luggage from the boot, I approached the door and gave a knock, which though gentle, clearly startled a short and frumpy woman, who I imagine had been half-dozing in front of the TV.

Bloody hell. Who's that at this hour?

When she came to the door, she seemed almost puzzled by my presence.

'Can I help you?'

'We have a room booked.' Nothing. 'Under the name of Mark Lane?'

'Lane … Lane … Ah, yes,' she said. 'Mr and Mrs Lane – please come in.'

'Oh, we're not married,' I said.

'You're not?' She looked me up and down. 'Well, you still have time for all that. Follow me and I'll show you to your room. It's not big and it's not fancy, but I hope it'll be to your liking.'

She reminded me of Grandma.

'Sink and shower in the room – toilet is down the hall. Any questions?'

'What time's breakfast?'

'Breakfast?' At that, she laughed and walked from the room, muttering to herself, *This ain't the Ritz, honey.*

Mark passed her on the way in, a suitcase in either hand, a bead of sweat shimmering on his brow. 'Serves me right for booking so last minute,' he whispered to me.

'I don't think she much cares for us city slickers,' I said, wrapping my arms around him.

'I don't think she much cares for people.'

I looked at the suitcase. 'How did you know what to pack?'

'You've left enough stuff at mine over the last few months … I just bunged it all in a bag.'

'Was that a hint?'

'Nope. I like having you around – I *love* having you around. And maybe one day …'

'One day what?'

But just as I thought Mark was going to ask me to move in with him, to take that tentative step forward, to turn me and him into us, he changed the subject. I was disappointed, sure, but at the same time, I didn't want to rush him. The trip alone was gesture enough.

Mark made love to me that night with an intensity I'd never known before. We were two love-starved animals, and I'm ashamed to admit we might have got a little carried away ...

'Quite the performance,' said the landlady as we left the next morning. 'Though I should be glad not to catch the next one.'

And so we set off for Polperro with a rap across the knuckles, and a spring in our step.

'Wouldn't it be wonderful to live here,' said Mark, as we walked down the narrow, gently sloping roads, past the squat cottages that crouched over a tributary of the River Pol, towards the harbour itself.

'Is this where you see yourself, one day, away from it all?'

'Maybe. I know I don't want to bring up kids in the city.'

It was the first time he'd mentioned kids.

'You think about that?' I said. 'With us?'

Mark stopped walking and turned to me, squinting against the sun. 'I'm sorry, I didn't mean to freak you –'

'No,' I said. 'You haven't. I think about that stuff too.'

'You do?'

I nodded and took his hand.

'Good, because this ... for me ... I –' He couldn't seem to say what was in his heart, but he wanted to. He really wanted to. '– I don't want it to end. The last nine months have been –'

'Wonderful,' I said emphatically.

'Wonderful,' he agreed. 'At my darkest, I never could have imagined I would find someone again, someone like you, and so soon after ... Sometimes I hate myself for it, but I guess we can't control when the right person enters our lives.'

He looked at me then as though he was trying to decide something, as though there were many roads open to him and he was unsure of which to take. Or perhaps he was trying to understand something, something about me.

'You know what I really, really want?' His eyes narrowed and I pressed my body to him in anticipation, our faces mere centimetres apart.

'Yes?'

'Well … I really, *really* want a zig-a-zig-ah.' He burst out laughing at his own joke.

'Thank God you're pretty,' I said and rubbed his hair like a child. His cheeks flowered red in response and, for the briefest of moments, the man became the boy.

We spent hours wandering the beautifully winding streets of the village, climbing forgotten paths up and over cragged terrain to the summit of the wild cliffs, where we looked out over a restless sea – waves curling, cresting and crashing against the rocks below. From up there, side by side with the man who would become my everything, all else seemed so utterly trivial.

'Look,' said Mark. A small fisherman's boat was pulling into the harbour. 'Wouldn't it be great to just take off somewhere, leave it all behind. Take to the seas with nothing but the clothes on your back and the wind in your face?'

Was he thinking about her?

'To disappear, you mean?'

'Well, no, not exactly. Not disappear. To start again. Like a do-over.'

I thought for a moment. 'I'm not sure I believe in do-overs. We get one life.'

'One life perhaps, but multiple acts.' He felt in his pocket for something and seemed a little panicked.

'You OK?' I asked.

'Yes,' he said. 'More than OK. In fact, I've got one last place I want to show you. If we leave now, we can be there before sundown.'

And so we got back in the car and made our way along the oxbow roads, Mark's foot full on the accelerator as he raced against the dying light. Each bend he took at speed forced my heart into the pit of my throat. I wondered if we would make it there – wherever there was – in one piece.

But I needn't have worried. Soon, we were pulling into the sleepy town of Marazion and looking out across the water to the sun dipping its head behind the majesty of St Michael's Mount – a tiny island half a mile offshore, but connected to the mainland at times of low tide by a narrow granite-sett causeway. At high tide, the sea washes over the path, as though there had never been a path at all, and the island lives up to its name.

'Quick,' said Mark.

The tide was coming in and the path was starting to disappear, so he grabbed my hand and we ran as fast as our legs would carry us across the wet sand, the icy wind slapping our faces and laughter punctuating our steps.

Each foot on the causeway sent great splashes of water leaping up. As we reached the middle of the path, it looked like we wouldn't make it across – *It's too deep*, I shouted – but Mark pulled me on, dragged me through the water that came up to our knees.

We made it. I dropped down on a rocky outcrop on the other side, out of breath and wet through.

'We're trapped,' I cried, looking out to the mainland.

Mark laughed. 'Not quite. There's a boat back.'

'So we didn't have to run?'

'More fun this way though, isn't it?'

'Oh, you're in so much trouble.'

He grinned. 'Possibly.'

Having both caught our breath, we climbed a long cobblestone pathway to the castle, which was on the verge of closing.

Just ten minutes, Mark pleaded, and we were waved on.

Last boat's soon, said the man. *Best be quick.*

A series of narrow pathways and steps led us up to the ramparts, where we were greeted with the most incredible view. In one direction, the shoreline, where the smoke rose from the chimneys of a hundred little houses and spread faintly across the bay; in the other, an endless, unbroken ocean that lay untroubled beneath a blanket of stars. And in that sublime, celestial moment, the sea became not a thing that kept us in, kept the island from the mainland, but a path in and of itself – a path to other lands, a path that

127

begged you not to stay put, but to venture forth, explore, connect. I looked out into the distance, out to the confluence of a great many worlds, and thought back to that pillbox, where I had sat and plotted and planned. Would that girl then recognise the life I've come to lead? Would she recognise the woman I've become?

'Incredible, isn't it?' said Mark, as he came up behind me and wrapped his arms about my waist.

'It's – It's not often I'm lost for words.'

There was a silence then as we both took in the view. I could feel Mark's warm breath on the nape of my neck.

'Well,' he said, 'do you think you could find just one?'

Mark's hands withdrew from me and I felt him step away. When I turned, there he was, down on one knee, with a diamond ring reflecting back the last light of the sun. It was elegant, it was beautiful; it was everything I had ever wanted in one object, in one gesture. He was everything I had ever wanted, and here he was offering himself up, staking a claim over my future, over our future. It felt too soon, a little rushed, and yet it felt right, absolutely right, and I knew, in my heart, just as Grandma knew before me, that there was no other answer in the world. I knew him, all of him, and in time he would know me, all of me.

'Yes!' I screamed – first at Mark and then out into the vast ocean, so that the whole world might hear too – 'Yes!'

*

Karen, Grandma and I returned to that beach in Camber every summer, come what may, hell or high water, until Grandma no longer had the strength in her legs to make the journey. It started with a small fall at home, a trip to the hospital, clipboards, pens, white jackets and disinfectant; a fracture, a break, a blood test, a scan, more scans, and then a final scan; it ended with a growth and a conversation that a doctor had been steeling himself for.

It's not good news, Mrs Webb.

No, replied Grandma, *I don't suppose it is.*

In a cruel parody of her arrival at the farm to look after Mother, Mother now returned to look after Grandma. It was happening all over again.

'How's Derek?' croaked Grandma, as we gathered around her bed one evening. By this point, she was too weak to sit up; her speech was too throttled, and she was forever slipping in and out of consciousness as the medicine eased her suffering.

'I wouldn't know,' said Mother, struggling to manoeuvre Grandma's arms into a tatty old cardigan. 'I barely see him. And that suits me fine.'

'Trouble in paradise, dear?'

'Trouble on earth.'

Grandma threw K and me a look as if to say *look what awaits you*.

'Well, that's marriage, dear. You've got to take the good with the bad.'

'There's so much bad that I've forgotten what the good looks like.'

'But you're happy?'

Mother thought for a moment. I don't think she'd ever asked herself that question. Then she looked at us, the daughters she'd all but abandoned. A certain melancholy came over her.

'I could be happier.'

Grandma waged a war with her own body to get the words out. 'We could all be happier,' she struggled, every other word followed by a deep intake of breath. 'It's what we do with the happiness we have. We must grab it with both hands or else let it go altogether.'

'Are you happy, Mum?' Mother was on the brink of tears as Grandma drew her hands to her face.

'I'm the happiest. And as for you … I'll have a word with Him Upstairs when I get there. That's if your father lets me get a word in edgeways.'

That is one of the very last memories I have of Grandma – a frail old woman in her final moments, waiting to meet her maker, and welcoming, with open arms, the chance to be reunited with her soulmate.

Piece by piece her mind faded gradually over the coming weeks; by the following month, she too was gone. The woman who had entered our pained little lives left, having taken the pain from us and having taught us how to heal.

We buried Grandma in a plot beside Grandpa. *Here lies Eileen Bertha Webb*, said the headstone, *Beloved Wife, Mother and Grandmother.* It seemed such a petty summation of a rich life. *That it?* I could hear her saying. *That all I get?*

When we arrived back after the funeral, I went outside, sat behind the pillbox, withdrew a cigarette from a crumpled-up pack and struggled to strike a match against the strong head-winds. Three times I tried before giving up, the cigarette balanced precariously between my lips.

'Let me,' said a voice. Mother crouched beside me and cupped hands around my mouth. I lit the cigarette successfully in the shadow of the makeshift windbreaker and looked up with just a hint of suspicion. 'Oh, you're almost eighteen,' said Mother. 'What do I care. Besides ...' She took another cigarette from the pack, pressed it up against the cherry on mine and placed it in her mouth. 'It's been one of those days.'

It had been one of those lifetimes. Jessica, Dad and now Grandma. Three generations had passed in the blink of an eye. Three people I had loved, three people I would always love ... gone. You love someone and they go. It seemed to me then that it would be far simpler if we had never loved at all.

'Too much death has visited this family,' said Mother, as though picking up the thought. 'If I believed in such a thing, I'd say it was cursed, and it has cursed us.' She looked at me, her eyes blood-red from weeping. 'But perhaps I am the cursed one, perhaps I am the curse.'

Did she want me to disagree?

'I just hope, one day, in the not-too-distant future, we'll be able to put all this misery behind us. I hope we can bury this sadness and each find the happiness we deserve. I tried to be a good mother, Annie, I really did, but I don't think I was cut out for motherhood. It fits some women like a comfy shoe and you wonder how they could have been anything other than the mother they became. But not me; I had to work at it, and still I managed to fail. I failed me, and I failed you girls.'

'You didn't fail –'

'Yes, I did. And that's OK. I could have been gentler, more open, less strict on you both. I could have been kinder to *you*.' Mother wiped a tear from her cheek and I remember thinking how pretty she looked when she cried. 'You deserved better. You deserve better. So, yes, I failed, Annie, but I suppose sometimes one needs to fail in order to go back and try again. I want to try again.'

I didn't really know what to say; I wasn't sure if I could forgive her, just like that, after all that time.

'Just think about it, OK?'

A chill wind whistled up and through the windows of the pill-box, prompting Mother to pull her jacket tight around her.

'They'll be waiting for us inside,' she said, stubbing out her cigarette. 'Ready?'

*

'Annie.'

'Yes?'

'I said *are you ready?*'

'Huh?'

Karen was stood beside me, peering through the slats on the fence at the foot of the farm. The odd car raced along the main road, headlights full-beam in the pitch-black night.

'Have you got the torch?' pressed K.

'Yes,' I said. 'I think so.'

I looked down and found the pink torch resting in the pouch on the front of my dungarees. In answer, Karen held aloft her butterfly net with a pride usually reserved for show-and-tell.

'You think we'll get one this time?' said K, running her little fingers through the latticework of the net.

'Only if you're quick.'

'I am quick.'

'No, really quick.'

131

'Give me the torch then if you think you can do better.'

'You know I won't be able to squeeze through the fence in time.'

K thrust her tongue into her bottom lip. I *really* hated that.

'Annie, look!'

In the brush opposite, a rabbit tentatively made its presence known. It emerged from a tangle of brambles and crossed the small grass verge on the other side of the road. A car swept past and still the rabbit didn't move; it sat there, motionless, staring at us, watching, waiting. It seemed to be trying to tell me something, but I didn't know what. It seemed to be trying to understand.

'Flash the torch, Annie.'

But I didn't; I just stood there and stared.

'Come on. It's gonna get away.'

'Shush,' I said and slowly inched forward to open the gate.

'What are you doing?'

'Be quiet and stay here.'

I closed the gate behind me, crossed the road and knelt down on the grass verge, a pen's breadth between me and the rabbit. Still it did not move. And as I looked into its glassy eyes, I saw pain, only pain. The rabbit was hurting, but it could not understand why.

'Annie!' yelled Karen, so loud I worried it might wake Dad. 'Help!'

I stood up quickly and turned around. Another car swept past, its headlights dazzling me.

'Annie!'

Karen was pointing to something emerging from the house and making its way down the long gravel drive. It was walking uncertainly, unnaturally. It seemed to carry a cloud. And as it drew nearer, as K's screams became more forceful, more persistent, more feverish, the figure resolved itself: a small child with a black veil over its face.

I awoke in the guest house in a hot sweat, a tangle of duvet around me, constricting me. I couldn't breathe. I tried to shake off the nightmare, shake myself back into reality, but my reality was no less disquieting – there, staring at me, several inches from my face, with a renewed blackness in his eyes and an intensity I hadn't seen before, was Mark. He had been looking at me, watching me sleep, and I had the strangest feeling in that moment that he meant to do me harm. Then just as I was about to cry out, just as I made to kick him in the chest with all my might, he grabbed my leg hard about the ankle.

'Who is Jessica?' he said. 'Why do you keep calling for Jessica?'

21

I suggested Mark see someone. A professional. Someone who might help him with his drinking. It is beginning to affect everything – his temperament, his work, his relationships. But he refuses to acknowledge there is even a problem. I'm just unwinding, he will say. You're unwinding all day, every day, I answer.

Sometimes I push him too far and I see a devil dancing inside him, waiting to come out. So I retreat, regroup and try again the next time. But what if the next time is the last time? What if he does something unspeakable?

Mr Rahman from the hospital phoned yesterday. I assumed he was looking for Mark, but no, it was me he wanted to speak with. We'd met once at a charity benefit, but that's it. I was surprised he even remembered my name.

What's wrong? I asked.

Mark apparently arrived in theatre in a state, stinking of the night before. He suggested Mark take some time off – to recover. He's used to giving prescriptions, but he seemed uneasy giving this one.

I'll talk with him, I said.

Thank you, he replied. I really think it's for the best.

Later that night, we went for a walk – down along Court Lane, round the old circle of Dulwich Park, past the Picture Gallery, and then right through Lovers Walk. We passed two teenagers pressed up against a lamp post in a clinch and in a world of their own before suddenly becoming aware of their new audience and scampering off. I smiled to Mark and he smiled back.

Rahman phoned, I said.

Mark stopped still in the darkness and I became very aware of how alone we now were. Just two figures on a narrow path among the trees.

He wants you to take some time off. He's worried, really worried.

Mark turned to face me, and the devil did too.

I braced myself, tensed my whole body, but the anger never came. Instead, he walked to me slowly, drew me in tight and said, I'm worried about you too.

22

Cameron approached the late Victorian terraced house in Oxford with just a hint of apprehension. Frank had been very specific on the phone: he did not want his wife playing any part in this. *Let's try to keep this between us*, he had said. Yet Cameron understood in his gut that Mark knew more of his wife's disappearance than he was ever prepared to let on. And who better to unlock the man than the mother? Jean held the key to this, whether in part or in whole. He had to speak with her, or his job would not be worth doing. Frank would thank him for it later.

As Cameron rang the bell, noting the little porcelain Siamese cats perched on the windowsill, the understanding in his gut turned into a sinking feeling.

'Hello, Mrs Lane,' he said when the door opened finally. A small woman, with a straw-hat of grey hair, poked an aquiline nose through the tiny opening, the door still latched to the jamb with a chain.

'Yes?' she said.

'I'm a friend of Frank's,' said Cameron. 'We went to school together.'

'Oh,' she said, still holding the door open only a crack, still unsure of her visitor. 'He won't be back for some time.'

'Well, it was actually you I was hoping to speak with.'

'Me?'

'May I?' said Cameron, gesturing to the door.

Jean smiled. 'I better put the kettle on.'

'He was always such a mother's boy, growing up,' said Jean, as she returned to the living room bearing two cups of tea and a plate of biscuits on a wooden tray. 'Tuck in, won't you.' Cameron took a biscuit and dunked it in his tea. 'Everywhere I went, he wasn't very far behind.'

'That must have been very nice for you,' said Cameron, realising that he'd held the biscuit in the tea for too long and it had started to break apart.

'Oh, it was. Mark was never much interested in the traditional boysy-stuff. Which, of course, came as somewhat of a disappointment to Frank, raised as he was. Press-ups, boot shining, that sort of thing. Frank was rather hoping that he'd follow in his footsteps, but not Mark. He wanted to help people, and medicine was a way for him to do that.'

'Are they close, would you say, Mrs Lane?'

'Please, call me Jean.' She thought for a moment and took a sip of tea. She must have found it bitter, for she winced. 'They've had their disagreements – being a teenager is a curse we all share – but they worked through them. Now ... well, I'd say they're closer than ever.'

'And the disappearance?'

Jean changed at the very mention. Her shoulders grew stiff, her back arched.

'What about it?'

'Did it bring them closer?'

Jean drew a blanket over her legs. 'Quite the opposite. It drove Mark away. Even now we hardly see him. He's engaged, I'm told, to a woman I barely know – I've met her once – and the wedding's a few months away. She seemed nice enough, I welcomed her as any prospective mother-in-law should, and I'm glad Mark is on the road to happiness again, but tell me: is that normal behaviour? I'm his mother.'

'Do you think he blames you?'

'For what?'

'For his wife walking out on him.'

'I should hope not. I did everything for that girl, went out of my way to make her feel welcome, to bring her into the family, but she always gave off the impression, to me at least, that she could never truly commit.'

'To Mark?'

'To this family. Unsurprising really, given she had never had one of her own. I guess if you're not used to it, being part of a family is work, and hard work at that. Frank thought the world of her, of course. So did Mark, but that hardly needs saying.' She stopped then and looked up at Cameron. 'Is that why you're here? Her?'

He nodded weakly.

'Talk to Pete,' she said firmly.

'I have.'

'And what did he say?'

'He implied, more than implied, that Mark had been, how shall I put this, stepping outside of the marriage.'

'Mark? Nonsense.'

'I'm afraid a colleague at the hospital all but confirmed it.'

Jean grew sullen, her indignation taken from her just as it was finding its feet.

'He wouldn't do that, he loved –'

'He may well have done. But I'm not here to pronounce on the limits of love; I'm here to understand.'

'Yes, of course,' said Jean, as she looked out the window. 'Do you do this often then? Pry?'

'No,' he laughed. 'Not for a while, anyway. I'm a joiner, really – have my own little business. I decided long ago that my hands served me better than my mind.'

'I wouldn't be so sure. You're sharp, sharper than me.'

'That's kind of you to say, but my wife does all the best thinking in our house.'

Jean laughed. 'Women always do.'

'Is there anything else you can tell me about Mark's marriage, anything that might indicate what caused her to leave?'

'I'm sorry ...'

'Cameron.'

'Cameron. I told the police at the time everything I knew. They were very thorough. Asked me all sorts, but I couldn't answer much of it. As far as I was concerned, they were happy. There was no suggestion that Mark was playing away – I still don't believe it for one moment – and she seemed to lead her own life, a full life. But ...'

Cameron leant forwards. 'Yes?'

'Shortly before the disappearance, she made a new friend. Mentioned her all the time – a yoga friend, I think. One might suspect there was a romantic element there. In fact, I'd put my money on it being her playing away, not Mark; especially with him keeping those long hours at the hospital. How would he find the time? But I wouldn't wish to speculate.'

'Can you remember her name? The friend.'

Jean closed her eyes and ran her fingers over her temples. 'Her name …' After some time, she opened her eyes. 'I'm sorry, it's gone.'

Cameron sighed, his breakthrough snatched from him in a fog.

'That's quite all right. Thank you for your time, and the tea.'

Jean smiled and got up to walk Cameron to the door. He gestured to the porcelain cats on the windowsill.

'Oh, those,' said Jean. 'Frank is allergic to the real thing. Marriage is all about compromise. So we do. Keeps us going after all these years.'

'Thank you again Mrs –, ' but he caught himself before he finished the sentence. 'Thank you, Jean.'

'Charlotte,' she blurted.

'Sorry?'

'Hope's friend. Her name … It was Charlotte.'

'Are you sure?'

'Positive. I never met her, of course, but that was her name. Sure of it.'

Cameron made a note on his pad, and scribbled a number on the corner of a piece of paper, which he tore off and handed to Jean.

'If you remember anything else, I'd be grateful If you would give me a call. Oh, and I'm not one to encourage secrets in a marriage, but my life would be a hell of a lot easier if you don't tell Frank you saw me today. I'm not sure he'd understand.'

'There are many things I don't tell my husband, and, I'm sure, many things he does not tell me. Secrets are a gift in the right hands. You were never here.'

And soon, as he got in his car and left the city, he might never have been.

140

23

Once upon a time, or so the story goes, a handsome sculptor named Pygmalion, the finest sculptor in all of Cyprus, despairing of the manner in which love was given so freely and taken so insincerely, turned his back on women for good, vowing, as he did, never to take a bride so long as there was strength in his hands to forge his art. For art is all, he reasoned. It is the thing through which we understand that which we cannot. Sculptures were the only beauty he knew and would ever need to know.

So one day, in his workshop, faced with a block of marble, Pygmalion set to work on carving a woman of unrivalled beauty. For many months, he locked himself away, chiselling here and hammering there, his arms heavy from the labour; and when he was done, as Eos threw open the gates of dawn, he stepped back and wept just to look upon his work – for there, having emerged from the milk-white stone, was the most perfect woman he'd ever seen. Full thighs, delicate lips, hair down to the small of her back and a heart-shaped face that demanded only love. She was not like the other women that Pygmalion had known; she was chaste, she was pure, she was virginal, and through her form and her poise, she managed, effortlessly it seemed, to communicate to him, to anyone who should chance to look upon her, an eternal ideal. She was the woman Pygmalion had believed he would never find. In a fit of madness, in the grip of a swarm of desire, he named the statue Galatea.

Each day he caressed Galatea's face, dressed her in the finest silks and placed his warm, soft lips to the cold, hard, unyielding stone. He had fallen in love.

Soon came the festival of Aphrodite, at which offerings were made, incense burned and music played in the great goddess' honour. Pygmalion too was in attendance and made a point of visiting Aphrodite's temple to atone for the many years in which he had not observed her splendour. At the temple, he fell deep in prayer.

'You gods,' he said, 'you who are capable of all things, I ask for only one: that you grant me a wife, a woman that I can love and who can love me, unconditionally.'

Aphrodite heard Pygmalion's pleas, and taken with his plight, paid a visit to the young sculptor's studio set high upon the hill. Upon entering she saw the object of his desire, understood his need and was amazed to see that the sculpture had been cast in her own image. Charmed and not a little flattered, she set about granting Pygmalion's wish.

Once the festival of Aphrodite had come to an end, the sculptor returned home and, as was his habit, planted a kiss upon Galatea's milky lips. But this time, as he did so, as the warmth of his lips met the stone, he felt a warmth radiate back at him. The stone had softened, had grown eyes to see, had found legs to walk and a mouth to speak. After his time of celibacy, of singledom and suffering, he was finally blessed with a wife with whom he would live out the rest of his days in the sweet ecstasy of companionship and love.

Pygmalion had won his ideal by imagining it into existence. It is a powerful lesson that we should each carry with us always: just by thinking and believing and loving, we can make it so. The mind and the heart can conquer the physical world.

As I saw Mark for the first time on that train, as I watched him enter the carriage and grip on to the rail, surrounded by a sea of commuters, I was not looking upon the Mark I know now; I was looking at a pure lump of stone that could be refashioned and remade. And so remade he was. Mark became my Galatea, my milk-white statue, hewn from a rougher, more primitive thing by my own hand – a hand that has only ever wanted the best for him, and will only ever want the best for him.

Then, he did not know his own mind. He was helpless, unformed, trapped even, in a loveless marriage with a woman who did not, could not, love him. But I came along, with my hammer and chisel, and I freed him from all that, from the burden of his past. He has never thanked me for it, why should he; he thanks me every day in his kiss, his laughter, his touch. He thanks me every day with his indelible goodness.

I fell in love with him, with the idea of him – don't we all fall in love with an idea first? – and in time, gently shaped that idea, gave it flesh, made it real, and so it was that he, in turn, fell in love with me, with Annie. It happened so gradually, an unwitting lobster in a warming pot, that he didn't even sense the hard marble softening. But soon enough the statue had a heartbeat, it had a pulse. The grief became joy, despair became hope, and the hole that his wife had left, the gaping maw within him, was filled, by me. And so long as there is strength in my hands and breath in my body, he can never know it was I who put it there in the first place.

What's past is prologue.

PART THREE

THE HONEYMOON

Three days after the wedding ...

24

Cameron sat in his office, far above the factory floor of his carpentry business, surrounded by reams of invoices – some paid, some not – and turned over in his hand, delicately so that the light could touch every surface, a wooden model boat. The craftsmanship was extraordinary, he thought, but then he would: he had made it himself, but not *by* himself. His father had cut and carved and whittled and sanded and varnished, had lashed the white cotton sails to the three masts, had cursed when a splinter slid under the bed of a nail, had laughed as little Cam managed to glue his palm to the hull and had smiled, satisfied at last, the moment his son gingerly applied the final lick of blue paint. They had built the ship together.

Away from the cruel playground, Cameron's childhood was a happy one, mostly. His mother was doting – the very image of the 1950s housewife, complete with chequerboard apron and hair curlers. She fussed but she did so with love. Never nuisance, love. His father was a different prospect altogether; *his* love was not given freely, but rather held tightly, secured fast by lock and key. You could see it glinting in the gloom, just, if you chanced to find him in high spirits after a glass of his favourite scotch. Then, in those dark hours spent in his workshop in the basement of the house, you might encounter a man who measured out his love, as one might a dram of whisky, through the time he spent with those dearest to him.

And so, late at night, as his mother half-dozed in the sitting room, her knitting unfurling on her lap, Cameron would creep to the basement and join his father in the workshop. The first of such evenings, Cameron made his way down the dimly lit stairs and found his father bent double over a lathe.

At some point, he must have become aware of the young boy's presence.

'Put those on,' he said, without looking up and back to the small, diffident figure lurking behind him, watching him work.

Cameron inched forward and picked up a pair of safety goggles from the nearest bench. The elastic made a satisfying *snap* on the back of his head as he secured them in place.

'Now take this –' His father passed him a small, curved chisel. '– and hold it right here. Keep it flat now. Steady ...'

The lathe seemed to gather speed, to whir and buzz, as Cam slowly manoeuvred the chisel towards a groove in the spinning length of wood. His eyes ran along the even grain, noting, here and there, the presence of numerous circular notches of varying widths and gradients, beautiful in their regularity and simplicity. He realised with some wonder that this was the makings of a table leg. With the slightest of movements, Cameron met the wood with his chisel, prompting a long, thin shaving to break free of the surface and curl up and out in a tendril towards him. He sought in that moment to smile at the old man, to try to see if there was but a hint of pride in his worn face, to catch the glint in the gloom; but as he did so, his tool slipped and careened across the wood.

His father shut off the lathe with a bang. 'Just look at this mess ...'

With tears on the verge of overcoming him, Cameron made to run away, but his father grabbed the back of Cameron's dungarees.

'And where do you think you're going? If you make a mess, you stay and you clean it up. Now, come on – we'll have to start over.'

Cameron blinked up at the man who still had hold of his clothes.

'And wipe those eyes.'

Cameron thought of all this as he continued to rotate the model boat in his hand. He thought of how his father had him fix a fresh block of maple to the lathe, how he had watched him turn it, shape it, each notch a puncture in the wood's flesh. Cameron's skill would grow immeasurably with each new block that was set before him.

Night passed and morning announced itself in a sprinkle of light through the lone basement window. Cameron's father held his son's labour up to the dawn. It was raw, a little rough around the edges, but it was a table leg all right. He smiled to himself.

'We'll make a chippy of you yet.'

When Cameron's skill approached that of his father's, the lessons ended, and play began. Thereafter, every evening they would whittle and carve and sand and finish for the pure joy of it. Cam's mother would creep down the stairs and find her husband and her son bent over the lathe, together. If his father did measure out his love in time, he had finally poured young Cam a full glass.

One evening, as Cameron sanded the cherrywood that would shortly form the quarterdeck of their latest project, a wooden sailboat, his father took his son's hand abruptly and led him upstairs to the sitting room where Cameron's mother lay sleeping.

'Thirty-two years that woman has looked after me,' he said, running his fingers thoughtfully through his shaggy beard. 'When I'm gone, she'll need someone to look after her.'

Cameron's shoulders rounded as though a great weight had been placed on his neck.

'In time, and not before, I want you to take over the business. My hands are not what they once were, but yours ...'

His father became drawn in thought. His slight build formed an even slighter silhouette against the pale glow of the living-room lamp.

'You'll soon be a man and that brings with it certain responsibilities, certain duties. You see, and I say this because it was once said to me at your age, for which I am glad: every man must lift the heaviest rock he can find and carry it up a long, steep hill.'

'A rock?' Cameron's small features bunched in confusion.

'Yes, a rock. Now some men choose a pebble and they summit the hill without so much as breaking a sweat. They make it to the top but what have they achieved? They have not grown, they have not prospered. But not you. You're better than that. You will bear a boulder and you will keep going. You hear me?'

Those words rang softly in Cameron's ear as he sat in his office and continued to turn the boat against the light, just as he once turned the wood on his father's lathe. He considered the boat, considered the gunports and the rigging, the bowsprit and the keel, and wondered in that moment, as one wonders at the vastness of the oceans and all that lies beneath, whether he'd dropped his boulder a long time ago, or else if he'd ever held one at all. He thought of Mrs Capel, the death that broke him, the case that made him leave the Force, and he thought about the life he'd left behind.

*

'She's here again.'

Cameron looked up from his paper and allowed a note of irritation to creep into his voice. 'That's the third time this week. Can't Bill take it?'

The young DC shook her head. 'She asked for you by name.'

'Of course she did.'

Cameron finished the remainder of his black coffee in one exaggerated mouthful and made his way downstairs to the front desk. No sooner had he set foot through the double-swing doors, a woman was fast upon him. Small, red hair, a nest of crow's feet sprouting from each eye.

'Detective, I need to speak with you.'

The din of the station – the processing, the protesting – receded the moment Cameron closed the door of the interview room behind them. Nervous at first but gradually assured, Mrs Capel settled her small frame into a hard plastic chair.

Cameron sat opposite, pen and pad in hand.

'It's getting worse, Detective.'

Mrs Capel raised her hand, then hesitated. Once certain of Cameron's full attention, she gently pulled back the shoulder of her sweater to reveal a small circular bruise, no bigger than a postage stamp. She held Cameron's gaze.

150

'I came home with the shopping yesterday ... He was in the garden, a phone to his ear. I didn't announce myself, perhaps I should have, I don't know, but I didn't. I went to the bedroom window and I opened it just a crack. His voice travelled. He mentioned Copenhagen, so I assumed it was work-related. I went to close the window again, but he looked up at that moment and saw me listening in. "Get down here," he yelled. He was waiting for me at the bottom of the stairs, anger everywhere. And that's when ...'

She rubbed her thumb delicately over the bruise.

Cameron made a note in his pad and then tapped the desk decisively with the head of his pen. 'Mrs Capel, I'd like for a colleague, a female colleague, to examine you – with your consent, of course. Is that quite all right?'

She shifted uneasily in her chair.

'No, I don't want that. It's too —'

'I understand,' he said. 'But we're going to need to take some photographs, for evidence, and I require a formal written statement from you.'

'No,' she repeated, more forcefully this time. 'I can't, he'll —' Her words tapered away. 'Can't you speak with him?'

Cameron sighed.

'Please,' she said. There was a wild desperation in her eyes. 'Just talk with him again. Your colleagues have tried, but you ... I think he'd listen to you. I wish he would just —'

'Just what?'

'Sometimes ... Sometimes when I'm lying beside him at night, and I can't sleep for fear of what he might ... I close my eyes, close them real tight until all I see are colours washing back and forth, and I wish ... I wish he would just die.'

With that, Mrs Capel broke into floods of tears. Cameron made to comfort her, but before he had the chance to extend a sympathetic hand, his attention was drawn to the hazy figure stood beyond the frosted-glass window. He couldn't be sure, but from the slight depression of her face and the fossa of her cheeks, she seemed to be frowning.

'She's mad,' said DCI Vernon, once Cameron had left Mrs Capel clasping her hands to the warmth of her tea. 'We've interviewed

151

the husband countless times; he's squeaky clean. But her ... We notified the CPS and they won't touch it. She has form – a long history of making false accusations, and not just against her husband ... Her sister, former colleagues ... She accused her own mother of stealing from her. I've got her psychological records if you'd like to see them but they don't make for pretty reading.'

Cameron looked at his boss as if to say *I know*.

'You've spent enough of your time on this. I need you elsewhere.'

'Yes, Ma'am.'

'I'm serious. I know you, and I know you want to help, but you can't help *her*. Give this fire any more oxygen and it'll consume us all.'

A greying man with thick, black, circular glasses perched on the peak of his nose, looked up at Cameron as he stood on the threshold of the barn.

'Can I come in?'

'Who's asking?' said the man, looking down again to the spread of graph paper before him. He corrected a line with his pencil, licked the tip. An old habit, Cameron supposed; his father would do the same.

'Detective Inspector Wilkes.'

The man tucked his pencil in his shirt pocket. 'Then I suppose you better.'

Cameron approached the table and looked down at the surface, at a giant sheet of paper containing all manner of lines, etchings, precision measurements, notations and marginalia.

'A conversion,' said the man, anticipating a thought.

'This barn?'

'Oast house,' he corrected. 'Not much call for them any more, save for residential use. It's funny: many started out as cottages before being converted, and now here we are converting them back again.'

'And this?' Cameron pointed to an area on the schematic that resembled an uroboros, a winding, self-eating snake.

'Let me see ... Oh, that. Well, the owners want a slide, for their kids, built inside the perimeter of the roundel, starting right up there at the top, beneath the cowl.'

152

'Just like in the old days,' smiled Cameron.

The man smiled in response and offered his hand to the inspector. 'Edward Capel. I'd suggest a tea or perhaps a coffee even, but I'm a little under-equipped.' Edward gestured to the empty expanse of the house's interior. Bricks and exposed beams, little else.

'I don't plan on staying long. A flying visit.'

'In that case, what can I do for you, Detective?'

Cameron rubbed the back of his neck, hesitated. 'It concerns your wife.'

'Veronica? What's she done now?'

'Well, nothing. Nothing that I'm aware of anyway, but she has been to see me. Four times in as many weeks, to be precise.'

Edward seemed genuinely surprised. 'What for?'

'That's where I'm hoping you can help me. You see, she showed me a bruise.'

'A bruise? What kind of bruise?'

'At the top of her arm. She said you'd put it there.'

Edward rolled his eyes up to the roof of the roundel.

'I'm ever so sorry, Detective.'

'You hit her?'

The man held his hands to his chest, a little too theatrically for Cameron's liking.

'God, no,' he said. 'I'm sorry only that you've been blighted with this nonsense, *her* nonsense.' Edward sat on the edge of the table and massaged his temples. His long grey locks spilt over his hands. 'I thought we'd moved past this, I really did. I thought she was better. You're aware of her history, I take it?'

'I am.'

'And do you think me capable of such a thing?'

'All men are capable of all things, Mr Capel.'

Edward sighed, then grew maudlin as he spoke. 'Twenty years we've been married. Twenty years. Her brother warned me before we got together that there was – how did he put it? – a *wild streak in her*. And there was. She was impulsive, passionate, carefree. It was one of the many reasons I fell in love with her. But it was never like this. I thought she would mellow as the years went by, but it's only gotten worse. Perhaps I am to blame.'

153

Cameron had difficulty squaring the man he saw before him with the role of the abusive husband. Mr Capel was charming, he was convincing, but then, Cameron reminded himself, the best criminals are. Actors playing a role.

'Have you been arguing a lot lately? Perhaps some choice words were exchanged, regrettable? Did you get angry, Mr Capel?'

Cameron eyeballed Edward.

'No. I –'

'Then how do you account for the bruise?'

'I – I don't know.'

'You don't know?'

'I don't like to speak ill of my wife, but she is – how do I put this – a fantasist. I've never laid a hand on that woman. Really, I haven't. I've been through all this before.' Edward's face grew pained.

Perhaps it was his ruddy cheeks or his slight air of disorder, but Cameron believed him. He never could quite put his finger on why.

'I'm not here to upset you.'

'Not at all,' said Edward, passing his hand through the air as though dismissing a fly or an over-attentive waiter. 'It's your job.'

'It is, and I'll be perfectly honest with you, I've got much better things to be getting on with.'

'Yes, yes, of course. I'll have a word with her ... wasting police time ... It's really not on. Just, please, I beg of you, don't take any formal action. She's been through a lot. Lost her mother last year, poor thing. I'll take care of it, speak with her doctor again, something.'

Cameron nodded, considered the man, wondered if he'd even done the right thing by coming here.

'I'll see myself out.'

'Oh, just before you go, Detective, take this.' Edward handed Cameron a business card. *Capel + Dock Designs*, it read, the letters running in a circle around the doodle of a small rowing boat. 'So you know where to find me.'

*

Cameron gently placed the model wooden boat that he had been turning over in his hands on the paper-strewn desk before him.

Sophie had offered to spend a day each week at the office, processing the invoices that threatened to spill on to the factory floor below, but the prospect unnerved him. He'd heard so many stories of marriages that had faltered in the wake of spouses working together. Even though he knew in his heart of hearts that their marriage was strong, stronger than it had ever been, he didn't wish to leave anything to chance – so what if it meant a few extra late evenings in the office; it was, after all, where he felt closest to his father. And lately, he seemed to be further away than ever.

'Cam, you will come back, won't you?' his mother asked shortly after his father's passing.

'I've got a career here, Mum. I can't just up and leave. What about Sophie, what about –'

'Your father always wanted you to take over the business. You know that.'

Cameron thought back to the promise he'd made as his mother lay dozing on the sofa. He thought about the boulder and he thought about the climb.

'I'll think about it, Mum.'

'You do that, but hurry; I'm not sure how much longer I can keep going on my own.'

*

As soon as Cameron had set foot inside DCI Vernon's office, she shut the door. He knew this was serious.

'Take a seat,' she said, gesturing to what was once an armchair, but was now an explosion of foam and ripped leather.

'Ma'am.'

'I'm afraid I have some bad news – about Mrs Capel.'

'Veronica?'

DCI Vernon seemed in equal measures concerned and surprised that the Detective should be on first-name terms with the woman.

'I know you paid her husband a visit last week.'

155

Cameron flushed red and a heat ringed his collar.

'Look, I –'

DCI Vernon cut him short. 'I'm not interested in the whys and wherefores. This has gone beyond that now.' There was a leaden gravity in her voice. 'I'm afraid she's dead.'

Cameron's stomach seized.

'A neighbour saw smoke pouring from the garage. He went to check and, well, he found them both sitting there, in their car, a hosepipe running from the exhaust.'

'Did he – ?'

DCI Vernon simply nodded.

'Her hands were tied to the interior roof handle. And we found this in her handbag.'

It was a Post-it note folded up into a square the size of a stamp.

I shall leave him a knife, a fork and a spoon. And it will be too much.

'I'm so sorry, Cameron. I know what you're thinking, but you did all you could.'

'But not enough.'

'This is not your fault.' The words were measured, emphatic.

Cameron held his head in his hands. How had he missed the signs? How had he allowed himself to be charmed by that, that … man?

'I'll give you some time to yourself.'

With that, DCI Vernon left her office and Cameron found himself desperately alone. His breath was a rattle that started in the belly and worked its way up and out through his throat. He feared that his body might break from the sheer force of each exhale. As the rattle grew louder and the room grew smaller, Cameron sat in the tatty armchair and wept. He wept for his father. He wept for his mother. He wept for the woman whom he did not, could not, save.

*

Cameron considered the little wooden sailboat that served as a reminder of a man who had stood so powerfully within his life,

156

and he wondered how different things might have been had he not left the Force; how different things might have been had his own sense of failure, of failing her, not pressed upon him to cut and run. He could no longer trust himself, no longer trust his own judgement – to sieve good from evil, right from wrong, the actor from the acted upon. What he could trust, what he knew, was a piece of wood and a plane. But as he studied the boat, noting an uneven bind here, a dash of rogue paint there, he remembered how disastrous his first attempt at turning had been, how he had wanted to run then too, how his father wouldn't let him, had brought him back to try again. And he did, he did try again. He stayed, and the little wooden boat, imperfect though it was, took shape and found its sail.

Every man must lift the heaviest rock he can find and carry it up a long, steep hill, his father had said. He remembered it clearly, the underlying message that his father had wished to impress: responsibility. Cameron had to start taking responsibility. He had spent far too long running from it, running when things got tough. He was tired of running.

An abusive husband had once slipped justice from right under his nose; he wouldn't, he couldn't, let that happen again. Mark would continue to be a prime suspect until proven otherwise. Besides, it was not as if he had a surfeit of leads.

Cameron looked around the office at the reams of paperwork, down through the glass window to the factory floor below where cabinets and tables lay unfinished, and he realised that in leaving the Force and returning to the family business, he hadn't heeded his father's words at all; he had merely swapped one pebble for another. But in taking Frank's case, in searching for Hope, for the missing woman, he had finally picked up his boulder, and he would be damned if he was going to drop it.

25

It's been three days. I'm officially Mrs Mark Lane, and I'm sat, on my honeymoon, at the edge of a villa overlooking the crystal-line Tyrrhenian Sea, watching out towards the sun-beaten bay of Naples, and still my husband has not touched me.

It's funny how you can be in one of the most beautiful places on Earth, with the person you love the most, whom you would do anything for, and who has vowed before a church-load of people to love you too, come what may, and yet feel so terribly, wretch-edly alone.

Mark has gone for a walk. I asked him if he'd like company but he didn't answer. Instead, he dug his hands deep in his pock-ets and raised his shoulders just enough to suggest a shrug. *I'm a bit tired*, I offered, *I'll see you when you get back*. His relief was palpable. Do all newlyweds spend this much time apart?

Mark has disappeared every evening since we arrived, and despite his insistence that we need to talk, we're still yet to really do so. He tried, to his credit, as we sat in the Gatwick airport lounge watching the yellow and white lettering flicker on the departures board, but he struggled to find the words. He struggled to articu-late whatever thought had burrowed its way inside him, whatever thought had upended his surety, his confidence in me, in us.

Annie, I –

Have you ever felt like – ?

There's something that –

But the words stalled. A sentence felt a long way off. So instead we sat in silence, watching, waiting for our gate to be assigned.

For all my probing, I still don't know what is troubling him; he won't, or simply can't, tell me and I've stopped asking. Perhaps

I am worried what he might say, what I might discover. Some things are better left unsaid. Though perhaps ... Perhaps I don't ask because I already know the answer.

When he's gone, I've taken to sitting out and watching the ferries come and go between the island and the mainland; each evening I witness the sun die behind Vesuvius, causing a blood-orange vapour to fan out like a carpet across the tide. The ferries journey on, unconcerned, bearing lost souls to the land of the dead. For we are all dead here; there is nothing left alive. Mark knows that too.

I hear the keys rattling in the door. He is back from his walk, and I can tell from his tight pacing, from the heavy timbre of his footsteps, that something has upset him. A thought, perhaps, that he has made a terrible mistake.

'How was it?'

His eyes refuse to meet mine. 'Yes, fine.'

'Fine? This is Capri – nothing here is just *fine*.'

'OK, it was wonderful, glorious, superb, the most incredible show on earth. Happy?'

I look at him long and hard. There is dirt under his nails.

'Are you?'

Mark pushes past me to the bathroom and begins to apply a thin layer of foam to his second-day stubble. He considers me in the reflection of his small, circular shaving mirror.

'I'm not in the mood for games, Annie.'

'What games? What's prompted this?'

He dips the head of the razor under the warm tap, and tests the sharpness of the blade with the flat of his thumb. A small prick of blood forms.

'Have you been drinking?' I ask.

'You can't help yourself, can you? You're just waiting for me to trip up. It's as though you're comparing me to someone – and whoever it is, I'm not him. It's too much. It's –'

'*Me*? You think I'm comparing *you*.' Mark sucks the blood from his thumb. 'I've been living in your ex-wife's shadow from the moment we met.'

He turns to look at me, turns with a fire raging inside him. But it shall do him no good, for there is a fire raging inside me too, and it has been raging for too long. I can hold back the flames no longer. I have tried to be kind, considerate, patient; I have tried to give Mark the space I thought he needed. But it has changed nothing.

'I thought after the wedding, when we were married, things would be different, but she's still here, she's … She's gone, Mark. She walked out on you, walked out on your marriage and started a new life. God, she wanted to get away from you so badly that she vanished into thin air. She's dead to you, Mark. Hope is *dead*. It's time you buried her.'

We all have tells: tiny, almost imperceptible signs that we have reached the limits of our understanding. And now Mark has reached his; a small muscle to the left of his cheekbone flickers like a sputtering candle.

Too far, Annie.

'Look, I didn't mean –'

'Yes, you did,' he says, turning back to the mirror. 'You did mean.'

'Darling, look at me. Mark, please …'

I grab his chin and rotate it until he's forced to face me again.

'I love you.' His face softens, just. 'There's a whole lot of past out there, for both of us. But it is just that: the past. You, me –' I take his hand and guide it to the base of my stomach. 'This, all of this, whatever we may decide to create at some point, is the future. And nothing else matters. OK?'

Silence.

'Do you remember what you said to me that day in Polperro, as we stood on that cliff and looked out to sea? The day you proposed?'

Mark looks blank.

'*Wouldn't it be great to just take off somewhere, leave it all behind.* Well, here we are. We've made our great escape. We're somewhere, and it's all behind us. You said we live one life, with multiple acts. Now do you want to embrace this second act, or do you want to relive the first?'

I ease the razor from Mark's palm and run it under the tap. He has never allowed me to shave him before.

In slow, measured strokes, I gently run the blade from his right cheekbone to the ridge of his jaw. I rinse the blade and repeat the action on the left side of his face, before tilting his head back with a push at the centre of his forehead. *Boink*, I say, and he smiles, just.

With his head back, I rinse the blade one more time and draw a perfect line with the razor from the cleft at the base of his neck, up and over the bobbing hillock of his Adam's apple to the top of his throat.

And as I do so, as the razor makes its slow ascent, I think how easy it would be to slip, how easy it would be to cut him.

*

Before we moved to the farmhouse, we lived – the five of us – in a small cottage that straddled two counties. The front garden was in Kent, the rear garden in Sussex. Dad would joke that we lived neither here nor there, both hither and thither, and would pretend that the wardrobe in the bedroom that K, Jessica and I all shared, a room slap-bang in the middle of the in-between, led straight to a mythical land where a lion was king and the world had been frozen by a white witch. It was only when I was older, when I rifled further through the abandoned books at the farmhouse, that I realised where he had stolen that tale. Not stolen, perhaps, but repurposed. For all stories are a variation on a theme, an echo passed through a giant cave that emerges at the other end substantially the same and yet irrevocably altered. Life was smaller then, happier. Tragedy, it seemed, was a distant unknown that had yet to visit us.

'Daddy. Hand.'

Dad reached down to the small, unsteady shape beside him; Jessica reached up tentatively and wrapped her whole fist around his thumb.

Jessica was two, but she'd learned the basics, and understood, even at that tender age, that her vulnerability, her helplessness

162

was the only key she needed to unlock the world. She *was* cute, anyone could see that. The worst part was she knew it. Boy, did she know it.

A tiny head populated by big features – big eyes, big ears, big lips and blonde hair that exploded out in tightly wound curls from beneath an oversized bucket hat. She was spunky, she was stubborn, she was loud and unshakeable, and yet marked by a cheerful optimism that found its physical expression in the light-ness of her feet. You would never have guessed she'd started walking only a few months previously, for she bounded with such confidence and conviction that Mother had taken to calling her Rabbit.

And so she hopped and bounded with untrammelled glee as we made our way – Mother, Dad, Jessica, K and me – to the funfair that had arrived in the village one hot summer's night. Dressed only in T-shirts and shorts, we trod the quiet country lanes, ever-green trees and hedgerows all about us, the faint scent of freshly cut grass in the air and the lights of the various stalls and rides and amusements flickering low in the distance. For some time we walked in silence. Mother sighed every now and then, but they were sweet sighs, happy sighs.

We turned at the corner of an old pub, when Dad, appearing to spot something we hadn't, stopped and crouched down behind Jessica, rested his chin gingerly on her right shoulder and encir-cled her waist with his hand.

'Look!' Dad pointed up to the sky, just beyond a row of ash trees. He turned to K and me. 'You too, girls.'

We all crowded in and looked up at the moon, at two moons: one darker, rounder orb seemingly suspended between the horns of a brighter crescent.

'You see that?' said Dad. 'Right up there?'

We squinted at the brightness.

'The new moon is holding the old moon in its arms.'

Mother smiled at me.

'Is the old moon tired?' asked K, confused. She was struggling, had been struggling, for a long time with the prospect of no longer being the centre of her parents' universe, no longer being the shiniest, brightest star in that universe; a fact I'd reluctantly accepted about my own standing a long time before. But for K ... Well, Jessica's arrival had catapulted K into the unenviable position of middle child.

'Yes, love,' said Dad, not quite realising the intent behind the question. 'He's tired. The old moon has done his job, and it's time for the new moon to take over.'

K's eyes narrowed to a point. 'But maybe the old moon doesn't *want* the new moon to take over.' Her initial confusion had turned to obstinacy. She stamped her foot, and just then the penny dropped with a thud. Dad looked at Mother, who scooped up K and held her tightly.

'Karen, listen to me. The old moon is just as loved as the new one. OK?'

K wiped a small tear from her eye and buried her head deep into Mother's shoulder. 'Yes, Mummy.'

Though K may have found herself outmanoeuvred, she was not one to be outgunned – not in the cuteness stakes. Had I been standing just the other side of Mother's shoulder, I might have seen her wink.

'Right,' said Dad, standing up and slapping his knee. 'Who wants first go on the dodgems?'

The fair was loud and bright. A carnival of noise and bad taste, of shimmering lights and sequinned suits, of hooplas and merry-go-rounds, of teacups and dodgems, waltzers and Wurlitzers.

'Goldfish for the young lady?' A man dressed in candy-coloured stripes, with a thick moustache and even thicker Scottish accent, pointed to the wall of small fish in see-through plastic bags behind him. 'Hook a duck, win a prize,' he promised.

Jessica tugged twice on Dad's trouser pocket.

'Oh, all right,' he said, handing over a coin to the man in exchange for a wooden pole with a silver hook on the end. 'But you're a big girl now, so here ...'

Dad placed the makeshift fishing rod in Jessica's hands and lifted her by the armpits up and over the lip of the stall so that she was looking down, a giant among ducks, on a great paddling pool filled with floating yellow rubber. Her eyes lit up at the spectacle.

'Now lower your rod,' said Dad, guiding her through the air in hot pursuit of a duck that'd caught her attention. 'That's it. Hook it under ... gently ...'

With Dad's steer, Jessica hoisted the yellow duck from the water.

'We have a winner,' declared the moustachioed man, who pointed to the starred *Prize* logo stamped on the duck's belly. He reached behind to the wall of goldfish and handed a bag to Jessica.

'You won't forget to feed him, will you?'

She shook her little head, her wide almond eyes fixed on the newest member of the Clark family.

This, for K, seemed to be the final straw.

'Why does *she* get a fish?' said K, smouldering. She was jealous, and I have to admit that I was a little too.

Mother tried to take K's hand, but she snatched it away.

'You can have a go too, darling.'

'I don't want a *go*. I want a fish.'

A storm was brewing beside the teacups, and it threatened to engulf us all. Even Dad was powerless to prevent this one.

K puffed out her cheeks, balled her fists at her sides and let out a tremendous wail. Her small frame dropped to the ground and, with renewed vigour, she began to pummel the grass, fist after fist. Mother's good humour dissipated in a breath.

'Karen Elizabeth Clark, get up right this minute. What on earth do you think you're doing? What has come over you? Well?'

The wailing stopped as K looked up, seemingly bemused by the use of her full name. Mother only deployed the full three names when she was angry, really angry.

'Right, since you seem incapable of behaving yourself, we're going home. David, keys. Annie, fetch your sister. Now.'

I looked around to the space behind Dad's legs where Jessica should have been.

'Dad, where's Jessica?'

He turned around and panic spread across his face like a plague. He was always so calm, so composed; I'd never seen him worried before, not until that moment.

What happened next was a blur, remains a blur. When I think of it, the film is studded with cigarette burns, the camera out of focus, whole frames missing, voices indecipherable, flared, submerged in water. It is a carnival, and it is chaos.

'Jessica!' he called. 'Jessica!'

Mother turned her attention away from K and took up the screams too.

'Girls, stay here, OK? Right here. Don't move.'

Mother ran to the nearest stall to ask for a message to go out over the loudspeaker. Dad grabbed anybody he could find, grilled them, described Jessica – her clothes, her hat, her goldfish. Every face was blank, fretful. They hadn't seen her.

'Annie.' K gestured to something in the distance, something headed to the woodlands behind the fairground, something vague, indistinct. It grew smaller with each passing second. And, before I knew it, so too did K – she had run after it. She was bound for the woods.

Come back here! I shouted, but her feet carried her ever further away from me. I followed her through the crush of bodies, around the ghost train, past the waltzer and caravans, until I arrived at the lip of the woods, where K stood frightened, her gaze caught by something on the ground. I drew closer. A bright red bucket hat.

'Go get Dad,' I said, and off she ran, back into the dancing lights of the fairground.

The wood was dark, brooding – the increasingly faint jangle of the fair a distant birdsong. I shivered in my T-shirt and shorts.

The dark has the power to wrong-foot us. It can bend and twist and distort and bind an image until it is no longer the thing that we once believed it to be. It can raise the dead, bury the living, and it can give form to our worst fears, our worst excesses – providing you let it. But embrace it, embrace its myriad possibilities and the dark assumes a different tenor; for it can facilitate a great release, a space to disappear, a canvas for fanciful thoughts. My sister wasn't afraid of the dark; she was drawn to it.

I called into the space beyond. 'Jessica? You can come out now.'

Nothing save for the rapid beating of my own heart.

And then, through the darkness, I could just make out a frenzied rustling in the thicket ahead.

'Jessica?'

The rustling abated temporarily at the sound of my voice before starting anew – quicker, more forceful. My blood ran cold and my legs went numb. I inched closer, unsure whether I was the hunter or the hunted. When I was within touching distance, I swept back a branch with my forearm, and, through the gloom, amid a tangle of brambles, two small glassy eyes reflected back at me a brilliant light, two brilliant lights – the headlights of a car that would one day, one day soon, change everything and take from us something that could never be returned.

For some time the rabbit sat there motionless, staring at me, watching, waiting. It seemed to be trying to tell me something, but I didn't know what. It seemed to be trying to understand. This image, this moment, this snapshot in time, has stayed with me ever since. It has taken on the character of a dream, ethereal, disconnected from reality; it has been repurposed in my nightmares; a scene shorn of its context and slotted into a different narrative: two young girls at the side of the road, hunting for rabbits with a torch.

'Annie!' It was Dad. 'We've found her.'

Startled, the rabbit darted off into the brush.

At the edge of the woods, Jessica stood beside Dad with that old familiar grin splashed across her face, her inexplicably-now-waterless goldfish in one hand and a giant pink candyfloss in the other, blissfully unaware of the panic she'd caused.

'Chased after a rabbit apparently,' said Mother. 'Might have lost her for good if Mr Gurtovoy hadn't grabbed her before she ran into the woods.'

'Rabbi—' agreed Jessica with a bite of her candyfloss.

K scowled. She almost seemed disappointed that Jessica had been found.

'Anyway, I think that's quite enough excitement for one evening,' Mother continued.

As one, we looked down at Jessica, who blinked up at us from beneath her blonde curls. It was impossible to stay mad at her – impossible for everyone but K it seemed. Jessica must have sensed this too, for she bounded over to her older sister and placed the goldfish at her feet in a gesture that Karen still talks about to this day.

'K,' she said, reaching out and up, the new moon carrying the old moon in its arms. 'Hand.'

*

Mark takes my hand, but the grip is slack. I squeeze, but he doesn't squeeze back. Not now.

Fairy lights line the edge of a promenade looking out over the restless sea. We walk the cobbled streets, our *passeggiata*, on the way to dinner. I had dressed in white, in a long white dress, to remind him of what he has not taken: me. Or rather what he has not taken *from* me. What is rightfully his, and rightfully mine to be given. But I don't just want to give it, not any more. I want him to take it with a force that I have never known. I want to be thrown up against a wall; I want to be owned. And worse still: this apathy seems to be spreading, like a mute sickness, a contagion. The locals don't look at me, and when they do it's as though the thought repulses them; it's as though *I* repulse them. There was a time when Laura and I would go out drinking, dancing; a time when we would stay out until 3 a.m. and catch a night bus back to my flat, half-cut; a time when groups of teenagers nursing cheap cider, would leer at us – *Go on, give us a kiss* – and grow aggressive when we declined. *Lesbians*! And now ... Now, I would give anything for that kind of attention. I would give anything to be objectified, anything for Mark to just fuck me, to own me; but he doesn't wish to, not in the way that I need to be owned.

Something happened at our wedding; something was said, a seed of doubt planted – by whom, I don't know – and ever since, that seed has started to grow inside of him, has gone from kernel to flower in three full days, has been nurtured and watered by our time alone together. But it is not a flower, for nothing beautiful, nothing good can come of it. No, it is a weed, and as with all weeds, it must be taken by the root before it strangles the garden.

As we continue on from La Piazzetta, round and down a series of narrow alleyways lined with sprawling deep-purple bougainvillea, we see couples – young, glamorous couples, arm in arm, carefree – and I remember a time, not that long ago, when that used to be us, a time when the world was our own.

We approach the restaurant, hidden in a warren of side streets, and my heel gets caught in a drain. Mark watches me struggle in my attempts to wrestle it loose.

Does he still love me, or is that now a fiction too?

'Signora, allow me.'

The host steps forward and offers his hand as I steady myself. Mark seems irritated by the gesture.

'*Grazie*,' I smile, which the host returns.

'Do you have a reservation?'

Mark interjects, 'Mark Lane.'

'Yes, of course, Mr Lane. Right this way.'

We're led to our table beneath a magnificent grove of lemons, some as big as rocks, made all the more enchanting by a stream of hanging lanterns, such that the lemons themselves seem to glow, seem to be the source of all light. We're led in and out of diners, couples mostly, couples in love, couples exchanging kisses and hands and stolen glances, unaware of anything other than themselves. Where once I would have delighted in the spectacle, today, this evening, I think it gauche.

When the wine has been poured, our main courses set before us and the waiters have disappeared beyond a smokescreen of lemon trees and trellises, Mark becomes increasingly distant, inaccessible. Mark becomes *detached*. He detaches himself from me. The silence builds between us like gas under compression; any moment now, I worry it'll implode, we'll implode. I need to equalise the pressure.

'Games,' I say, seemingly apropos of nothing.

'Games?'

'Earlier, when we were getting ready, you said you weren't in the mood for games. How about now?'

Mark eyes me suspiciously.

'What kind of games?'

'Game. Singular. We can always move on to Kerplunk if we get bored.'

He smiles reluctantly, as if against his better nature. 'I'm listening.'

'Truth or lie,' I say. 'We take it in turns to make two statements, the juicer the better. The other has to guess which statement is true and which is false. Simple. Oh, and each truth should be something we have never told the other before, to make it fun.'

Mark swirls his wine, and then sits back, considers me carefully as he did hours before in the mirror's reflection; save that now he is looking directly at me, the first time he has done so in any meaningful way since the world shifted inside that car.

'You first,' he says.

'OK.'

I think for a moment. A waiter walks past, bearing a cake with a forest of candles and *Buon Compleanno* carved into the centre of the icing; it is set before a distant table, prompting the far end of the restaurant to burst into song.

'When I was fifteen, I set fire to the new maths block with a box of matches and a whole lot of newspaper. I was suspended for two months, until Mother pleaded mitigating circumstances.'

'Which were?'

'The usual bereavement stuff that often served as a passport out of trouble.'

'Right. And Number Two?'

'I once entered an Avril Lavigne lookalike contest, and lost.'

'Age?'

'Old enough to know better.'

Mark rubs his chin thoughtfully. He seems to be participating, which is more than I could have hoped for.

'Well … I can't imagine Little Miss Goody Two-Shoes committing serious arson, even though your reasoning for it checks out. It's almost like you're trying too hard to couch a lie in detail. So, I'm going to say the second one is the truth: you lost the lookalike contest.'

'Nope!' I struggle to contain my joy at his underestimating me. 'Oh …'

170

Mark grows distant again. *Is he angry at me for not having told him this before? Is he starting to question how much he even really knows me?*

'It was a long time ago, a difficult period in my life. I'm not proud of it, but it happened. I was a different person then. I'm a different person now.'

Thoughts seem to course through him like errant trains. I wish he'd let me ride just one of them.

'Come on, your turn,' I say. My eye is drawn to his thumb; it looks sore from the razor.

Mark takes a long sip of wine, drinks in the silence.

'At university, I was part of an all-male a-cappella group.'

'Baseball jackets, doo-wop haircuts, that kind of thing?'

Mark smiles. 'Not quite so cheesy, but headed in that direction, sure.'

'Interesting. The Mark Lane Quartet. I can picture it now … And the second?'

He shifts in his chair and his eyes are drawn to a table on the far side of the restaurant, the woman celebrating her birthday. Blonde. He sucks in a breath and then returns his gaze to the table; not to me, to the table.

'I have only ever loved one person.'

He looks up at me flatly, challengingly. He looks at me like he has just lit a stick of dynamite and he's waiting to see the full extent of the damage. In his eyes, he is daring me to select this as his truth. And yet, if I do so, if I fall into the trap that he has laid before me so artfully, it can mean only one thing … A fact I don't wish to face, a fact I'm not ready to face, will never be ready to face. Moreover, what is his truth, might not be mine.

'The first is true,' I say a little too triumphantly.

But he does not respond, his face does not move. And then it dawns on me, slowly and with some wonder, that he is never going to tell me whether I am right.

We arrive back at the villa and sit on the terrace, together but apart. There are no ferries journeying now, for even Charon must sleep. Mark pours me a glass of wine; we talk little, share little.

171

We sit in companionable silence for a while, counting the stars and the beads of condensation running down and around the rim of our glasses.

'Look,' says Mark after a spell, pointing to the sky, to a dark round orb suspended between the horns of a bright crescent. 'The new moon is holding the old moon in its arms.'

I smile, for the present and the past, and for the confluence of the two. I am back there at that fairground, back there beside the woodlands, a small hand reaching up through the darkness, stretching for the light. A rabbit stunned in the brush; a rabbit found, a rabbit lost.

Mark fiddles with his phone, scrolls through his playlist. Distracted again, I think. But no. Having found what he was looking for, he presses play: 'Wonderful Tonight'. But if he thinks that of me, of this evening, of the way I look in my white dress and mules, he hasn't said so, in body or speech. Has he lost the ability to communicate, to communicate desire? Have I?

Then he gives me a look that allays my fears, a look I've seen before, a look that fans out across the tide on a blood-orange vapour and finishes in my lap, finishes with me. He takes my hand, wordless, and leads me to the bedroom, where he stands a metre before me at the foot of the bed, the unused bed. Music drifts in with the fragrant breeze through an open window.

Without moving, his lips or his body, he gestures for me to abandon my dress. So I do. One shoulder, then the other. The dress slides to the floor in a whisper, and he realises that I'm not wearing any underwear. I think I see a note of delight in his smile and a gathering passion in his stance. But no sooner has the smile blossomed full on his lips than it withers swiftly on the vine. Delight becomes disgust and the budding warmth, a distant coldness. He looks at me like I am a creature, like I am appalling, like I appal *him*.

'Put it back on,' he says, 'I'm tired.'

Every fibre in my body is screaming for me to challenge him, to ask him why he is behaving like this, but the courage escapes me. He has taken it; he has taken that thing that I have always held dear, that thing that throughout my life has been in short supply; he has taken my self-belief. Perhaps, I start to think, I deserve this.

He watches me callously as I pull the dress up over my calves, my thighs, my belly, my breasts. He seems to enjoy the pit of humiliation in which I now find myself; he seems to enjoy my shame and my unwitting participation in a cruel parody of the wedding night that never was.

26

The nightmares have started again, every night without fail.

Tess and I are playing, as sisters do. Silly games. Twister becomes snakes and ladders, snakes and ladders becomes Monopoly. Until the board games bore us. Tess suggests hide-and-seek, which I loathe. I suppose it was the prospect that I would never be found that terrified me, that the seeker would tire of the search, that the seeker would stop caring, would have other, more interesting things to do. I would be forgotten.

But we played. Two rounds, then three. We ran all over the house like mice scurrying in search of the smallest hole. Down the backs of sofas, behind curtains, under coffee tables. Ready or not, here I come.

Let's go again, Tess said excitedly.

I don't know … I'm getting pretty hungry.

Please? she petitioned. Butter wouldn't melt. We'll eat after, she said, as if to sweeten the deal.

Fine. One more.

You can hide this time, she said.

And so as she counted down – Niiiine, eiiiiight, seveeeeen, siiiix – off I went upstairs, in search of a hole to hide in.

Ready or not … she called as she reached one. I'm coming!

Towels and spare duvet covers licked at my face as I hid, curled in a ball, at the back of the airing cupboard. The heat was oppressive. The heat was cloying.

As tiny footsteps approached, I worried the grumbling from my belly would give me away. Where once I was afraid I would never be discovered, now I was terrified I would. I stayed silent, held my breath, even as a thick bead of sweat ran down my forehead and into the corner of my eye. It stung. The footsteps grew closer and stopped at the cupboard door where they lingered for some time. The game was up, I thought. But Tess did not open the door. Instead, I heard a rustle as she reached for something, the sound of wood on wood, followed by silence. By now the sweat is running into both eyes and I'm light-headed from holding my breath. Just as I think I might pass out, the footsteps retreat down the hardwood stairs. She's gone, I tell myself and breathe out finally, in a rush of relief. I wait a few minutes, then a few minutes more. Ten minutes pass, then ten more. My cotton socks are sodden with perspiration. She's given up the ghost.

I go to stand and push at the door, but it does not budge. I push again, harder, more forcefully. I kick at it, use my shoulder as a buttering ram, but it does not give. I knock, then shout, then scream.

No one comes. I am trapped and my nightmare has come true.

It's just a nightmare I tell myself. It never happened. But I have dreamt it so often that I'm not sure any more. What if it is not a dream, but a memory?

I tried to call Tess, to root this scene in reality, but she didn't pick up. She never does. The last time we spoke, really spoke, was two years ago, around Christmas. She dropped by the house to borrow money. Mark opened the door, but he wasn't best pleased. When is he ever?

All she ever wants is handouts, he said. You never see her unless she wants something.

That's not true, I said. But the moment the words left my mouth, I knew them to be false.

I gave her the money and she hasn't called since.

I tried again to talk to Mark about the recurring dream. Your mind is playing tricks on you, he said. You have always had an overactive imagination. But he knows that is not true, as much as he'd like me to believe it. I'm worried that one of these days I might start to; that his version will become my version, his story my story and that there shall be no other.

27

'Something's wrong.'

'What do you mean?' says Laura. I can hear a man murmuring in the background.

'Who's that?'

Laura is distant, evasive. 'Who's what?'

'That man in your bed.'

'Oh, that.'

'Yes, *that*. Well?'

'Another story for another time.'

Just hang up, says the voice, clearer now. *She know what hour it is?*

'One sec, Annie.'

A commotion breaks out on the other end of the line.

'Bad time?'

'No, it's a great time. I'm just moving into the other room. What's up?'

'It's Mark –'

'If you tell me you two have broken up already, I want my gift back – toasters don't come cheap you know.'

'I didn't realise service stations sold toasters.'

Laura giggles. 'Come on then. Don't leave a lady waiting.'

'Lady?'

'Oh, shush.'

I can hear movement out on the terrace, where Mark is having his morning coffee. He coughs and turns the pages of a newspaper.

My voice is a whisper. 'He's changed.'

'What do you mean *changed*? You've been married four days. Changed how?'

'Changed – changed his mind.'

'About getting married? It's a bit late for that An—'

'About me.'

There's a silence on the other end of the phone as Laura grapples for a response, any response. She's not often lost for words.

'Wh-what makes you say that?'

'He's here, but he's not here. He's elsewhere. I've tried, Laura, I've really tried. Tried to get him to see me, to really see me, to notice me. But he's not interested. It's like he's a ball of regrets. He's no longer Mark, no longer my Mark. I don't recognise him.'

I can feel the tears prick the corner of my eyes, but I refuse to cry any more. I don't have the strength.

'Something was said at the wedding to him, but I don't know what. How can I answer to a crime I don't know I've committed?'

'Why don't you ask him outright?'

'And say what? *We've barely spoken and you've refused to fuck me for the third night in a row since we got married. Is everything OK, honey?*'

'Well, maybe not *exactly* that,' Laura demurs.

'Well, what then? I'm all ears.'

'Annie, listen to me. I'm sure it's nothing. You're a newlywed, you're emotional, and you're seeing daggers in the dark. We'll be getting you fitted for a tin hat soon. Besides, all this emotion, all this stress, do you think it might just be a bad case of PMT?'

'Perhaps. Though it's not due for another week or two *in theory*.'

'In theory?'

'I've not stopped taking the pill ...'

'Ah. So no Capri baby?'

'Let's get my husband to love me again, shall we, before we talk babies?'

The absurdity of that statement forces the gathering tears into free-flowing tears of laughter. We laugh together until even the laughter can't hide the underlying sadness.

'I love him,' I say, after a time. 'I really love him.'

'I know you do. And he loves you, I'm sure of it. OK?'

'OK.'

Are you coming back to bed? That distant voice again – it seems familiar.

'Honey, I've got to go. I'll speak to you soon.'

'Wait, I –' But the line goes dead and I am alone once more.

*

The sun sits oppressively high above the hills as a squat yellow bus races down a long road littered with hairpin bends, down to the rocky sea. The wind catches in my lungs and a thrill of adventure ripples through me and I find myself, almost instinctively, placing a hand on Mark's inner thigh where it lingers. He does not smile or wrap his arms around my shoulders and pull me in close as he might have done a mere week ago, but neither does he remove the hand from its perch, which is progress, I suppose.

At the bottom of the road, close to the Marina Piccola, but away from the sunbathing masses, a parade of unmanned rowing boats gather, tethered to the shore by thick trusses of rope. Mark hires one and proceeds to row us out from the island, out from the beach clubs full of glamorous women and midday spritzes, and out past the luxury yachts adrift in the jewelled sea – and yet not too far, for I can still discern individual towels and loungers, floats and blow-up balls – just enough so that we can look back at Capri's full splendour, at its promontories and sweeping cliffs, at its rugged beauty. We sit there together in silence as the boat gently lollops in the ocean, washing between the tides. It feels, for the first time, like I am on my honeymoon, albeit a honeymoon for one.

'To think this was once Emperor Tiberius' playground,' I say eventually, half to Mark, half to myself, and more in consternation than awe. 'The past feels so present here.'

Mark doesn't answer. I'm not even sure if he is awake beneath his sunglasses. The boat's rocking has cast a spell over us both.

'Darling?' I press, but then regret the word. Had I become my mother? Did Mark think me as cold, as unyielding?

'Yes.'

'What are you thinking?' That awful question that no man wishes to hear.

Mark stirs, pulls himself upright and lifts his straw boater just enough to allow the back of his hand to pass across his clammy forehead. He gazes back to the shore as though considering his escape route.

'I'm thinking it's about time I go back to work.'

'To the hospital?'

'No, to the coal mine.' There is irritation in his voice.

He seems to think his own tone too harsh, his speech too rash. And then he seems to think me worthy of opening up to once more, after hours on hours of walled silence.

'I feel … I feel robbed of my purpose, Annie.'

He removes his sunglasses and clamps an anxious palm to his chest.

'I look back and I think what have I achieved in the past two years, actually? I thought a new relationship, us, would be enough. But it's not. I got wrapped up in the dates, in the newness and the excitement – the proposal, the wedding, the prospect of a family. But now … what's left?'

He looks at me, looks through me, and I feel like something snaps inside, retreats.

'We're left,' I petition.

'You cannot be my purpose,' he says flatly. 'What if, one day –'

'Mark, I'm not going anywhere.'

'But –'

I pull him up short, 'Listen very carefully: I. Am. Not. Going. Anywhere.'

He looks at me, really looks at me, with those little marbles, whose centres are as blue as the sapphire sea. 'I've been promised that before.'

I freeze, feel his words get the better of me. 'I can't keep having this same conversation, Mark. Round and around we go.'

'You're not listening.'

'I have done nothing *but* listen. And I'm sick of it. Sick of trying to be the perfect wife.'

Mark sneers. 'Perfect?'

'I didn't say I *was*; I said I was trying. Which is more than can be said for you. You've barely acknowledged me since the airport.'

He falls silent again.

'I don't understand what changed, what changed in you. Talk to me, please.'

Mark sighs. I'm nervous about what he's going to say, and then he says it, casually and without hesitation. Here it is. The heart of the matter, the root of the root.

'I spoke with our mystery guest at the reception. Cameron. Or rather, he spoke with me.'

The figure by the car. Of course. He hadn't left after all.

'What about?' I say, but disingenuity has never been my strong suit. There's only one thing he could have said that Mark does not know, not fully.

'What really happened to Jessica?' he says. 'And this time, the truth, Annie. Nothing else will do.'

28

Six weeks before the wedding, Mark stopped answering my calls again. When he did pick up, he seemed distant, unconcerned with me, with my life.

I'm getting a promotion at work; they're making me Associate Professor.

That's good.

They want me to start teaching a class on Greek Mythology.

Myths? But you're a historian.

Fact and fiction are fast friends … Want to come over?

Maybe tomorrow. I'm tired.

And that was that. I celebrated alone that night: a bubble bath, a Chinese takeaway and a voicemail from a solar panel salesman who was very sorry to have missed me.

I tried to talk with him, with Mark, but he said there was nothing to talk about; he simply closed up in his usual fashion, as men do when they're forced to contend with complex emotions that extend beyond anger, mild sadness and post-orgasm elation, then showered me in assurances. *How could anything be wrong? I'm about to marry the woman I love.* But I knew better: it was Hope. Was he ever going to let her go?

I suggested we visit the Richmond Centre, together; if he couldn't talk to me directly, perhaps it would help to share his grief with strangers, with those who have endured private tragedies too and yet each found the strength to share their tragedy with others. *It had helped me*, I said. *It can help you.* Mark being Mark, I was expecting more of a struggle, but to my great surprise, he agreed. In the end, I don't know if he did it for me, or for himself. I don't suppose it much matters.

'No, it's fine,' said Mark, twelve pairs of eyes on him, twelve sympathetic smiles.

'Are you sure?' James could sense his hesitancy.

Mark laughed a little nervously. 'This is not a spectator sport.'

'No, it's not. But neither is it a grief auction. There is no prize for the highest bidder.'

There are no prizes at all, said one of the other attendees, to titters and whispers. James waited for these to pass.

'Over the years, I've seen many people walk through those doors and walk out of them again having never said a word. The Richmond Centre is not a space where you have to talk; it's a space where you *can*. There is a difference.'

'Do *you* have to talk?' said Mark, irritated.

James didn't falter. He smiled. 'I find it helps.'

At that, Mark nodded, caught my eye. A look can say so very much.

'It's the not-knowing,' said Mark finally, just as James seemed poised to move on to another patient, attendee, client, call them, us, what you will.

'Why she left?'

Mark opened and closed his fists, one at a time.

'It's more than that.'

'How so?'

Mark paused for a moment, collected his thoughts. My heart paused too, skipped a beat, thudded loudly on the next. Blood rushed into my ears.

What are you going to say?

'Not knowing why she left is one thing … Our relationship is over, I've accepted that. But what if it was something *I* did? What if I'm destined to repeat – ? What if I lose –'

He paused once more and looked up at me. He was scared to lose me, just as I have been – just as I am – scared to lose him.

'I wish I could talk with her one last time. Tell her I'm sorry for whatever I've done. I wonder sometimes had I been a better partner, a better husband, whether she would have left. Maybe we were always destined to go our own ways, to find happiness with other people. But maybe not. Maybe things could have been different had I just been more attentive, more understanding, more flexible. The worst thing is, I'll never know. I have so many questions for which I'll never have the answers.'

James leant forward, hands on both knees. 'You want closure.'

Mark nodded and a silence blossomed in the room. James' words had dried up, Mark's too. But where they had each lost their voice, I had, unaccountably, found mine.

'I think we all go through life expecting a Hollywood movie, with a clear beginning, middle and end.' Faces turned to look at me. 'But it never quite pans out that way.'

James gestured with his hands, encouraging me to go on.

'The subplots are convoluted, and more often than not, total dead ends. And don't get me started on endings. Sometimes they never come, not in the way we want them to, not in the way we expect or need them to. Sometimes things are left undone, things, important things, left unsaid, and scenes unfinished. But I've come to learn that's OK. There is a desire within us all for closure, but sometimes the unfinished is an ending in and of itself.'

Mark looked up at me. He seemed to intuit my meaning, which, admittedly, I'd delivered with all the subtlety of a sledgehammer.

'When we don't get the closure we crave, we feel out of control,' I added.

James clasped his hands together, as though in prayer, and pressed the tips of his fingers to his lips.

'And is that how you feel, Annie? Out of control?'

I thought about it, long and hard, so long that the clock on the wall seemed to become my enemy, counting down the seconds, time slipping more than passing. This was not supposed to be about me; this was about Mark.

'I used to,' I said eventually. 'I used to feel powerless. I used to feel that things happened *to me*, rather than through me, or because of me.'

'And what changed?'

'I did.'

'In what way?'

I started to feel on display, exposed. James the Poacher had laid another one of his traps and I was damned if I was going to get snared. That is ... until I looked up at Mark and pictured myself stood before him in just six weeks' time, sharing my vows, which would begin with an *I* and end with an *us*. It would always end with an *us*.

'Last time I was here, I told you about a game my sister Karen and I would play at our farmhouse, as kids.'

'That's right,' said James. 'The rabbits.'

'The rabbits,' I repeated. 'Well, the reason we played that stupid game, the reason we would creep downstairs and try to catch rabbits at night, with our torch, was to bring back Jessica.'

James looked at me blankly, went to speak, stopped himself, regrouped before marching onwards. 'I don't understand.'

'My sister. My other sister. Her nickname was Rabbit. Jessica Rabbit. My mother's name for her, silly really. And ever since, when I've seen one, a rabbit, I've felt close to her, as though she is alive again. So that night – you'll think me mad – with the incident, and the car ...'

'You're among friends, Annie.'

' ... the car that collided with the stunned rabbit ...'

Mark shifted uneasily in his chair, swallowed hard. I was crying.

'Well, I went out into the road, and I picked up that injured rabbit, as I wish I could have picked up Jessica, and I carried it inside, back into our home, where it belonged, where she belonged. It was so small, and in so much pain. I carried it to the basement. I fed and watered it. For weeks. The body was a mess, legs crushed, a mass of blood on its fur –'

No one knew quite what to say.

'And why do you think you did that, Annie?'

I couldn't answer this truthfully; if I had, Mark might have seen the real me, instead of the me I wanted – I want – him to see.

The truth is, I'd spent all my life thinking it was because I wanted to save that rabbit, nurture it back to life. But it wasn't that at all. Not if I really think about it. No.

I wanted to punish that rabbit. I wanted to heal it just enough to keep it hovering in absolute pain, in a liminal state, between this world and the next. I wanted to see another living thing suffer the

186

way we had suffered, the way our family had suffered. Suffering should be universal, most religions are founded on the notion, and yet some are forever destined to suffer more than others, some presented with Gordian knot after knot, while others skate through life trouble-free, the world on a string. Every so often that string should be cut.

When I was fourteen, rebellious, foolish, I stuck out my foot as our class marched from the changing rooms into the playground. It was child's play, nothing else. Having seen the foot too late to correct her path, a classmate tripped over it, went crashing across the ground, face first into the rough, weather-worn tarmac. I'll always remember the way she looked up at me, blood seeping from her grazed thigh, a look that said, *Every sort of wild animal is kinder than you.*

That thought has stuck with me ever since. There is a streak of cruelty in me, something feral and unruly that I don't, *won't*, often allow to see the light of day. I suppress it, I dress it in kindness and love and desire and passion, until the cloak conceals the dagger. People will usually see what they want to see. But sooner or later I'm worried I'll forget to be kind, to be endearing, to be thoughtful and patient and goodness itself. I'm worried that one day I shall forget to be Annie, the Annie they expect, the Annie they know and love. I'm worried the cloak will slip and everyone will know me for who I really am, for the animal, the monster who takes, only takes. I'm worried all this will be over and the slice of happiness I've managed to carve out for myself will be ripped from me, and I'm worried … I'm worried what else I might do to preserve it, to preserve me.

I was once actually the person I want the world to see. Before we moved to the farm, back at the old house. I was once goodness itself. I was carefree and playful and endearing. I was kind. I was all the things I was expected to be, all the things a little girl should be. Suffering had not visited us yet, suffering had not visited me.

And then one day a small girl, the smallest of us all, followed her sisters out of the house, through an open door, to the end of the path where under the cover of night they played with a torch and a butterfly net with reckless abandon; and that small girl, excited by the game, drawn to the dark and the bright light that streaked it, gave chase to a rabbit that had fled the grass verge for the road. The last thing she saw, as she turned back, too late, was the life she would leave behind and the suffering she would leave in its place. The rabbit scampered off into the brush.

And me? Well, I was the one who left the door open. I was the one who killed her.

So how did I answer James and the twelve haunted faces that looked on expectantly? With the only language that can conceal, with the only language they could understand: silence.

29

As the boat rocks gently in the ebb and flow of the sapphire sea, Mark's words lap the edge of the hull and threaten to drown us both.

'What really happened to Jessica?' he says.

My instinct is to run, but there is nowhere to go. I am trapped. *Did he pick this moment deliberately?* I wonder. *Did he hold his tongue until he knew there would be no escape?* The isolation – the shoreline now a distant scratch against the sky – scares me. His presence scares me.

'Annie?'

'I've told you what happened. I told everyone at the group,' I say, but I know already that it rings hollow.

'You told me she died,' he says.

'She did.'

'And you –'

'It wasn't my fault,' I say desperately.

He looks at me as he looked at me last night, at my naked body: with disgust.

'You killed her.'

'I didn't. It was –'

'An accident,' Mark mocks me.

'What did Cameron tell you?'

But Mark doesn't answer.

'I know where he's got it from: Mother. The dog in the manger. I caught them talking at the wedding. She blames me, I know she does. She has blamed me my entire life. For Jessica, for Grandma, for my Dad, for everything that has ever gone wrong in *her* life, for everything that has ever impinged upon her happiness.

That has been, and always will be, her primary concern. K and I have been afterthoughts.'

Mark looks at me blankly; neither sympathetically nor with great kindness, but like an understanding is beginning to form.

'What happened to Jessica was an accident. I left the door open, yes. But it wasn't deliberate, despite what you might have heard. It was an accident. I have spent so many years harbouring the guilt of that evening, and I may never entirely be rid of it, but I can't go on like this.'

'Why didn't you tell me?' Mark asks.

'I was scared you'd react in exactly the way you have. You see me as some sort of monster, not as the woman you fell in love with.'

'I don't think you a monster,' he says, 'but I don't like being lied to.'

'I haven't lied to you. I fucked up, but I was a child, Mark; and I have had to live with the consequences of that night ever since.'

Mark takes a deep breath and runs his thumb and forefinger across the length of his forehead, just as he did in the taxi four days previously.

'And your dad?' he asks.

'What about my dad?'

'How exactly did he die, Annie?'

30

It is said that storytelling is like juggling; each ball a motive, a character, a plot that is cast up and returned in a dizzying, seemingly endless parade. The juggler must not drop one ball, lest the illusion be broken; the teller must not abandon one motive. If a ball should fall, down will come cradle, story and all.

Some stories are not easily told. They're there, wriggling eel-like in a sea of stories, and the closer you get to them, the more you try to grab them, to make sense of them, to comprehend, the faster they slip through your hands. But there's one that I need to tell, and not for me, but for him. The other him.

There was a monster beside my dad's bed.

It wasn't the kind from kids' books, the type you'd expect to find beneath some bridge, or holed up in a dark castle perched on the edge of a cliff. It had no razor-sharp teeth, no teeth at all in fact; it had no eyes to speak of, no mouth to speak with. But what it did have was a heartbeat, a heartbeat that came as regularly as yours or mine, yet unlike ours. You could *see* its pulse: thin, scratchy green lines that rose and fell in gentle undulations, like a mountain range across the monster's face. Sometimes, when my dad laid very still, a calmness heavy on his eyelids, the line would run flat for a spell before vaulting upwards again. Those were the times that scared me the most.

Its hands, a sprawl of wires, reached out to my dad, grasping the length of his body – though he never seemed to mind. For the first time in an age, he looked peaceful, I think, pain-free, as though the monster had taken his burden from him. Part of me, a very small part, didn't want him to wake up.

And a voice. Yes, the monster had a voice. Not a fiery boom or a maniacal laugh, but a bleep, yet a bleep like no other, because each one was a note of hope. And hope was all I had.

'Annie?'

I couldn't face her – not then. I was ten, and I was stubborn, and I was breaking.

'We were worried about you. Karen said you'd gone for a walk and ...' Mother's voice trailed off into the middle distance. The room fell still, save for the rasping sound that sprang from my dad's chest. Mother approached me from behind, placed a warm, clammy paw on the nape of my neck and sighed a sigh that could have cleaved a hole in the floor. 'I know this has been tough on you, it's been tough on all of us, for God's sake. I just –'

'Mum?'

'Yes?' Hope raged like a bonfire.

'I'd like you to leave.'

And with that her face sank. The network of gently worn lines on her forehead ceased to offer any signs of life. Without a word, she turned and left me. And I was grateful for the silence.

I sat there for what could have been days, hours, minutes, and contemplated the fragile form on the hospital bed. How weak he seemed, how ... *unliving*. He was little more than a bag of bones where once he had been so strong, so imposing. Karen could probably have lifted him up now. I didn't want to see him like this; I wanted to remember him as he was: so full of life, so full of stories.

Every night, before the sickness took hold, he would creep upstairs as my Mother lay quiet on the sofa. He would sit on the rocking chair at the foot of K's bed, kick his feet up to the mattress and let his whole body relax into a yawn.

'Right,' he would say, 'which one do you fancy tonight?', before scooping a handful of books from the shelf.

But I never wanted a story from a book, not from Dad.

At times, I wondered whether the stories would burst from him; during the day, they lay in wait, coalescing into a carnival in the pit of his throat, until darkness came and the stories made their great escape. There were tales of daring, of great courage and conviction; of dragons, tormentors, skeleton kings and pirate maidens; of creaky old houses, Native American burial grounds and spacecraft; of woodworkers, innkeepers, slavers and miners; tales of love, adventure and hope. But the greatest story he had to tell didn't exist in some book, no matter how dusty or revered. His greatest story was him. And that story was coming to an end.

'Annie?'

I looked up. 'Dad? Dad!'

I must have jumped up on his bed and wrapped him in my arms because he made some joke about me tugging on his catheter. I didn't know what a catheter was. He was croaky, but he was Dad. He was suffering.

'Now listen,' he said.

I didn't want to listen; I wanted to call a nurse.

'Annie …'

'Yes?'

'Remember the jellyfish?'

*

'Come on, girls – to bed. Your father's tired.'

'But, Mum …'

'No buts. Your father needs his rest.'

K and I were crouched by Dad's legs in the living room. The night was drawing in as he sat in his patterned armchair, book in hand, beneath a pool of light cast from the lamp behind him so that a halo, a crown, appeared to encircle his head. He was then, as he is to me still, a saint.

'I'm fine, Chris, honestly. I'll just finish this chapter …'

He didn't look fine. I knew that, even then. He had deteriorated quickly that summer. His legs, once great oak trees, were awkward and swollen; his breath, once full and determined, was rasping, always rasping; and his sallow skin, once taut and glowing, hung from him like wet wallpaper. He could barely walk, much less carry us. I wished he would get well again. But I knew he wouldn't. He was fading fast.

'So what about the jellyfish?' I asked.

'Let's see, shall we ...' Dad wet his forefinger and turned the page, his black-rimmed glasses perched on the tip of his nose. 'The immortal jellyfish or the *turritopsis dohrnii* ...' Dad looked up to check K was listening. ' ... has the rare ability, during times of environmental stress, to revert to the polyp stage.'

Karen's expression hovered somewhere between bored and confused. 'What does that mean?'

Dad removed the glasses from his nose, folded the arm pieces and placed them in his shirt pocket. The small action provoked a coughing fit. More blood, more rasping.

'It means ...' He managed between breaths. ' ... the jellyfish can grow *younger*. It can age in reverse. Like Benjamin Button.'

Karen's eyes lit up. 'Really?'

'Really.'

'Can't you do that, Daddy?'

He smiled sweetly. 'I'm working on it.'

Mother, who until now had been sitting absently in her armchair, looked up from her fashion magazines. 'Right, you two; you've had a good run of it. To bed now. I'll come and tuck you in.'

There was no use arguing, so we kissed Dad on the cheek and clambered up the stairs.

Halfway up, K whispered, 'I wish I was a jellyfish.'

'Would you really want to be all gooey?'

She thought for a moment. 'Maybe not. But if I were ... I could go back in time and save Dad.'

'I don't think it works like that,' I said.

Karen thrust her stubborn little nose in the air and narrowed her eyes. 'Well, it should.'

'Come on. Let's brush our teeth.'

Shortly after, when K was tucked up in her sheets, the lights low, the window open just a notch to let in a light summer breeze, Mother arrived. I sat on a little chair beside K's bed, mapping Mother's once youthful face to the one that greeted us now. She looked tired. She looked lost.

'Can you tell us a story, Mummy?' asked K.

'It's late, darling. Maybe tomorrow.'

'But Daddy always tells us a story before we go to sleep.'

'You've just had a story.'

'No, a *proper* one.'

Mother sighed and then relented, which surprised me. I couldn't recall her ever having read us a bedtime story. 'Well, OK, but just a short one.'

Karen clapped her hands excitedly as Mother went to the bookcase and selected a book at random.

'Not that one, Mummy,' said K.

'Well, what do you want then?' She was irritable.

'Something fun. Something with a princess.'

Mother turned once more to the bookshelf but, for what felt like a small eternity, she did not move. Her back was straight, her shoulders square, her hair gently roused by the breeze. But she did not move.

'Mum?' I said with a lump in my throat. No response.

'Mummy?' tried Karen. But it was no use – she had crossed into another world, a world in which, I supposed, her reality was an altogether happier one. She *was* lost.

Suddenly, as a starling flitted from its branch on a tree outside Karen's window, a loud crash could be heard downstairs. Shaken from her reverie, Mother turned on her heel and ran, faster than I knew her capable. I tried to follow but she shouted back, *Stay there.*

'What's going on?' asked K, sitting bolt upright.

'I don't know,' I said. But I did.

I climbed into bed with K and watched the starling outside dance from branch to branch until the sound of an ambulance siren cut through the night. The starling disappeared.

*

'I remember,' I said. The machine seemed louder then, menacing.

'You do?' Dad replied.

I nodded.

'Remember how the jellyfish could age backwards so that it could live forever, so that it could never really ...' He didn't want to say the word, none of us did. So I said it for him.

' ... die?'

'Yes. Well, sometimes living forever is just being remembered. And being loved.'

'But I do love you.'

'I know,' he said. Tears were in his eyes. 'Then I shall live on. But you have a lot to give – a lot of love – don't waste it all on me.' He laughed for perhaps the first time in weeks. But there was a deep sadness there. 'Promise me?'

'I promise.'

'And look after your sister. She needs you; your mother, too.'

His gaze drifted to the corridor behind me, where a figure hovered uncertainly. Mother came into the room and once again placed a hand on the nape of my neck but this time I didn't wish it away. It came as a warm comfort to me.

Mother fished around in her pocket for a few coins. 'Why don't you go and get yourself a soft drink from the canteen, love?'

She was trying to get rid of me, and from the look on Dad's face, he wanted the same. I took the money, gripped the coins so tight that red marks stained my scrunched palm and left the room – but not the conversation.

'Chris,' I heard him say, as I hid just out of sight in the corridor, my ear pressed towards the half-open door. 'I can't do this any more.'

The voices became hushed, frantic. There was a note of panic, of pure horror in Mother's voice. Something was being asked of her, and she resented him for asking it. And all the while the rasping and incessant bleeping of the machine seemed to grow louder and louder and louder, seemed to drown their words in a wall of sound, until I thought the machine itself, the monster beside the bed, might have consumed them both.

And then, just like that, the machine fell silent. The monster lay at rest.

31

'I'm sorry,' Mark says as he pulls me into his chest, as I bury my head like I once had, in an embrace that stretches across time – from that hospital bed to this boat. 'I had no idea.'

'I didn't do it,' I sob amid a torrent of tears, amid a fist that pounds on Mark's chest and refuses to let up. 'I didn't. You've got to believe me.'

Mark strokes my hair, tucks the loose strands behind my left ear. His way of trying to impose some order on this chaos.

'It's OK,' he says in hushed, soothing tones as he cups my face and looks sympathetically into my eyes. His touch is delicate, reassuring; an auctioneer holding a priceless china vase. He seems grateful to me, grateful for my having shared this. 'I believe you.'

I pull back, unsure if he means it, truly means it, or whether he is just trying to placate me in this moment. It's hard not to suspect the latter.

'I just wished you'd told me, Annie. I wished you'd talked to me. There should be no secrets between us. You're my wife. And when I heard those things, I started to wonder who I'd married.'

'Is that why the game in the restaurant bothered you? Another instance of my life kept from you?' Mark remains silent as I wipe the residual tears from my cheek. 'There are always going to be things from our pasts that the other doesn't know, not fully at least. But you're right: I should have told you about Jessica, I should have told you about Dad, about his end. But can you look me in the eye, truly, and tell me that you have told me everything?'

Mark looks at me, sheepish. He takes the point, and he takes it on the chin.

'I guess not.'

'And that's OK,' I reassure him. 'We've got a lot of road ahead of us to discover these things. And we will be better at sharing. We must.'

Mark nods and this time I embrace him.

Hoot hoot, he says softly.

Hoot hoot, I reply.

*

We arrive back at the villa just as the sun begins to set behind Vesuvius. Once more that blood-orange vapour fans out across the tide. But this time is different; this time the vapour does not reach us.

Mark takes my hand in his, guides me firmly but surely to the bedroom, where the thin curtains blow about in the gentle coastal crosswinds. His palm finds its way to the cradle of my head and he draws me to him. Our lips meet, burn, and that thing that I'd thought long gone, banished to a distant time, that unruly desire that once resided so resolutely within us both, between us both, re-emerges as though it had never been gone at all.

Mark pushes me back on the bed, regards me with a white-hot fire, lifts my soft linen dress and disappears between the warmth of my thighs as I lay here and think on all that we have, and all that I came so close to losing.

32

2nd December

He resents the fact I haven't been able to give him children. He has never said it – how do you say such a thing? – but I fear he looks at me and sees a cold and barren place where no seeds may ever grow.

The doctor has said as much, confirmed at last. I am infertile. To speak the words, to write them even, hurts. Each flick of the pen a flick of a knife which turns and turns in the pit of my stomach. It is a shame that I carry with me, and carry with me always, but I hoped Mark would lighten my burden; that he would reassure me in some way. But he hasn't. He doesn't. His focus is elsewhere. He looks at her, Nurse Nelly Nightcap, I just know it, of course he looks at her, she's beautiful ... He looks at her, during one of their late-night shifts, and sees abundance in her youth. An escape from all this. From the cloying mundanity of me. From my failure.

This morning we were in the kitchen. The first frost of winter had settled on the raised planters in the back garden. Mark had his head buried in a newspaper, as he often does when he wants to shut out the world. The world. Me. There is little difference. I brought up adoption again. He'd remained silent before, the last time it was raised, but perhaps this time would be different. Perhaps, I thought, there is a world in which Mark will be able to think of an adopted child as his own.

He'd consider it, he said, so I laid the papers in front of him, showed him how easy the process was to begin, showed him where to dot the i's and cross the t's. Look, honey, I've already filled most of it out. To his credit, he did look. He looked and then he tore the document in two. A great betrayal, apparently.

Sneaking around behind his back. I'm not to do it again. Yes, dear.

I hate the person I've become. I hate who he makes me. How can my love for him inspire such hate? I'm missing my classes, clients are falling away. I'm distracted. How can I practise peace and inner calm when my outer world is a mess, when my inner world is falling in.

Charlotte called. She suggested a weekend away. Not with Mark, with her. She knows a place in the woods, a place to recentre, reconnect with nature. I don't know, I said. But she insisted it would do me good, that it would give me some headspace. I'll think about it, I said. And what do I do about Her? I asked. She suggested I confront him, give him a choice. At least you'll have your answer. And what if it's not the one I want? Then you face the front, and you don't look back.

So this evening, as he settled on the sofa, I issued Mark an ultimatum. It was me or her. But when I put it to him, when I dared to take a breath and speak my truth, this truth, he grew monstrous, terribly monstrous. Told me many things, horrific things. Said I was a curse cast upon the family, that his father hated me, his mother too. The former I knew was a lie. Frank adored me, and I him. But Mark's barbs were forged to cut. And so they did.

I'm leaving, I said. I can't put up with much more of this. I can't keep trying to pretend everything is OK when it's not. It's not, Mark, it's not.

Good, he said matter-of-factly.

33

The suit and tie had been a mistake. He knew that now as he sat at the back of the yoga studio, waiting patiently for the current class to come to a sweaty end. He tugged on his tie, tried to loosen it, but it was no good; the heat was all-consuming. His socks felt like two wet towels wedged into his shoes, and the perspiration marched in thick beads on to his drawn brow. As the sixteen students entered their final pose – straight back, seated on their ankles – Cameron felt at any moment as if he might faint, which worried him at first before deciding it a blessing. Perhaps the air would be cooler down there, less oppressive?

'Thank you, everyone,' said the instructor, who eyed with suspicion the strange man in the suit, and must have wondered, surely, who had allowed this man in before she arrived. 'I'm seeing lots of progress. Keep at it.'

A number of students went over to thank the instructor, chatted briefly, and then left. The room thinned out, and thanks to the newly opened door, the air did too. Cameron could breathe again.

'Do you always watch hot yoga dressed like that?'

Cameron smiled. 'Sometimes I participate. My dead body pose is coming on in leaps and bounds.'

She was pretty, Cameron thought, and bore a striking resemblance to the woman he'd come to find: blonde, strong cheekbones, blue eyes.

'Sorry, I didn't catch your name?'

'Cameron. It's Kate, right?'

If the instructor was moderately suspicious before, she was outright chary now.

'You're not here for tuition, are you?'

'No, I'm not.'

'Then I think it highly inappropriate your being here.'

Cameron couldn't tell if Kate was always like this, or whether she'd erected a wall just for him, one at which he would have to slowly chip away.

'I'm looking for information. Perhaps you can help.'

'Depends what kind of information you're after.'

'Hope Lane.'

Kate's eyes lit up at the name.

'She was an instructor here too,' continued Cameron.

'Yes, I remember Hope. Fun, bubbly, bags of energy. She taught this class before me – I was her replacement. In fact, she was my teacher before –'

'Before she disappeared.'

'Before she disappeared.'

'That's sort of why I'm here.'

'You're a detective.'

'In a manner of speaking, yes.'

'Well, *Detective* –' Cameron could hear the distain in her voice. 'I'm not sure what I can tell you beyond what you must already know. We weren't friends or especially close. She turned up, taught her class and left. Charlotte would know more.'

Mention of the name sent a shiver of excitement coursing through Cameron. 'Charlotte attended her class?'

'That's how they met. Grew very close in a very short space of time. Would go out for drinks and meals together after work. Just those two, no one else. Of course, she stopped coming after Hope's disappearance. Probably couldn't face it. And that's all I know. We never spoke.'

'What did she look like? Charlotte, that is.'

Kate thought hard for a moment.

'She looked …' Cameron made to write a note in his pad. 'She looked: ordinary.'

He relaxed his pen. 'Ordinary.'

'I'm sorry, I don't know what else to tell you. Average height, average build, averagely long and averagely brunette hair. Ordinary.'

'No distinguishing features? Marks? Scars? Tattoos?'

Kate shrugged. 'Not that I ever saw.'

'And Hope. How did she seem before she went missing?'

'A little erratic. Irascible, perhaps. Not very patient with the newcomers.'

'And this was unusual?'

'It wasn't Hope. She was so giving of her time, very gentle and encouraging.' Kate put her hands on her hips and sighed deeply. 'I probably shouldn't be telling you this, but I heard rumours, and they were just rumours, that all was not well at home.'

'With her husband?'

'Again, they're just rumours.'

'What sort of rumours?'

'That he'd fallen off the wagon.' Kate leant in, lowered her voice to a whisper. 'That he'd been violent with her.'

*

'Frank?' Cameron's voice echoed back at him. *It must be a bad line.*

'Cam, can you hear me?'

'I can now.'

'Good. How are you getting on?'

Cameron couldn't bear to concede that he'd encountered too many dead ends to mention, that all he'd unearthed was the name of some mysterious brunette who nobody seemed to know anything about. He didn't want to disappoint Frank. He didn't want to disappoint himself by facing the truth. Some lies were worth telling.

'Strong progress,' he said. 'I'm following up on a number of leads – some more promising than others.'

'I knew I could count on you, Cam.'

The trouble with lies is that one begets another. They multiply like rats, one stacked on the other, until, before you know it, it's rats all the way down.

'And I am sorry about all that, last month.'

'I don't think I've ever been chased out of a wedding before.'

A silence opened on the other end of the line, which Frank eventually filled gruffly. 'I told you to keep a low profile.'

'I tried. But your new daughter-in-law is quite the firecracker.'

'You had a word with Mark too, I gather?'

'Annie's mother had some interesting things to say; the girl had an eventful childhood, and I wondered how much Mark had been told. Very little was the answer.'

'Well, that's what I wanted to talk to you about. I'm wondering if we've been looking in the wrong place.'

'Oh?'

'Annie.'

'I see.'

'I'd like you to pay her a visit. She may know something, may have tried to find Hope herself. She's an inquisitive sort, and I imagine she'd want to see what she was getting into, before she had got into it, if you follow.'

Cam wasn't sure he did follow. 'How can I find her?'

'I'll send you the address. Mark's moving in with her shortly once the sale of his Dulwich house goes through. A farmhouse, I think, somewhere in Kent. Annie's family home. Maybe let them settle a bit, Mark and her, and then stop by, unannounced preferably.'

'Moving in together *after* the wedding. How traditional.'

'Mark's idea. I think he needed time to say goodbye to the house and to his old life there with Hope.' Cameron thought he heard Frank choke back something. 'With the sale of the house … he's finally given up. Given up on her. No trace remains.'

'I'll pay Annie a visit,' said Cameron. 'I just don't know how happy she will be to see me.'

'Do you believe in God, Cam?'

The question wrong-footed Cameron. His mother had always taught him not to discuss sex, religion or politics. Much like picking one's nose at the dinner table, it wasn't polite. And so he didn't know how else to respond to the question with anything other than nervous laughter.

'What's so funny?' asked Frank, irritation marking his voice. This was clearly not the reaction he was seeking.

'I really don't know what to tell you, Frank. I'm a man of this world, not the next.'

Cameron hung up and looked from his disguised position across the street to the house opposite, the one with the Japanese maple in the front garden, bowed. With the French shutters open, he could just about discern a lone figure packing boxes of various shapes and sizes with the last of his belongings. Mark's belongings. An idea came to him in a flash. Perhaps, thought Cameron, he *had* been watching the wrong house after all.

34

I can't recall the last time the house was teeming with this much life, this much play and cheer and bonhomie. Perhaps when Dad was still around, perhaps when he and Mother would host book clubs while K and I sat in our rooms inventing questionable dance routines to Spice Girls' songs or rummaging through Mother's closet and parading in her black court heels and coral lipstick. If you look hard enough, there's still a dash of mascara on the corner of the landing, and a faded section on the bannister where we'd slide along happily. Spit-spot. Of course, we made nuisances of ourselves, but we were young and understood little of the adult need for company and the keeping-up-with-the-Joneses veneer of respectability. Life was simpler then, for we'd lived very little of it; the rest was yet to come.

Now, friends and family gather once more in the kitchen, the living room, by the roaring fire and under the ageing timbers, to celebrate yet another milestone in our relationship, a mere two months on from our wedding and not a moment too soon: our moving in together. We have spent so much time living in each other's spaces, but for the very first time, we have a space of our own. It'll be an adjustment – how could it not be? – I have lived here for far too long for it to be otherwise. There are bits of me, of my family, everywhere, etched into every floorboard and on every wall. The chip in the bannister where K slipped head first in her new socks; the white-paint shoe print that Dad left by the back door; the splinters of glass coming away from the downstairs loo window where a crow flew straight into it as we lay out on the lawn, picking dandelions. All things that I could never bring myself to fix. To do so would be to delete memories given physical form. But this house is not a mausoleum. It must evolve as I evolve. So gradually Mark is putting his stamp on the place too. And it is a happier place for it. A lamp here, a side table there. They're not to my taste, but that's OK. This is no longer my home; it is ours.

And so here we are, hosting a house-warming of sorts, although I've never much liked the term, which I discovered only recently is steeped in a tradition of guests bringing firewood to newlyweds' households and lighting fires in every vacant cavity in order to drive out residual spirits or ghouls. A cold house is a cursed house, apparently. But there are no spirits here; they left a very long time ago. I am the last of the line.

So yes, the house is alive again. I welcome more guests, though I needn't; they welcome themselves, and help themselves to Prosecco, canapés, bowls full of Twiglets and pitted olives. I was always terrible at laying on a good spread. Not my mother; she was born to it.

'You've looked after the old place,' says Mother, as she careens past me in the living room, old fashioned in one hand, cigarette in the other.

'You're smoking again?'

'Perceptive as ever, Annie darling. Anyway, where's that handsome man of yours? Haven't scared him off already, have you?'

She was both joking and yet deadly serious.

'He's in the garden with Pete and some of the boys.'

'Don't mind me,' says Mother, dancing off into the distance and nearly crashing full into my cousin Jeanette. She shouts back across the room, both arms held aloft, her waist cinched in by a sparkling green dress. 'I'm just going to say a little *hello*.'

At her departure, a voice, all too familiar, sidles up behind me. 'Still fabulous as ever.'

I turn to see K, beaming.

'You made it.'

'I made it.'

We give each other the most enormous hug. The last time I saw her was at the wedding; while Mark and I were on our honeymoon, K had moved, and quite some distance at that.

'How's Berlin?'

'Cold, very cold, but great. Hannah sends her love – sad she couldn't be here.'

'Wow. So you two are back on again? God, I can't keep up.'

'For now. We're trying to make the long-distance thing work.'

'Prognosis?'

'Gloomy, with certain chance of heartache.'

'Oh, I'm sorry, K.'

'Yeah, me too. But maybe it's for the best. I've started a new chapter, and as Mum would say: *The past stays put, you hear?*'

We laugh. How many times had we heard Mother utter that phrase?

'So how's married life?' says K. 'Tell me how wonderful it is, how spellbinding and enlivening; tell me that I'm missing out, that maybe, just maybe the conventional path is for me after all. Make me deliciously jealous.'

'To be honest with you ... not much has changed.' That was a lie; *everything* has changed. 'We're still the same people, in the same relationship, doing much the same things, except now I'm Mrs Lane, and I have this on my finger.'

I lift my hand to show the gold band.

'So you took his name after all? You mean to say I'm the final remaining Clark?'

I guess I was wrong: K is the last of the line, of this line.

'It would seem so.'

'Oh, Mum sent me the wedding photos by the way,' says K.

'Stunning, aren't they?'

'You and *Mark* look stunning. I look like an egg.'

I laugh. 'Nonsense.'

'Fine. A very well-dressed egg ... And did you notice a certain someone in the background of the outdoor shots?'

'Who?'

'Your favourite gatecrasher. Whatever happened to him?'

'Cameron? No idea. Mark suspects he was a freeloader. You know, those people who turn up to events, drink all they can, eat all they can, and then disappear.'

'Liggers?'

'Exactly.'

'Maybe I should give it a go,' mused K. 'Hell of a way to stumble through life.'

'You've got form, after all. The way you used to stand by the Pick n Mix in Woolworths, slipping them into your mouth instead of your bag ...'

K laughed. 'Hey. I was hungry.'

'Speaking of, let's get you some sausage rolls. Correction: veggie sausage rolls, I haven't forgotten.'

'A glass of red wouldn't go amiss either.'

'You got it. I'll be right back.'

I pass out of the living room, into the hallway, smile at my colleague, Sean – a classicist like me, unbearably stuck up. I didn't mean to invite him; I'd entered his email address on the round robin by accident and he was the first to respond (*would love to, thanks, Annie*) – and fight my way through more bodies, huddled and awkward, to the kitchen. Mark enters from the garden and we lock eyes across the room. He mimes placing a rope around his neck and swinging from it, literal gallows humour, and kisses me in the middle of the kitchen for which I'm forced to go up on my tiptoes. Sometimes I forget how tall he is, how imposing.

'Having a good time?'

'I am now,' he replies and pulls me in close. Mark is one of those people that when they hold you tight, the sheer force of their clasp squeezes smiles out from your face. 'K here?'

'Just arrived. Have you seen the red?'

'You mean this red?'

Mark lifts a bottle from the island, upends it above a glass, finds it dry.

'Never mind, I think there are four more bottles in the basement. I'll just pop down.'

'I'll go,' says Mark.

'No,' I say a little too abruptly. Mark's eyes narrow, a jot. 'No, it's fine,' I repeat, casually this time, languorously, so as not to arouse suspicion, further suspicion. My cheeks burn as I kiss him once more. 'I'll just be a sec.'

'So you and Pete, huh?'

'Me and Pete,' Laura replies. She seems impressed by my sleuthing. 'How did you – ?'

'Never mind that. I'm asking the questions.'

Laura sits up straight on the kitchen bar stool. 'Yes, Ma'am.'

'How? What? Why? When?' Laura moves to speak. 'Oh. My. God. Is that who was in the background when I called you from Capri? Pete? You were in bed with Pete.'

'Yes.'

I'm a little surprised she has kept this from me, a little hurt.

'Oh, Laura, you know what he's like.'

'He's changed.'

It's so hard not to roll my eyes.

'Stop it. He has!'

A few guests leave – air kisses across the room as they make for the door – but the party is still very much in full flow. I sort of wish it wasn't. Marriage has made me tired, has made me long for my bed at nine o'clock in the evening. It's exhausting looking after someone else's needs too.

'Besides,' continues Laura, 'Mark was not entirely an angel in his bachelor days – and after, by all accounts.'

'Did Pete tell you that?'

'Oh, come on, Annie. This can't be news to you.'

I look over at Mark, hovering by the French doors. He's holding court with an old colleague from the hospital. She's pretty, I suppose, in an obvious kind of way.

'My point is,' says Laura, 'people *can* change. Pete has changed. To tell the truth … OK, Annie, you have to promise not to take this the wrong way.'

I worry what she might say.

'Promise,' I offer.

'Well, when I sat there in the church that day, and I saw you walk down the aisle, saw the way you looked at Mark, I was jealous. There, I said it. I was jealous.'

'But why?'

211

'I mean, I was happy for you, of course I was. I *am* happy for you. But seeing what you had reminded me of what I didn't. And then at the reception, after you'd left, Pete and I got talking, and we discovered we had a lot in common.'

'A desire for one another's genitals?'

Laura laughs. 'It was more than that.'

'Seeing him feel up someone by the tree wasn't the most auspicious start.'

More laughter. 'Well, no. But that was then and this is now. I think I may have tamed him.'

I've lost count of the number of times I've heard this said of wild men.

'I mean it, Annie. He might be The One.'

'Wow. I never thought those two words would come out of your mouth.'

'I'm worried anytime now three small words will follow them,' she says quietly, as if to herself.

This is the first time I've seen Laura so open, so unguarded. Vulnerability looks good on her.

'OK,' I say. 'If he makes you happy, then I'm happy for you.'

Laura gives me a hug. Her hair smells like cinnamon.

'Thanks, babe. Are *you* happy?' she asks with a knowing look. The billion-dollar question, and one that my grandma had put to Mother all those years ago.

'I wasn't. The honeymoon wasn't exactly the adventure I'd dreamed of. For a time, I was worried I'd lost him, that my mother had set him against me.'

'How?'

I hesitate. 'She intimated I was to blame for Jessica's death.'

'Oh, come on, Annie. That wasn't your fault.'

Does she really mean that, or is it what she thinks I want to hear?

'I try to believe that. Every day. But then Mother, pissed as she was, goes and suggests otherwise. She blames me; I've always known it, and now I've had it confirmed. Anyway, I guess after hearing something like that, Mark started questioning everything I'd told him, started wondering how much of it was a lie. How much of us was a lie.'

212

'And now?' asks Laura, concerned. 'You two seem close again.'

'I managed to straighten things out, I think. I hope. More of a plaster than a suture. Things have got better. He loves me, I know he does. And he's back at work, back in theatre, which seems to have answered a need in him. But it's like there are two Marks, and I'm never quite sure which I'm going to get. He chops and he changes. Though he probably feels the same way about me. I chop and I change about most things, but not about him.'

'You are the quintessential Gemini.' Laura reaches her hand into a bowl of Twiglets.

'Now you believe in horoscopes?'

'Someone's got to. Also, who the fuck serves Twiglets in this day and age?'

'Me, apparently.'

'Are you glad you did it?' asks Laura.

'The Twiglets?'

'The wedding.'

Mark catches my eye again from across the room. His old colleague continues to run her fingers through her hair as they talk. Mark seems embarrassed that I'm a witness to the encounter, and just then it occurs to me that instead of driving the spirits out, we seem to have welcomed them in.

35

As I packed my things in preparation for my fortnight away with Charlotte, Mark hounded me. He tried to take my clothes, to hide them from me, so that I couldn't leave. Please don't go, he said. I'm sorry; it's been a rough few weeks. He looked pathetic, he looked tired. I'd never seen him plead before. I hated that I enjoyed it. No, I said, It's been a rough few years. You don't mean that, he said. Think of all the good. Rome, remember Rome? We were in love. We are in love, and this can be salvaged. Whatever it is, I'll put it right.

I think he sensed that what was pitched as a fortnight was, in truth, forever. I'd made my mind up – I deserved more, and I would get more. His pleading turned to anger. Venom. Humiliated at his prostrating himself, he really wanted to hurt me this time. Having realised this was it, he saw nothing left to lose. And he went for the jugular.

You're really fucking stupid, aren't you? he said. Four years of trying and no dice. You never thought to dig a little deeper ... Well, let me help you pick up the shovel: I had the snip the day we met. Do you really think I'd want to have children with you? he laughed.

It was disgusting. He was disgusting. *He was lying, of course – he hadn't. It's funny how we try to hit hardest those we desire the most.*

And you're a really fucking stupid bitch if you think I'm going to just let you leave, he said. I stopped then and I looked at him, read the fury in his face. I believed him.

Mark ... He grabbed my wrists. Mark, you're hurting me. Mark ... And it was all I could do not to sob. Had I found a

215

voice within me or a whit of strength, I wouldn't have called for help, I'd have screamed over and over and over again:

This is not my husband. This is not my husband. This is not my husband. This is not my husband. This is not my husband. This is not my husband. This is not my husband. This is not my husband. This is not my husband. This is not my husband. This is not my husband. This is not my husband. This is not my husband.

It was only when the tears came that he stood back, shocked at his own power. He was appalled of what he had proven himself capable of. There was a monster lurking within him and only now had he stepped in front of a mirror and seen it for himself.

Hope, I ...

Go, I said. And he did.

Tomorrow I will start again. And tomorrow he will be sorry. I shall leave him a note, and it will say all there is to say. A full stop on us.

36

Cameron's father had told him that universities were where people hid from the real world. He had said that they were places where knowledge was doled out to those and only those who could afford it. They were not crucibles of ideas, but graves, mausoleums. They were places where ideas went to die. Had Cameron gone to university then, had he not entered the police at the tender age of sixteen, his father would have considered him a failure.

And so it was that Cameron chuckled lightly to himself as he walked into the Strand campus of King's College, London.

What would his father have made of this? he wondered.

As he climbed the stairs up and around to the right, the faint sound of choral music seemed to flood towards him in great waves. He traced the sound, followed its path back to its source and stopped in front of two great, solid oak doors, to which he pressed his ear and listened. The music, the singing ... it was beautiful. It was the sound of a hundred voices convening and offering up one single, collective, impassioned plea; an offering of love and a request for reciprocity. The sound of a long-suppressed sigh finally being released. An exhale. A petition.

Cameron gently pushed open the doors and edged his way into the chapel. As the music and the voices soared, so too did his eyes – up from the chequerboard aisle, up past the pews and red balustrades entwined with gold detailing, up past the ornamented arches and along to the semi-dome of the apse, where they rested on an image of a seated Christ surrounded entirely by his angels.

He stood there – for how long, later he could not say – and felt within him a great sense of loss. He thought of Mrs Capel, the woman he couldn't save, and of Hope, the woman he never knew, and he wept. Not for the sheer fact of their absence, for he hoped them to be in a better place where suffering could not touch them, but for all the wondrous things in life that they could, and would, no longer hear nor see.

Frank had asked him whether he believed in God, and he'd said no. It was the truth, and yet there was a space within him that was yet to be filled. He'd always thought that space reserved for a child, which never arrived, but perhaps it was for something else – something bigger than him, something bigger than Sophie and whatever they might make together.

Cameron felt his phone vibrate and the spell was broken. He wiped his eyes and fumbled in his pocket.

She's squeaky clean. No history of violence, psychological disturbance or any convictions whatsoever. Sorry. That's as much as I can do ... Good luck – Vernon.

Cameron replaced the phone in his pocket and slipped back out the great oak doors. The music followed after him, but it was quieter now, dimmed.

'Excuse me,' Cameron called after a man, a lecturer he assumed, bearing a battered old copy of Dante's *Inferno* under his arm. The man stopped in the corridor and pushed his circular glasses up the bridge of his nose. 'Can you tell me where I might find Professor Lane?'

'Lane?' The man looked confused, a touch flustered.

'A Professor Clark then perhaps?'

'Oh, Annie,' said the man. 'The History Department is just up the stairs again and to your left. She may be in her office, though I'm yet to see her today.'

'You know her well?'

Cameron thought he saw the man stifle a laugh.

'I don't think anybody here could be said to *know her well.*' It was Cameron's turn to look confused. 'She very much keeps herself to herself.'

'Would you say she was a bit of a loner?'

This time the man could not hide his mirth. The subject had clearly tickled him.

'There are hermit monks in Meteora who might describe Annie as *a bit of a loner*. I've worked with her for five years and we've barely exchanged two words. But then this is academia; it doesn't exactly attract the most sociable people.'

'When did you – ?' But the man cut Cameron short with a glance at his watch.

'I'm terribly sorry but I really must get going. I'm due in a seminar on the other side of the building.' The man walked off along the corridor, calling back to Cameron. 'Up the stairs and to your left. You can't miss it.'

Cameron knocked on the door of the office, just above the silver plaque that read *Professor A. Clark*. Cameron supposed she intended to continue using her maiden name in her professional life. Or perhaps she hadn't quite got around to changing it. After all, it hadn't been long since the wedding.

'Hello,' he called, and knocked once more.

Silence. He peered through the frosted-glass window, but it was no use; the refractions of light danced on the pane and gave the impression of movement where there wasn't any. He knocked once more, and after getting no reply, gingerly pushed on the handle.

Inside, the office was a mess. Paperwork lay piled high and strewn over every surface. There were trinkets and postcards, dozens of photo frames dotted along shelves between dusty old tomes of poetry, prose and plays that threatened to pull the supporting brackets from the wall. A sneeze, he thought, might bring the whole lot crashing down. Similarly, the walls heaved under the sheer volume of various portraits and landscapes; covered in prints and posters – every inch home to a Giotto, a Canaletto, a Degas or a Goya. There were depictions of historical scenes, some real, some imaginary. There were renditions of popular folklore, of fairy tales and of myths.

Cameron turned and looked up, where, positioned just above the door, and illuminated from above by a spotlight, lending the image a certain ghostly quality, was a painting of a young brunette woman in a black draped dress, kneeling before an ornate golden box into which she peers tentatively. The image captured Cameron in a way that the choral music had just moments earlier. The young woman's curiosity seemed to be mirrored in his own.

'Hello?'

Cameron's thought was broken by a figure now standing in the doorway.

'Sorry, I'm looking for Professor Clark,' she said, gesturing to the bound papers held in her outstretched hand. 'An essay.'

Cameron smiled at the young woman, who seemed to bear a striking resemblance to the painting above her head.

'You're a student of hers?'

The young woman nodded. 'A first year. Greek Mythology.'

Cameron could only recall one Greek myth. The one about a king who is punished by having to continually roll a boulder up a hill. As soon as he reaches the top, the boulder falls back down to the bottom and he has to start all over again. School did not agree with Cameron, and he did not agree with school.

'What kind of teacher is she?' Cameron asked.

The student seemed taken aback by the question and why he should be asking it.

'Passionate,' she said after some time.

'About myths?'

'About the lessons they can teach us.'

'And what have they taught *you*?' Cameron realised in that moment he had unwittingly placed the student under a microscope. He softened his approach. 'Which myth is your favourite?'

The student thought for a long while, until her eyes alighted on a print to her right, depicting a man with feathered wings soaring past the sun.

'Icarus,' she said. 'The boy who flew too close to the sun.'

Several times Cameron had not heeded this simple principle. Too many times in his career the wax in his feathers had almost melted, and he had almost plummeted. He had been lucky.

'And what does that one show?' Cameron gestured to the painting hanging above the door, the one with the young woman – this student's doppelgänger – kneeling before a golden box.

The student turned and looked up. 'That's Pandora's box. Well, technically it would have been a jar, but sometime long ago it was mistranslated as a box.'

The name Pandora rang a bell; Cameron had heard it said many times before in the context of unleashing something terrible, but he was unsure of the myth. He must have looked confused for the student continued.

'Yeah, you know. Zeus gives her a box as a wedding present but forbids her to open it. Eventually, curiosity gets the better of her, she unlocks it and out pours all the evils of the world. The last thing to escape is Hope.'

Cameron's eyes widened at the name and a cold chill ran down the length of his back, finishing in his shoes. 'Why Hope?' he asked.

'No one knows for sure. The question is: is Hope one of the evils, or a counterpoint to them? Is Hope ultimately a good thing or a bad thing?'

'And what do you think?' asked Cameron.

'I think it depends on how the individual chooses to perceive it.'

'And how does Annie perceive it?'

The student was amused. 'Professor Clark? You would have to ask her.'

37

It was dark by the time Cameron arrived at the farmhouse. Two candles perched on a windowsill glinted through the gloom, throwing a pool of light on to the gravel path outside – just enough so that he could see his own breath hanging in the air. He knocked twice, forcefully, on the wooden door, and then turned to look back at the field, which spread before him like a Persian rug, knitted together with fences, squat brick walls and brown, frosted December earth that ran up to the pillbox in the neighbouring field. *I could see myself here*, thought Cameron. Though he suspected Sophie might have her reservations; she wasn't the farmer's wife type.

A rustling inside startled Cameron from his reverie: the footsteps of a figure approaching the door.

'Who is it?' called out Annie.

'Cameron. We met at your wedding.'

Silence. A hedgehog scampered behind him.

'I owe you an apology,' said Cameron. 'And an explanation.'

A longer silence followed in which Cameron rocked back and forth uneasily between the heel and toe of his feet. After some time, he was starting to abandon all hope of the door ever opening, when, suddenly, the sound of a barrel bolt sliding back from the door jamb punctured the stillness of the evening.

The figure emerged, dressed in a long dressing gown – dyed pink, Cameron suspected, by an errant red sock – and stood there awkwardly in the weak glow of the hallway light, hands folded firmly across her chest. *Defensive.*

Cameron seized the opportunity to pull a bottle out from behind his back.

'For you,' he said. 'I'm assured it's a very good vintage.'

'Thank you,' said Annie, at once timorous and imposing.

'May I come in?'

'My husband will be back any moment.'

Cameron clapped his hands together. 'Wonderful. I dare say I owe him an apology too.'

Annie made to speak, but too late; Cameron strode past her into the hallway, rattling the lone, tatty umbrella on the hatstand.

'Lovely place you have here,' said Cameron, as he surveyed every inch of the hallway, and what little he could see of the kitchen from his vantage point. 'I hope I'm not intruding.'

'Well, actually –'

'Good. I do hate to come unannounced.' Cameron removed his gloves and his long mohair overcoat before gesturing to the living room. 'Shall we?'

On the drive up, Cameron was uncomfortable at the notion of playing the part of the obnoxious, uninvited guest, and yet, to his great surprise, here he was, in his element, a duck to water. Besides, he'd done it once at the wedding, he could do it again now.

Annie, visibly exasperated, acceded by way of a nod and followed the almost stranger into the living room, which he too appraised with an auctioneer's eye. That same eye cast around the fripperies of the room until it rested on a framed photo of Annie's father, nestled among various house-warming cards.

'A handsome man,' said Cameron, replacing the photo. 'You have his nose.'

Annie smiled at the intended compliment, and Cameron thought he saw a softening then, but he couldn't be sure.

'You had a little gathering here recently,' he said, his gaze drawn to a pyramid of empty beer cans by the wood basket. 'I'd ask the occasion but –' His gaze tracked back to the cards.

Annie cleared her throat in an attempt to reclaim an air of authority. Cameron could see that a quiet anger simmered within. Still, she remained calm, collected, but most of all defiant.

'Is there something you wanted? It's a little late and I was just about to –'

'Yes.' Cameron held her eye, and his nerve. 'I came to apol-ogise for our unfortunate meeting. I had no right to crash your wedding, uninvited –' He appreciated the irony of this apology. ' – and I certainly had no right to anger you.'

'What were you doing there?'

'I have been looking for someone.'

'And you thought that someone would be at my wedding?' Annie was snappish now.

'Not exactly.'

'Then what?'

Cameron scratched the back of his head as he always did when he was on the brink of broaching a difficult subject.

'Mark's first wife. Hope. I'm sure you've heard the –'

It was Annie's turn to cut her visitor short. 'I'm aware of Mark's past, if that's what you mean.'

'Then I'm sure you're aware she's been missing for more than two years now, presumed dead. In the eyes of the law, one cannot get married again if one already is – unless that spouse is dead, of course.' Cameron thought he saw a flash of panic in the upward thrust of her chin. He tried again, more delicately. 'I'm trying to trace her, on the assumption she may still be alive. I wondered if you could help me.'

Annie shook her head, defiantly. 'How? I never knew the woman.'

'Perhaps you'd heard something, or found something. Something that might point to her intentions.'

'She left a note, if that's what you mean.'

'I'm aware of the note.'

'But you don't believe it?'

'The authorities might be satisfied but I am not. I don't believe in accepting the first truth you're presented with. There's often another one lurking beneath.'

'So you think Mark was lying?'

'I haven't said that.'

'As good as.'

Cameron sighed. It was like arguing with an older sister. He tried a different tack.

'You and I have a great deal more in common than you realise.'

Annie smirked. 'Do strangers doorstepping you late at night also catch your ire?'

Cameron had had enough. He'd tried to play nice and it was getting him nowhere. 'No, but people with something to hide do.'

'I thought you'd come here to apologise?'

'I had. Apology's over.'

Annie stalked over to her phone and picked it up. 'I want you gone right this minute, or I'm calling Mark.'

Cameron took a seat on the sofa and put his feet up on the coffee table.

'I don't think you want to do that,' he said slowly, confidently.

'And why's that?'

'What I have to say might best be kept between us. For now. Besides, I know he's recently gone back to work, finally. You'll struggle to recall him from theatre. I don't think surgeons take phone calls mid-operation. Of course, you can try the police too, if you like. But I don't think that's going to help you either.'

Annie hesitated before slamming down the phone, frustration seemingly having got the better of her.

'Take a seat,' said Cameron. 'You seem a little flushed.'

This was the part Cameron liked. The bait had been set, the rod cast, and any moment now the fish would swim to the lure. But the struggle seemed to have gone out of this one. All he had to do, he thought now, was dredge the water with the net.

'Come on,' he said. 'Don't be shy.'

Reluctantly, Annie sat in the armchair opposite, where she cut a diminutive figure against its wide, sprawling floral pattern. She placed her hands on the arms and gripped them tightly.

'My investigation has turned up some very interesting information, very interesting indeed.'

The colour drained from Annie's face.

'I spoke with a few of Mark's neighbours – John and Diane to the left, Jake and Alan Carswell to the right. I doubt these names will mean much to you.'

Annie looked blank.

'Thought so. A while before Hope's disappearance, they all recall seeing a woman standing by the post box opposite, once a week, sometimes more than that, often for hours on end, often at night, a few mornings. Diane called the police one evening, but by the time they arrived, the woman had scarpered. She stopped coming after that, so Diane put it from her mind. That is until several months later, when the same woman was seen regularly dropping Hope off at her house. She never went inside.'

'This is an intriguing story,' snapped Annie, 'but I fail to see the relevance.'

Cameron leant in. 'This is where it gets good.'

Annie's eyes darted to the door, but her feet stayed put.

'I asked what this woman looked like. They all gave me exactly the same description.'

'Let me guess: a slim brunette? Am I supposed to be unique?'

'Not unique, no. But something else occurred to me as I stood outside Mark's house, from the same vantage point as that woman.'

Cameron stood up at this point and began pacing tightly around the living room, one hand in his pocket, the other on his chin, and his head faced squarely at the floor.

'You had a sister, didn't you?'

'I *have* a sister: Karen.'

'Another sister. Younger still, or at least she would be, if –'

Annie swallowed hard. 'Jessica,' she said.

'Very good. And perhaps you could remind me of her middle name.'

Annie seemed to grip the arms of her chair even tighter. Had she a little more strength in her wrists, she might have torn each arm in two. For a time, her eyes were fixed to the floor before springing up again to regard her accuser. Her judge, her jury, her executioner.

'I'll give you a clue. It begins with a *C*.'

'I know what it is,' said Annie, a renewed resolve punctuating her words. 'Her middle name was Charlotte.'

Cameron stood stock-still and considered Annie. The constant pacing had rendered him a little dizzy. Perhaps his blood pressure was low. He should get that checked.

'Hope had a friend called Charlotte,' he said. 'She used to attend her yoga classes. Started doing so twelve months before she disappeared.'

Annie was exasperated. 'It's a common name.'

'Perhaps. Mind if I take a look around?' said Cameron, but he didn't wait for an answer. 'Of course you don't.' He strode out into the hallway and through to the kitchen, with Annie in close pursuit.

'Just what do you think you're doing?' she barked. 'This really is –'

'I'll just be a moment, and then I'm gone. I assure you. My wife is waiting for me with a late supper, and it's coq au vin tonight. Not one to miss.'

With Annie only ever an inch behind, he worked his way around the house, room by room, but stopped short of entering her bedroom. He thought that would be rather gauche. Satisfied, he walked back down the stairs, each one groaning under foot, and then stood at the bottom, looking up at Annie, stood waiting on the landing.

'It really is a lovely house,' he smiled. 'I'm sure you and Mark will be very –'

His words trailed off as his eyes alighted on a narrow door, which he'd written off as a cupboard. But now he wasn't so sure. He grabbed for the handle, pulled, and there, opening out before him, was another set of stairs, descending into darkness, into the basement.

'Now what might we have here? Be a shame to leave without taking the *full* tour. Annie, be a dear and join me down here, won't you? I can't seem to find the light.'

Cameron stood facing the basement entrance. The staircase behind him creaked with Annie's footsteps, until she reached the bottom, when all fell silent. His thoughts ran away from him in the quiet, and he wondered whether she might do something silly, whether she might pick up a vase and –'

'Sure,' said Annie, composed. She ran a loose hair behind her left ear. 'Let me lead the way.'

She descended into the darkness a little and found the pull switch. The light spluttered into life.

'Well? Are you coming or not?' she said challengingly.

As Cameron looked at the half-lit basement, suddenly he was a boy again, walking down the stairs, watching his father bent over his lathe, turning something in his workshop, inviting little Cam, dungarees and all, over to watch him, placing a chisel in his hands, tendrils of shavings curling up and out, a dram of whisky, a sleeping mother. Boy and man. That seemed so long ago now, so very much had happened since.

The basement was spartan. On the cold concrete floor stood only a depleted wine rack, a box of Christmas decorations and a small, old fashioned trunk with brass clasps and leather bindings. Cameron walked to it with mounting unease.

'There's nothing in there,' she snapped. But Cameron opened it anyway, rifled through an assortment of ephemera – magazines, ticket stubs, journals, a torch, a child's dress, paints and paint-brushes. Nothing of any real interest, not to Cameron at least.

'Who's the artist?'

'My father is. Was,' Annie corrected herself.

Cameron smiled. 'We really aren't so different after all.'

Annie didn't answer; she was too busy focused on a patch of wall at the far end of the basement, a strip of wallpaper that was coming away at the bottom left-hand corner, crinkled and upturned, steamed away by the nearby heat pipes. Cameron noticed this, noticed her panicked expression, turned, felt a fris-son of fear ripple through his companion, felt the fish tug finally on the line, felt her tug on his shoulder in a small attempt to stop him lunging forward and taking the corner in his hand, to stop him pulling and pulling and pulling, to stop him seeing what lay beneath, what had been etched into the paint a long time ago, to stop him discovering the writing on the wall.

As he went down in a final, decisive hard slap against the cold concrete floor and felt the warm trickle of blood run down and around the crown of his head, he thought he heard, distantly, as though a whisper, his father's voice calling to him from the lathe.

38

I once thought the truth was immutable, I once thought it was cast in stone, engraved in bronze, that it was unchanging, a constant in the otherwise shifting sands of friendship, of court-ship, of marriage. I once thought the truth was sacrosanct, that no matter how much one tried to suppress it, to deny it, to bury it deep, that it would bubble up, rise to the surface; that the truth will out. And yet, as I have come to discover, that is the biggest lie of them all, a fiction we're fed from birth, bound up in the foolish notion of good and evil, of two opposing forces engaged in an eternal battle for supremacy, from which there can be only one victor. And it is *good*, we're told, that must prevail; that there is no place in this world for evil.

But how can anything be so utterly binary? At some point the two battle fronts – the black and the white – must meet, must descend from their hills bearing their standards and converge in this struggle, limb embroiled in limb, until the defining essence of each becomes lost; until grey, the noblest of all colours, emerges. It is here, in the melting pot of right and wrong, fact and fiction, in the victory of union, that truth exists, if at all. The truth is not fixed, it is as shifting as the sands. It is the product of a negotia-tion, and it is all a matter of perspective.

Stories make us and break us, shape us and elevate us. Stories have raised civilisations and levelled others. Stories are power, they are triumph, they are the lies we tell ourselves to find the strength to carry on. We yearn, so desperately, for stories, no matter how fanciful or escapist, to reflect something of us, some-thing recognisable, and in so doing that they might reveal something unseen, something about us, or within us, that we hadn't considered. Sometimes that is the case, but not always. For when the mirror is held up, we only ever see a distortion; we only ever see an image that is simultaneously true and not true, real and unreal. And so when I held up the mirror to our relationship, to Mark and me, I saw only that which I wished to see, and only that which I wished to be seen. I found my light, as the influencers say, the light that would tell the best story. It is all a matter of perspective. And this is mine.

We met on the train, on our commute. That much is true. We met again, we met fully, properly, outside the Richmond Centre. That much is also true. We dated, we laughed, we fell in love, we fucked liked teenagers and fought like cat and dog. We married on a sunlit autumn day and had a mildly disastrous honeymoon, until the tide turned and we found each other again, just before the waves threatened to break over our heads. That is all true. My word is my record, where once it was my bond. But it's not quite as simple as that.

I didn't believe in love at first sight, thought it a dismal notion that was all-too-often vaunted over and above a more slow-burning, creeping kind of love – that this widespread primacy somehow invalidated all the relationships I'd known and enjoyed to date. I thought it a Hollywood invention, a fable passed between school desks, a promise that could not be delivered upon. And yet, I was wrong. The day I first saw Mark on that train, the moment I saw his arm gripping the bar for support among a crush of bleary-eyed commuters, the long lock of dark-brown hair that grazed his eyebrow, I fell – I hate to admit it – utterly, madly in love with him.

The more I looked at him, the more I thought I understood him: the job he held, the people he met, the procession of ex-girl-friends who left love-starved voicemails on his phone ... But understanding wasn't enough. A great fire had been lit within me and it needed feeding with wood and petrol. I needed to see the man beneath the image I'd constructed and forced upon him. I needed to see the real Mark. And had it stopped there, had my fascination with him bedded down in my imagination, had I marvelled at the fantasy and not sought the truth, things might have been different. She might still be with him.

She might still be alive.

Their house was the kind of house that every little girl dreams of. Large front garden studded with roses of all different hues: reds, oranges, lilacs, yellows, pinks. There were hollyhocks and lemon trees, phlox, lupins, honeysuckle and lavender. There was a Japanese maple, a deep, hungry red, that bowed in welcome. There was a black-and-white tessellated path, a mint-green fence and door, and a bicycle perched up against the porch. But there was no sign of any children – no scooters or skateboards or helmets or basketball hoops. It was a family home waiting on a family.

Two figures moved about behind the windows, behind the French shutters, in a hive of activity. He was handsome, she was pretty. They had everything it seemed. Well, almost everything. They were together, but not really; each operated as if in isolation, in a vacuum. That is to say, dimly aware of each other's presence but thoroughly uninterested. Bored, perhaps. There was no love between them, I could see that from my position opposite, partially obscured by the hanging branches of an oak tree. I could see them, they couldn't see me, and they certainly couldn't see each other. I doubted they had even looked, properly looked, at one another in years. At one point in time they must have, long ago. They must have shared a bond, a connection that they believed would endure, would see them through the very best and the very worst, in sickness and in health, for richer, for poorer. The rings on their fingers told one part of the story, but their bodies told another.

They ate breakfast together, they dined together, they shared a glass of wine in the evenings. They would talk, but not really. They would laugh but it was joyless. Once a week, they would make love – Sundays at 10 a.m. – but neither of them would cum, and they'd given up faking it. It struck me that they'd spent so much of their lives living out the same week on repeat. Breakfast, work, dinner, breakfast, work, dinner. The Sunday fuck was thrown in just to remind them that they were still alive, until that too became routine, until that too reminded them both just how trapped they were.

How do I know all this? I studied them over many months; studied their patterns, their movements, their routines.

At first, I just wanted to see where he lived, nothing more, so I waited outside North Dulwich station one evening for him to return, followed him a little, matched my pace to his long strides. I liked the way he walked – loping yet with purpose. I liked the way he brushed his hair back from his forehead, the tip-tap of his brogues on the pavement, the pause at the traffic lights while he checked his phone, the whistle when he thrust his hands in his pockets to feel his keys as he approached his house, their house. Of course, she never greeted him at the door; Mark had stopped expecting that a long time ago.

How powerful it felt to be an observer from the street opposite. I thought of it as a social experiment: me the intrepid explorer, anthropologist, venturing bravely into the lives of others. And it was fun, a lot of fun. It was like watching a film first-hand, or reading a novel in which all the characters were real. Their life was a script they had no idea they were writing, a script that I could impose meaning upon, could control, co-opt. I would stay for hours, morning and night, just to watch them go about their miserable lives on this beautiful set, together yet apart. A few times I saw him try to make an effort with her – reaching out in his own subtle way. A new flower in the vase, a new vase for the flower, a hand on her hip, a cup of herbal tea, a dress for her birthday. He was trying to tell her he loved her, that he hadn't given up. But his gestures always fell on stony ground.

After some time, I decided he deserved better, much better than this cold, unfeeling woman, who only ever looked out for herself and didn't care one iota for this man whose only crime was trying to make his wife love him again. And so, I stepped into the novel, on to the movie set, started imagining myself in that kitchen, in that living room, in that bed. I started seeing myself as the wife, the perfect wife. For *I* would be grateful for the small gestures, grateful for the time he spent with me; I would make him laugh, dry his tears, soothe his worries; I would see the flower, see the vase, feel the hand on my hip; and I would always, *always* greet him at the door. I would make sure he felt loved, that he felt safe, every single day. He would know my love, and I would know his. The things I could do for him, the things I would do.

Still, it wasn't enough. There's only so much a person can glean from a kerbside vantage, there's only so much you can see from afar. I needed to get closer. But not to him, not yet. The best way to understand him, I decided, was to understand her.

Every Tuesday at 7.30 a.m., as he ate his cereal, readied himself for the train, the little princess would set out for work dressed head to toe in black spandex, a cropped jumper thrown over the top in a display of faux-modesty – there was nothing modest about this woman. One day I grabbed my yoga mat and the only pair of jogging bottoms I owned without a hole in the crotch, and I followed her – up through Lordship Lane, past Goose Green, right at Rye Lane – to a rundown warehouse in Peckham Rye. As I walked behind her, studied her lines, watched her wave every so often to someone she seemed to know, I struggled to understand what Mark had ever seen in her. She *was* pretty in an obvious way, with high cheekbones, freckles and blonde locks trailing down her back, but I felt cheated. There are millions of women just like her. There is but one me.

Two dozen people filtered into the studio, mats and water bottles in hand. It was hot in there, stiflingly so. To breathe was a struggle. She took her position at the head of the class, led us through a range of positions and cheered us on as we filed out of the room at the end, a mass of sweaty bodies and aching limbs. I was the last to leave, the last to roll up my mat, to compose myself. I saw my chance – and I took it. The rest, as they say, is history. Herstory. My story.

'Hi,' I said, extending my hand to hers. 'I'm Charlotte.'

39

October ... sometime ...

It's been ten months. Ten months of darkness. Ten months without air. Ten months with rats and damp and cold and cobwebs. Ten months down here alone with the thoughts in my head. Thoughts of Mark, thoughts of life before ... But the main thought, the one I keep returning to, the thought I thought I'd never think is a simple one: I might be better off dead. Except there's no might about it, not any more, not ever.

She visited me again today, for the first time this week I think. Not that it matters, time has lost all meaning. It passes or it doesn't. I'm still here. Along with the tinned food and the bottled water and the fresh bucket she always brings and leaves out for me like a sick dog, today she brought a little something extra. I recognised it immediately.

I found this, she said. In the living room. Thought it might keep you occupied. You must be very bored. She was right, but I wouldn't give her the satisfaction. Well, aren't you going to say thank you, she said, kneeling down before me. But my lips wouldn't move, or maybe I'd forgotten how to speak.

Suit yourself, she said and carried it back to the open door.
Wait.
She turned, looked at the diary.
This? You don't want this, do you? Oh, you do. Well, you should have spoken up earlier. The squeaky wheel gets the oil. So what do you say? And think real hard before you answer because I may not ask again.

Every fibre in my body told me to remain dignified. But there's no dignity down here, not when you have to empty yourself into a bucket. Thank you, I said quietly.

Better, she said and threw the diary across the floor. I'm ashamed to say I scrabbled for it, in the dirt and damp. Though even shame is beginning to pass now. Shame is for the civilised.

In the car we had laughed and joked. I was escaping, I was happy. Free at last. But something wasn't right. Charlotte didn't seem herself. Where once she was fizzing with energy, the life and soul of the party, she seemed quiet, withdrawn, in her own head. What's the matter? I asked. Nothing, she replied. We'll be there soon.

As we headed up a winding gravel path to a farmhouse, Charlotte grew animated again. Oh, you'll just love it here, she said. Some space to yourself. Some space to shut the world out. To reflect.

You grew up here?

Mostly, she said.

Lucky.

She fell silent.

Inside, my bag was taken from me, my coat hung up, a wine glass placed in my hand. I was led through to the living room where Charlotte lit a fire. It warmed us both through. Better already, right? I had to agree.

The late afternoon spread into evening. The wine came and the wine went. I pointed to a photograph on the mantelpiece. Your Dad? I asked. She seemed upset. Her good humour fell.

I'm sorry.

My glass was refilled, emptied and refilled again. She didn't seem to be drinking, or if she was I can't remember. My eyes swam, that much I do know. Then talk turned to Mark.

You're doing the right thing, she said. Never liked him.

I pointed out she'd never met him.

Don't need to, she said, to know he's bad for you. You've told me enough. What kind of woman would put up with that?

I wondered. She thought me a fool. Maybe I am, maybe I have been.

Still, you're here now, she said. You will build new things. The past stays put, you hear?

I heard.

I'm not sure what happened next. I saw an envelope with a name, not her name, not the name she'd given me. There was a struggle, a long struggle, I think. And then I woke up here ... my left wrist handcuffed to a heat pipe. There are burn marks up my arms, my back. I'm in constant pain, but no pain is worse than that of not knowing why I am here, why I am being punished.

She watched me as I flicked through the diary, as I read the strange, most recent passages, trying to piece together a past that I did not recognise, featuring a man that I did not recognise. The brutality, the violence, the slammed doors, the drunken abuse, the grabbed wrist. That wasn't my Mark, not the Mark I remembered. He was loving, caring, dependable, charming. He was all of those things and more. He had his difficulties, his own personal demons, our marriage was like any other: good days and bad days. But the good far outshone the bad.

This was my diary, and yet it wasn't. These later entries, these later words; they were not mine. This was not him, this was not our relationship. No, this was pure invention. The handwriting was strikingly similar to any untrained eye – the same looped 'L's, the same sloping 'P's and 'I's with a dot just a little too high – but it wasn't mine.

You, I said, looking up at Charlotte, hovering there in her jeans and T-shirt, so casual, so indifferent to my suffering. You wrote these?

She sniffed the air, defiant.

Why? I petitioned.

A contingency, she said, in the unlikely event the police were still looking for you after all this time. I couldn't have them thinking your relationship with Mark was a happy one, could I? A contented wife disappearing is a mystery; an unhappy one an inevitability. Fortunately there was little need; they gave up long ago. You were barely missed. A footnote in history. Now you and that diary have two things in common.

I looked at her blankly.

I have no further use for either, she said.

Just as Charlotte closed the basement door and shut out the only light I had seen in seven days, she told me something that inspired both hope and fear in equal measure: tomorrow she plans to move me.

40

Once upon a time, or so the story goes, Eos, Goddess of the Dawn, she of golden arms and rosy fingers, dewy skin and hungry heart, mother of the four winds and daughter of the bright sky, happened upon the Trojan prince, Tithonus, as he lay in sweet slumber beside the rush of the Ionian Sea. So peacefully did he sleep that Eos was loathe to wake him, but wake him she did, to gaze, if only briefly, into his crystalline eyes. The moment she saw him, really saw him, and he her, they fell into a tangle of mutual infatuation, and each knew, as sure as day follows night, as sure as Helios follows Selene, that love had them fully in its grasp and there was no letting go.

Days, weeks, months, years passed as that love grew into a hot blaze. But Eos could not relax. She was a titan and he a mortal. Time would visit a great unkindness on the young prince, and one day the fire would stop. This much she knew. Unless … But she dismissed the thought, thinking it too foolish, too impish, until that illicit thought grew too, burned as brightly as the fire but never brighter, until the thought consumed her, until it was all she could do not to at least *try*. She had to try.

So into her chariot she climbed, as she did every morning, and once her labours were done, once her rays of light had dispersed the mists of night and scattered the morning dew, her winged horses – there Firebright, there Daybright – bore her on to Mount Olympus to seek an audience with Zeus.

'Oh, King of the Gods, God of the Sky, I beg of you to grant me a favour, just one favour that would make my immortal life that bit more bearable.'

'A favour?' answered Zeus irritably. 'What kind of favour?'

'I have taken a lover, but he is mortal – eventually Thanatos should come for him, Hades too. And then he shall be gone from me, our love a past that I cannot reclaim. I wish to live it, to live it always. I ask of you then, make him immortal, so that we may live forever, always.'

Zeus looked across at his wife Hera, knew what it was to feel such longing, such fire. Theirs was a love that had too often spoken its name.

'That is all you ask?'

'That is all I ask.'

'Very well,' said Zeus. 'So be it.'

Eos returned to Tithonus, and was welcomed with the passion of a thousand suns. They made love, they danced, they sang together over the honeyed sounds of the lyre, which he played, would only play, for her. They journeyed, they married, they had children – two wonderful boys who were as strong and brave and handsome as their father, and whose light they'd inherited from their mother.

For many happy years, all was joy, only joy. But the world turned, the seasons came and went, and Tithonus developed lines across his forehead, became weaker with each passing Winter, found his once vibrant locks peppered with grey. His muscles slackened, his spine hunched, and his movement grew awkward, laboured. Enough was enough. Eos returned to Mount Olympus and set upon Zeus with a fury he had not seen in her before.

'You promised,' she said, as she collapsed to her knees before him and held aloft a single fibril of grey hair. 'You promised.'

'The Trojan, I presume?'

Eos nodded, a pool of tears collecting at her knees and dampening the hem of her saffron-coloured robe.

'You asked that I make him immortal. Is he not immortal? You said nothing of his remaining young, you said nothing of eternal youth. That would have been a second boon, and you assured me you sought only one. On that basis, your wish was granted. Now go. Enjoy your long lives together.'

Day by day, she was forced to watch Tithonus' once Herculean frame, his rippling torso and giant, powerful shoulders, reduced, by degrees, to a sack of bones, too weak to move; to witness his once crystalline eyes cloud over, unseeing now; to hear his once booming voice commuted to a scorched whisper. What little she could discern amidst the rasping and the rattling of his lungs, seemed to her utter gibberish punctuated occasionally by the clear, if desperate, plea for death, for mercy, for release as he hovered alone at the quiet limit of the world. But Thanatos never came, Tithonus' call was never answered. Instead, he withered further still, while Eos, gentle, unthinking Eos, whose light was never taken but given freely, remained undimmed – a constant, a pole star in an ever-changing world.

Finally, Eos could stand it no more; she refused to bear witness to the horror of his body, to attend to the tortured wailing that erupted from his scarred throat. She took action, what little she could, and summoned all her strength, called on all the godly powers invested in her, and transformed the wracked Tithonus into a grasshopper, who with a rub of his legs and a beat of his wings, hopped away into the night, his ordeal brought to a close.

Eos gazed up through watery eyes to her sister, Selene, quietly driving the moon across the canopy of the black sky and then back to her sons, who'd rushed in to see their father one last time.

'You must take heed,' she said, as she drew them both near, clasped them to her bosom. 'The gods themselves cannot recall their gifts.'

When Hope came to me one day, miserable, the long-suffering wife of a man who no longer saw her, a man who buried his head in his work or in the skirt of another woman, I took pity on her. How weak, I thought, to allow a good man to slip away; how dull she must have been to lose him, to forfeit his interest.

In the months during which our friendship had blossomed, I witnessed her marriage wither and decay like Tithonus; from the sidelines, in my capacity as confidante, advisor, I willed, no, *encouraged*, its demise, lest their doomed relationship should linger too at the quiet limit of the world. I told her she could do better than him, but the truth was that he could do far better than her, and I had someone in mind for the role.

When her unhappiness peaked and her suffering became unbearable, she wished for an end to it all, an escape that would take her far, far away from Mark. And so into the water I threw the lifesaver, and the struggling woman grabbed it, reluctantly at first and then with both hands: some time out of mind.

I drove her to the farmhouse, lit the fire in the living room. We sat and chatted. She grew weary, then agitated. The wine had done its worst, had started to speak through her, and in its grip, she voiced her doubts – about Mark, about leaving him. I tried to calm her, to reassure, but she was beyond reassurance. She had wished to be free, and I had gifted that to her. Did she thank me? Of course not. She asked for the gift to be withdrawn. So I told her, plain and simple, and in no uncertain terms, that just like the gods, I cannot recall my gifts. The wheels had been set in motion. She got up, distressed, and that's when she spotted the envelope, addressed to me, Annie, the real me. Not Charlotte. I panicked, became flustered, tried to explain it away, but she saw through me, through it all. Her whole face arched up into a question mark and fell into an answer – an answer she did not like.

She began to strike me, her arms flailing maniacally. There was something primitive in her eyes. I ran, first to the stairs, and then thinking better of it, through to the kitchen. She followed. I picked up a water jug, warned her not to come any closer, but my warning went unheeded. She stepped to me, advanced with wild abandon, and I swung and I swung and I swung. The first two missed, the third found its mark, and she hit the ground with a giant thud. She lay there, and to an onlooker it might have seemed that she was sleeping sweetly, were it not for the blood seeping from the gaping wound on her head. I marvelled at what I had proven myself capable of – of hurt, real hurt. But the thought passed through me and at a clap I was back at the gate, a rabbit in the road, a car sweeping round the bend … I panicked and picked up Hope, just as I picked up that wounded rabbit, and carried her down to the basement. How lucky she was to still be breathing, rasping through tired lungs. How lucky she was still to be alive.

I visited her often, fed her, clothed her, bathed her with a sponge and soapy water, and smiled when she still called me Charlotte.

I slopped out her bucket and read her bedtime stories – tales of daring, of great courage and conviction; of dragons, tormentors, skeleton kings and pirate maidens; of creaky old houses, Native American burial grounds and spacecraft; of woodworkers, innkeepers, slavers and miners; tales of love, adventure and hope. Hope.

She spat at me once, spat at my face as I bent down to change her sodden trousers.

'You're evil,' she said.

'No,' I replied. 'I'm saving him from it.'

And so my stories changed, from fantasy to reality. I raised the mirror. I told her about our first date, our second, our third, how he fucked me on their marital bed, pinned my hands behind my back until it hurt, how I couldn't walk in the morning, how I ached still. I told her of the moment I met his father, then his mother, how our relationship was hurtling along at a million miles an hour. I told her how in love we were, how I hoped he might propose any moment now so we could start our new life together. I told her how the police had given up their search; how she was, for all legal intents and purposes, dead. And in that small moment, all fortitude sped from her body like a phantom driven out by a prayer.

I brought her a diary, her diary, to relive her past and continue her story so that she may not be forgotten entirely. She thanked me, grateful at last. But it would be short-lived, for she would be moving in the morning, she would yearn for the basement, for the doting, for my gentleness and patience, and then she would know real suffering.

You see, I have a box. Annie's Box. It's 7 by 8 feet; it's cramped, it's dark, and it's buried far beneath the earth in a location known only to me. Like Pandora's, it contains all the evils of the world along with my deepest, darkest secret.

I have a box that I have sanded and decorated and fitted and adorned.

I have a box that is girded by lock and key.

I have a box, and one from which Hope shall not escape. For Hope was not the sugar that made the medicine go down. Hope was not the salve. Hope was the ultimate ill, the radix of a broken heart and the root of all misery. Hope was not the light, but the darkness. And now she has company. Misery loves company. He too struggled, briefly, before all the struggle went out of him, quit his body in a great exhale. The uninvited stranger, the interloper, now the permanent guest. My guest, but her bedfellow. She may not have found a new man in life but she was gifted one in death.

On the night before my wedding, I crept out of bed under the cover of darkness. The stars shone just enough to pick out my steps down the gravel path, down the rolling hill of the field and across the fence; just enough to find my way into the pillbox on the abandoned lea, to lie down on the hard earth within, press my ear to the floor beside the protruding metal pipes and listen to the sound of heavy, guttural rasping, for the very last time.

My heart beat fast against the soil as I told her of the wedding, of the guests, the dried flower centrepieces, the columns of champagne that would be hoisted in our name and in celebration of our love, of the car, the vows, the promise of forever, of the husband who had forgotten all about her, of the end to her suffering. I would be married in the morning, by which time I would have taken everything from her.

Had I lain there for longer that night after the pipes were stuffed with mud, scratched from the soil by mine own hands, had I been there as the final rasping came to a close, I might have heard, somewhere in the distance, the sound of a grasshopper beating its wings.

PART FOUR

THE HAPPILY-EVER-AFTER

41

The scent of lavender from the nearby fields catches on the air, as Karen, dressed in a bright white suit, makes her way down the aisle towards Hannah, who stands under the bough of a great oak tree in the heat of the midday sun, waiting for the woman, my sister, with whom she intends to spend the rest of her life. K smiles as she looks ahead to Hannah, to her future; she smiles at Mother who walks proudly beside her in a summer frock, ready to give her away, the very image of a very modern mother for a very modern wedding. There are no flower girls – the flowers are all around us – no maids of honour, no best men; just two best women, exchanging vows and sealing their love before fifty pairs of seated eyes.

'But I thought you two were going through a rough patch?' I said when K first told me the news.

'We were. But that was Berlin, the distance between us. When I decided to move back, well … Things took a turn. We realised as soon as we were in each other's lives again that we didn't ever wish to leave them. All the petty squabbling, the arguments we once had over who last replaced the loo roll went out the window, and the only thing that mattered was the fact I loved her, that I will always love her, and that she makes me happier than I ever thought I could be.'

'Then I'm happy for you,' I said, and I was. She too deserved her happy ending. I was living mine.

Had anyone asked me several years ago whether I believed in happy endings, in a resolution that was anything other than cheerless, anything other than a bag of bones interred in the ground or a scattering of ashes on the wind, I'd have answered *no*.

I'd have said that happiness is an ever-dwindling resource that peaks at the instant of one's birth and then is spent, often carelessly, in the pursuit of a good life. And then, well, as that life ebbs, as the thing we have all been running towards proves itself forever just beyond our grasp, we look down at our wasted limbs, our sallow skin and bent frame, all happiness lost to us, and realise that we would have been happier had we never chased happiness at all, had we stayed put and allowed the very thing we sought to find us.

But now ... Now I'm not so sure. Had I stayed put, had I not pursued my happily-ever-after, had I not done everything within my power to claim Mark for my own, then I would still be sitting in my small flat in London, swiping left and right in an endless game of chance to find Mr Right Now.

Had I not pursued my happily-ever-after, I would not be sitting here today, beside the man I love, who clasps my hand like a collector holding a precious timepiece; a man who looks across at me and smiles, just as his mother did at *our* wedding, with the punch of a thousand headlights; a man who reaches down with his free hand, lovingly, adoringly, to the small bundle of my belly and rests it there as he thinks on our future, our very own ending, and realises, at last, that I have been able to give him what she never could.

42

'Oh, Annie, you're so wicked,' said Beth, as she leant across the table to me and dropped a sugar cube into her espresso. Her nails are so long, so perfectly pointed, that she could slice open a cantaloupe without a second thought.

'All I'm saying is: the woman thought a wax was something you rub on your car. Her poor husband ...'

The table roared with laughter, and I was enjoying it. I was enjoying being the person they wanted me to be, expected me to be. The person I *could* have been.

'Are all your colleagues so frightfully tragic?' asked Mathilde.

'Classics doesn't exactly attract the young, glamorous types.'

Beth smiled wryly. 'Present company excluded, of course.'

'Of course,' I conceded.

'Especially with those new blonde locks of yours.'

'You do look annoyingly good, Annie,' said Mathilde, before turning to Beth. 'Your handiwork, I presume?'

Beth bowed.

'I was sat in that chair for four hours,' I said.

'One mustn't rush perfection. Speaking of ... how's Mark?'

'On a tight leash, I should imagine,' added Mathilde who threw in a raised eyebrow for good measure.

'That's all behind us now. It wasn't easy – it wasn't easy to admit there was a problem, not at first – but we worked through it together. I guess old habits die hard.'

'I thought they might have died with her.'

Beth gave Mathilde a look that said *too far*. Sometimes the conversational ball volleyed to the other side of the net can land with an excess of topspin.

'What? Are we just going to sit here and pretend that she's still out there somewhere after more than three years?'

'She was your friend,' said Beth sadly.

'*Was*,' emphasised Mathilde. 'And yours too. If she's still out there, then why hasn't she been in touch? Either she's dead or selfish. You choose one, though neither is particularly pretty. Besides, even before she went missing, it was always *Charlotte this* and *Charlotte that*. When we saw her that is, when her time wasn't spent elsewhere. No, she was done with us long before we were done with her.'

Hope had always spoken of Mathilde, of her laser-cut bob and leopard-print jumpsuits, her enormous hooped earrings and white-sequinned handbags, had spoken of her in a way that would indicate a skelf; a nuisance more than a friend. It wasn't until Mathilde came calling at Mark's door as we readied his house for sale, until I answered, paint-splattered and wearied, that I realised just how wrong Hope had been. There, on the doorstep, a new friendship, a real friendship, was born. Hope appreciated so very little of her adornments, discarded them like a spent match. Her life was wasted on her. And so it was wasted.

'Actually, I've heard something,' said Beth.

My heart beat a little faster. 'Heard what?'

'Well, apparently Mark's father hired some sort of investigator, an ex-policeman to track her down.'

Frank. I should have known.

'And?' urged Mathilde. 'What did he find?'

'We don't know.'

'What do you mean we don't know?'

'He went missing too, about eight months back. His car was discovered in some woods in Kent, torched.'

I had taken great care, of that I was sure; not a trace of him remained. Once his body was moved to the pillbox, I took the car keys that I'd fished out of his coat pocket, fetched some kerosene from the disused labourer's shed that bordered the stream at the foot of the farm, retraced his steps down the gravel drive to his car and drove it five miles to the other side of the nearby wood. There, I watched the flames dance in balletic fashion before me, in arabesque and pirouettes, as his notebook, into which he'd fed all his leads, all his suspicions, suspicions about me, was consumed entirely by the fire. Four weeks later, a policewoman, a detective, I think, an older woman, contacted by Cameron's wife or else Frank, I suppose, came by the farm to enquire as to whether I had seen a man out alone a month previous. *No*, came the answer. And it came so easily.

'They don't have a single lead, of course, though I'm sure there are no shortage of people harbouring a grudge from his police days,' continued Beth. 'And no one knows what he was doing out there. He left behind a wife too. A young one. No kids.'

My heart returned to its slower, rhythmic pounding.

'Is this true, Annie?' asked Mathilde. 'Has Frank said anything?'

I did my best to conceal my unease. 'Nonsense, surely. It sounds like something out of a film.'

Beth pushed her empty espresso cup away from her. 'Hey, I'm just telling you what I've heard. A lot of loose tongues at the salon.' She looked at her watch. 'Well, this has been fun, but I better get back before Mrs Jenkins wakes up for her blow-dry.'

'Wait. Before you go ... I have some news.'

Beth and Mathilde looked to one another and then back to me, expectant. Beth's eyes narrowed to a point, traced up and down, as though weighing the possibilities, weighing me.

'Shut the fuck up,' said Mathilde slowly. 'You're not? Are you? You are ...'

My smile widened. 'I am.'

A fug of screaming filled every inch of the little corner café. The girls threw themselves at me in a crush of arms that swallowed me whole.

'Oh, I'm so very happy for you!' said Beth.

'You're going to be a mum!' cried Mathilde. 'God, I hate you.'

'And I love you too.'

'What did Mark say when he found out?'

I bit my lower lip. Mathilde stared at me, puzzled.

'I'm telling him tonight.'

'Are you nervous?' said Beth.

'About what?'

'About telling him. He's not exactly been pushing the idea.'

Mark had always been reluctant to discuss children. *We're not ready*, he would say. *We don't need another complication in our lives – not yet. I'm back at work; you've got another promotion. Things are going well. You can see that, surely?* And I would nod and smile and agree, but only because I feared I'd lose him again – if not in body, then in spirit – as I did on our honeymoon. He seemed so very far from me then. I didn't want that again. I wanted him close. I needed him close.

The truth that I did not dare utter was that I *was* nervous to tell him, but I had put it off long enough. A child will bind us in ways that marriage couldn't. He might not see that now, but he will.

'He's ready to be a dad,' I said defiantly. 'He wasn't then, he wasn't with her. But he is now.'

'And are you ready to be a mum?'

The question fell on me from a great height. I was so concerned about telling Mark, about what his reaction might be, that I didn't stop to consider whether *I* was ready. I mean, is anyone, ever?

'I think so,' I said.

'You're going to be a terrific mum,' said Beth warmly. 'Just look at Karen; how wonderful she is. That's your doing, that's your influence.'

I'm not sure my mother's lack of parenting should be the barometer by which my own suitability for steering a child through life is measured, but Beth meant well.

'Thank you,' I said.

'She's right,' said Mathilde. 'Besides, you mother us. We were like two lost lambs before you came into our lives.'

'Speak for yourself,' said Beth.

Mathilde cupped her hand to her mouth, so as to form a dividing line between us and Beth.

'She watched *Erin Brockovich* last weekend and suddenly she's on an independent woman trip. It won't last.'

'I heard that,' laughed Beth.

As we got up to leave, she took my hand and held my gaze firm. 'You two make far more sense than he and Hope ever did.'

254

'Darling. Would you come in here a moment?'

The stairs groaned under Mark's weight as he made his way up to our bedroom, what was once my parents' bedroom. He looked tired as he bent down to kiss me where I sat on the ottoman at the foot of the bed.

'Long day?'

Mark didn't answer immediately. He unbuttoned his baby-blue shirt and removed his trousers until he stood, slightly bowed, in just his boxers and a white vest.

'Six hour surgery. Some poor roofer fell from the fourth floor of a council block.'

'That's horrible. Is he going to be OK?'

Mark looked at me and shook his head slightly. I didn't understand how he did it; how day after day he could deal with trauma, real trauma, and leave it behind in the hospital. He has an extraordinary ability to compartmentalise anguish, so long as that anguish is not his own. I get upset if one of my bright students turns in a bad essay, and I'll be upset for the rest of the evening. Mark must think me silly, but he never says anything. He's good to me in many ways that I never fully stop to count.

Mark went to the bathroom to brush his teeth, and called back to me through foamed mouth. 'Have you picked up my suit from the dry-cleaners?'

'I collected it this morning.'

Mark spat into the sink and turned off the tap. He re-emerged in the bedroom, a line of toothpaste down his vest.

'What have we got them by the way?'

'A stoneware cook set. K asked for it specifically.'

'Colour?'

'Terracotta.'

Mark laughed as he climbed into bed. 'I feel like the president receiving his briefing.'

'Would you like me to call you Mister President?'

His eyebrows shot up. 'Do you even have to ask?'

'Well, Mister President, before you get too excited and impossibly distracted, I have some news for you. I've been waiting for you to get home.'

'Oh?'

'Your anniversary present has arrived a little early.'

Mark sat up straight in bed, then scanned the room as though trying to locate the present.

'Well, what is it?'

I took a deep breath and fought back a knot of nerves before the words came out.

'I'm pregnant.'

At first, the words didn't seem to register; Mark stared out through the window to the old chicken coop. His eyes darted left and right in quick, sudden movements as though he was trying to read a script before him, but the sentences were swimming. And then the flitting stopped. He looked around, looked at me finally, grinned from ear to ear, and then opened his arms wide to me. I fell into them.

'I'm going to be a dad,' he whispered.

'You're going to be a great dad,' I replied. And just like that I wondered why I ever feared telling him. We were going to be a family at last.

43

The *clink-clink* of a butter knife tapping against a champagne flute rings throughout the marquee tent, and a hushed silence falls upon us. Several heads turn to the front, to the top table, as mine turns to my right, to my neighbour, to the woman holding the knife: Mother.

A prick of panic creeps down my lower back, all I can think of is the last time she delivered a speech. The embarrassment, the shame ... I don't want that for K. She deserves better. But it's too late. Mother has clambered to her feet and she holds the room in the palm of her hand. The microphone hisses on the table before her.

'I'd like to start by thanking you all for coming,' she says. 'I know many of you journeyed from slightly further afield to, well, a field.'

There are a few ripples of pitying laughter, nothing more. My stomach tightens as I brace for worse. Had there been crickets around, had evening fallen, we might have heard a gentle chirrup.

'I'd also like to thank those who couldn't make it today,' she continues, before pausing for effect. 'You've saved us about fifty pounds a head.'

The drummer in the wedding band rolls off a *ba-doom-boom-tssss*, which gives rise to more laughter, genuine this time. K and I look at each other in astonishment.

'Of course, this is not just any wedding. Today you get two brides for the price of one.'

Ba-doom-boom-tssss.

More laughter. Mother is enjoying this; and, I have to admit, so am I. Hannah and K laugh into their napkins.

'I'll leave the rest of the jokes to a professional, but I did wish to speak from the heart for a moment, if I may. You will all be most surprised to learn that this is not Karen's first wedding.' A few unnerved, furtive looks among the gathering do little to deter her. 'That's right: she is technically a bigamist. When she was a little girl, her father married her off to a Ken doll in our back garden. All her favourite toys gathered around, watching – unflappably, it has to be said – the union. Karen was blissfully happy. And I recall that moment now because although her father couldn't be here today, it warms me to think that he got a chance to attend one of her weddings.' Mother turns to K. 'Darling … had he been here, he would have been so proud, as I am, to see the strong, powerful woman you've become.' She turns to me. 'He would have been proud, as I am, to see the strong, powerful *women* you have become. He raised two very fine daughters, and though I'd like to claim some of the credit, the truth is that I can claim very little.'

Mother grows mournful. There is a note of regret in her voice, a tightening of the shoulder.

'I believe this is the bit where I am supposed to offer some sort of advice to the newlyweds. Well … I'm not sure I'm the right person to offer advice of my own, but if I could say just one thing, it would be this …'

Mother pauses, looks down for a moment and fishes a scrap of paper from the inside of her bra, which she straightens out with the flat of her hand.

'Let your love be stronger than your hate or anger. Learn the wisdom of compromise, for it is better to bend a little than to break. Believe the best rather than the worst. People have a way of living up or down to your opinion of them. Remember that true friendship is the basis for any lasting relationship. The person you choose to marry is deserving of the courtesies and kindnesses you bestow on your friends. Please hand this down to your children's children. The more things change, the more they are the same.'

Mother thrusts her flute into the air, and leads the tent in a toast.

'To the health and happiness of the happy couple, and to their very happy ending.'

In the past few months, Mother too seems to have found her happiness. I could chalk it up to her latest boyfriend or the menagerie of jewellery he has gifted her or the house she won from Derek in the long-contested divorce settlement, but to do so would be to do her a great injustice; to do so would be to refuse to look beneath the surface. No, it's something more profound than that, more *real*. I think she has drawn happiness from us, from me and K, from her girls, from our happiness with our partners and from the lives and foundations we have begun to build in earnest. Perhaps she realises, finally, that Dad, that Jessica, Grandma too, are all alive and well in us; that their passings were not ends but beginnings. None of us would be where we are now, or who we are now, without them. For better or worse. Perhaps, she has finally accepted that, and found in that acceptance a release.

I think back to when Mother sat with me and shared a cigarette beside the pillbox on the day of Grandma's funeral. How she said that she'd failed us, that motherhood fits some people like a comfy shoe but not her; how failure is just a prelude to trying again; how she wanted to be a better mother to us; how *she* wanted to try again. In the intervening years, she has not been the perfect mother – she could never be accused of that – but here she is, for the very first time since Dad's death, trying. She has placed her foot inside the shoe, and found, at last, that the shoe fits.

*

When Mother said this was not your average wedding, she was right. But not for the reasons you might immediately assume. Looking around, as I stand a mere four metres from a Ferris wheel, it is almost as if K, shaped by that night at the funfair, intended to recreate it, down to the last detail, save that this time all eyes are on her.

In and amongst the undulating lavender fields that seem to stretch out to the horizon on all sides, there are tombolas, teacup rides, men in striped candy-cane jackets and straw boaters tending to hook-a-duck booths. There are hooplas and candyfloss machines and coconut shies, and what wedding isn't complete without a mini-golf course with its very own revolving windmill. This is a wedding built not on convention and propriety, but on fun.

As I look up at Laura and Pete swinging precariously from the top of the Ferris wheel, a familiar hand finds its way around my waist.

'Oh, K, you look so utterly beautiful.' I stand back so I can take it all in.

'It must run in the family,' she says. 'We Clarks make very good brides.'

'You're keeping the name then?'

'Someone has to.'

Mark joins us, gives K a kiss on each cheek. 'I was just chatting with Hannah, collecting my bet.'

'Your bet?'

'Sure. I bet her there was no chance of you wearing a dress.'

K laughs, looks down at her white suit. 'Did you bet her I'd be in white too?'

'I didn't fancy the odds.'

'Oh, shush you,' says K, as she slaps Mark playfully on the shoulder.

He looks across at Pete now alighting from the Ferris wheel. 'Excuse me, ladies, but I have another bet to call in.'

My eyes follow Mark, follow his path to Pete, to Laura.

'What happened with you two?' says K.

'What do you mean?'

'You and Laura.'

'Nothing *happened*, precisely. There was no great falling out. We drifted.'

'In the space of six months?'

Some friendships were never meant to last forever. Some friendships serve a purpose. They work until they don't; they fit until you outgrow them. Laura was the person with whom I spent wild nights out and miserable, self-pitying nights in. She was the one

260

who would come over with a bottle of wine and a pack of cigarettes when two tabs of diazepam just wouldn't do. She was the one I would confide in when I didn't know who else to tell. But it was a friendship of convenience – for her too. Laura enjoyed, perhaps revelled in, playing the role of consoler, and I enjoyed being consoled; but there existed little below the surface of this exchange, little to suggest that we meant more to each other. That morning in Capri when I picked up the phone to Laura and it became clear her priorities had realigned, from me to Pete, I realised that it was time to move on, that she could no longer give me precisely what I needed. And that's OK. We try to cling on to the things that once made us happy when the best you can do is let them go entirely.

Laura walks over to me as K disappears into the arms of her new wife and into a throng of well-wishers.

'Hey,' says Laura.

'Hey,' I say, by return, but it becomes painfully apparent that we have so very little left to say to one another. This is the first time we have spoken in four months.

'I tried calling,' she says, 'but I, well …'

'Oh. Yeah. I got a new number. I thought Mark would have …?'

'No,' she says flatly. 'No, he didn't.'

'You look nice,' I say.

'Thanks,' she smiles.

Silence. *Someone should say something, anything.*

A dull ache fills the pit of my stomach.

'I gather you've taken up yoga?' Laura says finally. 'How did that happen? You always said that was for spoilt rich kids and people with too much time on their hands.'

I shrug lightly. 'I guess some things change.'

'And I guess some things don't,' she says pointedly. 'Anyway, it's getting late. Pete and I should make a move.'

'Well, it was good to see you,' I say, but Laura doesn't repay the kindness. She takes Pete by the hand and walks off with the very last of our friendship.

Mark spots me alone, returns, gives me an enormous hug.

'Are you OK?' he says.

I wipe away an errant tear. 'I will be.'

I'm not mourning our lost friendship. I'm mourning the person I used to be.

'They're leaving,' calls a voice suddenly. Hannah's sister, I think, but I can't be sure. 'Quickly, everyone. To the front.'

K didn't want a big send-off. No bouquet, no expensive car, no sparklers, no frills. She was never one for goodbyes; she'd much rather slip out of a party unannounced than exchange valedictions with every single guest. I supposed it was the finality of the gesture: every goodbye could well prove a final farewell. If you never say goodbye, then there remains always the possibility of picking up right where you left off.

We gather around at the gates as K, candyfloss in one hand, Hannah in the other, climbs into the taxi. She smiles at me from the back seat as we stand and we cheer and we clap. I think I see a very small sadness wash over her. Is she thinking of Dad? Of Grandma? Of Jessica? Was it the wedding she had imagined all those years ago on our lawn, in her little white dress with the red ribbon around the waist, surrounded by her careworn stuffed toys, and with Dad toasting the happy couple: Karen and noble Sir Kenneth Carson? How happy she was then, and, that momentary sadness having passed, how happy she is now. She glows once more, and this time it is all for real.

But before I can finish the thought, a searing pain ripples through my abdomen, and into my back, reveals itself in my contorted features. I grimace, bite back the throbbing heat inside and look down to see a small patch of red spotting the front of my cream summer dress. The patch spreads slowly, becomes a gaping ravine, and for a split second I am at the farm again, my feet dangling precariously into the dyke, a great chasm that has swallowed everything, with a lure so strong that even the light cannot escape. My future is in there still, somewhere, but it's not the one I'd envisioned.

I rummage in my bag, find a starched napkin from the wedding breakfast, blistered white in the dying light of the sun, and bend down to wipe the wetness from my legs. As I do, a child, clinging to her mother's thighs, her eyes and her eyes alone drawn away from the spectacle, watches me silently.

My eyes are drawn back up again, to K in her smart white suit, sat beside her partner, her wife, and I swallow down the hurt and the racking pain, hold back the disappointment I feel at myself, cauterise the anger. For K must not see my suffering. No, she must hear my clapping, hear the concert of clapping as we wish her well on a brand-new adventure. She will get her happily-ever-after, even if I have lost mine.

44

Once upon a time, or so the story goes, there were three sisters, long before there were two, when soon there would be one.

45

I look over at the man I love – the man who vowed to love me to my last – and I see a great void. His blue eyes, which I once declared little marbles in his head, don't look at me in the same way any more. There's affection, sure, but it's dimmed or else hiding. And there's a stillness in his arms that he can't seem to shake. He lifts the fork to his mouth as we sit here in this unforgivably chichi restaurant that I didn't pick, in the name of our first anniversary; and yet his arms are perfectly still. The fork moves, but he's motionless.

The band strikes up and the waiters seem to waltz to its rhythms – stumbling and pirouetting around us in an eddy of colour. I think on all the things they must have overheard at diners' tables. The proposals, promotions, infidelities, redundancies, births, deaths and marriages. The anniversaries.

The decay.

And that's when I see it, a flicker so slight as to be imperceptible to anyone other than his wife: a sadness creeps into the corner of Mark's mouth. His perfect mouth. I tell myself that the steak is overdone or that the wine must be corked, but I know neither to be true.

It dawns on me that one day he'll look at me and that dimness in his eyes will be a sea of black. I shall look at him, but there will be black – as though, all at once, the lights in New York City have gone out.

'Everything OK, darling?'

Mark smiles, but it is forced. There is a world behind that smile.

'Perfectly,' he says, and he says it, almost, perfectly. Had I not known him, had we met for the first time this evening, a first date, two intimate strangers sharing a meal and a bottle of wine, I might never have guessed he was acting.

'You sure?'

Mark drops his fork to the plate with a clatter that rings out through the room. An elderly couple at the table beside us turn and look.

'Must you ruin this, too?' he says angrily.

'You're right,' I say quietly. 'I'm sorry. Let's enjoy the meal.'

Mark picks up his fork, and the eyes of the couple occupying the table beside us consider each other once again. A relief; I hate public arguments, and Mark knows this only too well.

'Let's play a game,' I say.

'What kind of game?'

'Truth or lie. Remember?'

'I do.'

'Well?'

'Don't we already know all there is to know about one another?' His chin juts out at a slight incline. It's a question that does not require an answer. He has all the answers he needs.

'I'm sure there are things, small things, that we may have overlooked. Come on, it'll be fun.'

Mark dabs his mouth with the corner of his napkin and then pulls it away to reveal a perfect impression of his lips. His perfect lips.

'Very well,' he says. 'I'll go first.'

His fingers interlock and his brows furrow in concentration. *What is he thinking?*

'When I was a boy, I had a recurring nightmare. I'm in a pond, soaked through, and I'm calling for my dad, but a lifeguard keeps telling me they can't get a message through to his base. I keep calling and calling, and eventually he appears, but his face is just camouflage. No mouth, no nose, no features. Just camouflage.'

'Creepy. Slightly concerned that'll turn out to be the lie now. OK, and two?'

'I used to have a catchphrase.'

I almost spit my wine out.

'A catchphrase?'

'I thought it made me memorable.'

268

'What was it?'

'Life's a beach and then you marry one.'

There's a spot of mischief glistening from within; he's yearning to smile.

'I guess I walked straight into that,' I say.

'I guess you did.'

'The first one is the truth.'

'Ding, ding, ding. We have a winner. Now you.'

'OK. At university, I once covered every inch of my house-mate's dorm in tin foil. I was very drunk and very sorry the next morning. Alas, she didn't see the funny side and reported me to the student welfare officer. I had to move halls.'

'Childish. I like it. The second?'

I look at him long and hard, my handsome, dependable Mark, and think on all that we have been through, all that may still lie before us.

'I have only ever loved one person.'

He smiles, a real, genuine smile that seems to wash out the old and birth the new. A smile born of love, real, genuine love. He softens. And for the first time in a long while, we discuss our hopes, our dreams, our desires. Mark listens in a way that he hasn't since he proposed, or, if we wish to travel a little further: since our first date that day in Holland Park, besieged by charging peacocks and recalcitrant kids.

We relive the highlights of our relationship in an endless procession of *remember-the-time-when* … I always remember; he rarely does, not that it matters, for those moments come alive again in their retelling. Our love comes alive again, and we hold it up for the entire room to see. We tell stories to reassure ourselves that we're right, that there is precedent, antecedent, that what we have done is just, that where we are going is real.

'Do you ever picture us growing old?' I ask.

'No,' he says calmly.

'You don't?'

He goes to speak but it's stifled by dessert arriving in a hail of sparklers: a slice of cake – the cake from our wedding – and a message inked in chocolate around the edge of the plate:

We each pick up a fork and joust for the corner with a glut of icing.

'I used to do nothing *but* think about the future,' Mark continues, 'until I realised just how unhealthy it is to place so much stock in what might be. I wasted so much time dreaming when I could have been living in the here and now, taking in every detail. And life never pans out the way you intend anyway.'

I'm not sure if he means that as a barb, but it stings. *Is he disappointed with his future? Is he disappointed with me?*

Mark senses his error, backtracks.

'What I mean is, can't we just appreciate what we have without wondering where we'll be tonight, tomorrow, next week?'

He places his hand on mine, turns the wedding band round and around on my finger.

'Do you picture us old?' he says.

'I try, but I can't. Do I imagine a future? Yes. Do I imagine us together? Yes. But do I imagine us old? No. In my thoughts, we are forever this age.'

Mark smiles tenderly. 'Do you picture me with abs?'

I close my eyes. 'Oh, yeah.'

'Skimpy bathing shorts, lounging by a Tuscan pool?'

'I wouldn't have it any other way.'

'Am I always well behaved?'

I open my eyes again, bite my lip a little at the thought. 'You certainly know your way around that swimming pool.'

Mark laughs and then pulls from beneath the table a package wrapped in red-spotted wrapping paper and finished precisely with a cream-coloured bow. A present.

'For me?' I say.

'No, for the waiter,' he jokes.

I go to reach for the gift, but he jerks it just out of my grasp.

'Not yet,' he says, as he signals for the bill. 'I have another surprise for you first.'

'There's more?'

'There's always more.'

We sit in the car outside as night closes in. The engine hums low and a quiet heat works its way up and into the opening of my dress. I'm with my father suddenly, dozing on the sofa in front of the fire, a blanket placed over me, a gentle kiss on the forehead, a *goodnight, love.*

'Do you trust me?' Mark says.

I swallow hard, but I hope that it doesn't show. 'Always,' I answer.

He removes a length of dense black silk from the glove compartment and twists in his seat to wrap it around my head, over my eyes, so that all I can see is black. Its tightness unnerves me.

'Where are we going?' I ask, excitement and nerves colliding within.

'If I told you that, it wouldn't be much of a surprise. Hold tight.'

The car peels off and I can feel the soft warmth of Mark's hand working its way up my inner thigh, which he grips firmly, just to let me know that I'm still his, that I would always be his, just as he will always be mine.

Eventually, the car pulls off the main road, and slows to a crawl. Gravel crunches under tyre.

'Almost there,' he says reassuringly. But I am not reassured. My heart feels as though any moment now it will break free of my chest.

'Seriously, Mark, where are we going?'

He does not say a word. This silence unnerves me the most.

Soon the car stops, and he gets out. He circles to the passenger door, opens it, takes me by the hand to help me up. A ripple of electricity runs through my back. My lips are pursed, expecting, willing, a kiss. But it does not come.

'This way,' he says, leading me, my hand aloft, as though presenting a debutante to a room of dignitaries or else taking a donkey to market. 'Just a few more steps.'

We stop and my heels sink into the gravel.

'Right, you can remove the blindfold.'

I reach to the back of my head and unpick the knot in the fabric. A gust of wind catches it and the silk flutters to the ground

271

as I look up to see an imposing oak door with a circular iron handle. The door to the farmhouse. Our farmhouse. He has taken me to the farmhouse.

'Is this some kind of joke?'

'You tell me,' he says. There is a note of menace, real menace in his voice now.

And then he grabs me, hard by the wrist, pulls me towards him. I stumble on the stones and my head crashes into the iron handle. I fall backwards, but he pulls me towards him again.

Inside, he pushes me up against the wall. But not like he did last time; there is nothing sensual about this, nothing pleasurable. I am not his equal, I am the subject of his contempt. His hand grasps at my throat and air becomes a precious commodity. I would trade the house for it; I would trade this life.

'Where is she?' he screams, so close that specks of spittle land on my cheek.

'I don't know what –'

He shakes me, cuts me short.

'Where *is* she?'

'Darling, baby, I –'

But he just looks at me, cold and unyielding. He looks at me like ... like he might just listen. Like if I found the words, the right words, they might just get through to him, like he might just understand.

'Everything I have done, Mark, I have done for you. Everything I have done, I have done for *us*. You were miserable before, you were miserable with her. You don't have to worry any more. I have given us this life. And one day, I will give you one more.'

He looks away, and his grip on my throat loosens.

'I want us to be a family. I want us to try again. Will you let me try?'

But just as soon as I seem to have reached him, a vast chasm opens between us and I lose him. He is past sense now, past reason; he is for the birds. With a force that terrifies me, he grabs my hair and drags me to the basement door now open before us, the stairs beyond descending into the black. For a woman so used to being in control, I have suddenly found myself out of it.

272

'No, Mark. Just listen, we can –'

But before I can get the words out, I feel a shove, hard and fast in my lower back, and I go, head over heels, tumbling down into the darkness.

When I come to, I am propped against the basement wall. Mark stands over me. I am helpless and he can smell it on me like a cheap perfume.

'Here,' he says, throwing a present across the floor. 'I believe it's traditional to give paper on the first anniversary.'

I look down at the gift, which has been wrapped with such care, such precision.

'Go on then, open it.'

And so I do. I unwind the cream-coloured bow, peel back the red-spotted wrapping paper to find a journal, Hope's journal, with my entries, but more importantly: with a new entry, Hope's final entry, penned after the kindness I'd shown in returning the damned thing to her, proving, as I'd long held, that no good deed ever goes unpunished. For there it is – the whole truth of it all. Of what I've done. Of what I'm truly capable of.

'Where did you – ?'

But he does not answer, not the question I want him to answer. I realise that it doesn't much matter; he knows all there is to know and that's that. The Fates have ordained that my thread should be cut, and who am I to argue; not even Zeus has power over life and death.

'Why?' he says flatly, almost emotionless. 'What had she ever done to you?'

I feel a hot stickiness seep down from my ear. I can taste it. Iron.

'You deserved better,' I say. Mark rushes at me, shakes me bodily like a rag doll.

'You call this better?'

'It could have been. If you let it, if you give it time. It's not too late. Darling, just let me up. We can pretend this never happened.'

Mark laughs, bemused. 'Let you up?' He laughs again, harder this time, almost maniacal. 'Let you up. Right.'

273

Mark sits down on the floor before me and opens the diary from which he reads. He clears his throat theatrically.

'And you're a really fucking stupid bitch if you think I'm going to just let you leave, he said. I stopped then and I looked at him, read the fury in his face. I believed him. Mark ...
He grabbed my wrists. Mark, you're hurting me. Mark ...'

Marks looks back up at me.
'I had to ...'
A wild anger mounts in him. 'You had to *what*? Write a few fake diary entries? File some adoption papers in her name? You were going to set me up. You were going to let me take the fall for her death.'
'It wasn't like that. I promise.'
'Save your promises.' The devil before me snarls, stands back up and paces the room.
'She was here,' he says. His voice catches. Tears begin to pool in the corners of his eyes. 'She was here. She was desperate. And you did nothing. You kept her here; you saw her in pain; you saw her suffering; and you did nothing. What kind of animal are you?'
I am the worst kind.
'I'm going to give you one last chance, Annie. Where is she?'
But he must have known before he'd asked that the answer, even if I offered it up, wouldn't lead him to her – not as he knew her. She was gone. For good.
So I say nothing.
Just before Mark turns out the light and closes the door, he looks at me one final time, those black little marbles aflame, New York City on fire, and he speaks clearly, simply with what I know to be the truth, the whole truth and nothing but the truth, so help me God:
'I have only ever loved one person.'
The door closes with a thud. A key turns in the lock. Separating us, dividing us, once and for all. He plans to leave me here, just as I left her. Justice, I suppose.

The darkness comes to me as a great comfort, a shroud or eternal womb promising protection from the light that does little save illuminate the truth. I am safe here. I am secure here. For whatever awaits me out there must be far worse than the end I shall surely meet in here. No, this is my punishment – for Cameron, for Hope, for the children I was unable to grant him – and I must bear it all bravely if I must brave it at all. Did Tantalus not endure the falling water, the rising fruit? Did Atlas not support the heavens? Did Prometheus not abide the eagle, Ixion the burning wheel, Sisyphus his boulder, Arachne her second life? I think a second life might be the cruellest of them all. This first has been cruel enough.

Just then I feel something collide with my foot in the darkness. I reach down to feel for it, to take its weight in my hands. The shape is familiar, and yes ... there's a switch. A bright light pierces the darkness and throws shadows over the vast recesses of the basement, over the cardboard boxes, the trunks, the rolls of wallpaper and carpet offcuts, the bottles of wine. There, in my hand, is a little pink torch. And to the right, face down on the floor, is something I'd always held so very dear to me: a battered, torn and stained copy of *The Velveteen Rabbit*.

I smile – for Dad, for Jessica, for Karen and her newfound happiness. I even smile for Mother, for Mum, who has suffered just as much as the rest of us. And I smile for the new family that I tried to build in the wake of a broken one – the only one I'd ever known. A new family worth killing for. A new family worth dying for.

And just like that I'm crying, but not for me; they are not wasted tears. I am overcome by the flood of the past. *We will build new things. New memories, new friendships, new ideas. The past stays put.* But it doesn't, does it? The past is always just bubbling under the surface, informing all that we are, all that we will become. What's hysterical is historical.

I settle on to the hard warmth of the floor, as I had done many years ago two storeys above my head, my black dress piniioned between my legs, my high heels kicked to one side, and I open the book gingerly as one might a clam. And this clam hides a pearl.

It is a simple story, deceptively so. A stuffed rabbit, given to a young boy one Christmas morning, wonders if he will ever become *Real*. To be Real, a toy horse tells the rabbit, is to be loved. When the boy cannot sleep one evening, his nanny places the rabbit in his bed and the two become inseparable – wherever the boy goes, the rabbit goes, too. And over time, through play and adventure, as the rabbit's hair is loved off, as his whiskers grow threadbare and shabby, the rabbit becomes Real. For the boy loves him. It hurts to be Real, the rabbit learns; but when you're Real, you don't mind being hurt.

I cannot say, hand on heart, that I grasped the tale's significance when I first read it all those years ago. It was a nice story about a rabbit, little more. But as I returned to it in later years, the ending smarted: after the boy falls fitfully ill and the doctor orders all his cherished belongings be turned to cinders, the rabbit learns that he was not Real at all. Only when he finds himself on the green mile of the bonfire heap, does he shed a tear, a tear that contains within it the rabbit's own salvation: a flower grows on the ragged patch of earth, from which a fairy appears and grants the rabbit the gift of life. Love, it seems to say, can only take you so far, but it cannot make you whole. Wholeness comes from the understanding that all is lost.

Where once Mark had made me Real, now, finally, he has made me Whole.

I look up through the light of the torch to the far wall, which lies partially uncovered once more, undressing the words, her words, desperate words that I was so quick to conceal again, but which Mark in his sleuthing, just as Cameron before him, had found scratched into the surface, engraved into the paint so deep as to be etched into the fabric of the building itself, shimmering in their naked honesty: *Hope, Hope to the last.*

ACKNOWELDGEMENTS

TK

A NOTE ON THE AUTHOR

TK

A NOTE ON THE TYPE

The text of this book is set in Linotype Sabon, a typeface named after the type founder, Jacques Sabon. It was designed by Jan Tschichold and jointly developed by Linotype, Monotype and Stempel in response to a need for a typeface to be available in identical form for mechanical hot metal composition and hand composition using foundry type.

Tschichold based his design for Sabon roman on a font engraved by Garamond, and Sabon italic on a font by Granjon. It was first used in 1966 and has proved an enduring modern classic.